AN UNEXPECTED PROPOSAL

Astrid didn't say a word, just bowed her head as they both said their silent prayers of thanks for the food they were about to eat.

Astrid lifted her gaze and found Ira already watching her.

She took a breath, hoping it would calm her, needing the air to say what was on her mind.

But Ira beat her to it. "I think we've been set up."

"I know we have," Astrid admitted.

"It's not so bad," Ira said.

Astrid studied his expression, trying to determine where his feelings lay.

"I suppose not," Astrid said. "It's easier being on the other side of it, though."

Ira chuckled. "*Jah*, I suppose it is."

"I seem to remember, though, the time at my house, you walked out."

He nodded. Then he looked up. His blue eyes had turned serious. "I'm not going to walk out tonight."

Had she just heard him say what she thought he had said? "What was that again?"

"I said I'm not going to leave tonight. Not until you promise to marry me . . ."

THE AMISH MATCHMAKER

AMY LILLARD

ZEBRA BOOKS
KENSINGTON PUBLISHING CORP.
www.kensingtonbooks.com

ZEBRA BOOKS are published by

Kensington Publishing Corp.
119 West 40th Street
New York, NY 10018

All Kensington titles, imprints, and distributed lines are available at special quantity discounts for bulk purchases for sales promotion, premiums, fund-raising, and educational or institutional use.

Special book excerpts or customized printings can also be created to fit specific needs. For details, write or phone the office of the Kensington Sales Manager: Kensington Publishing Corp., 119 West 40th Street, New York, NY 10018. Attn. Sales Department. Phone: 1-800-221-2647.

First Printing: October 2022
ISBN-13: 978-1-4201-5176-3
ISBN-13: 978-1-4201-5177-0 (eBook)

10 9 8 7 6 5 4 3 2 1

Printed in the United States of America

SPECIAL THANKS

I'd like to thank reader Cherese Akhavein for helping me name the puppies in this book. I can't tell you a lot about them without revealing too much of the story to come. But be watching out for Huck and Hoss in the following pages! And thanks, Cherese, for picking out such perfect names for the pups!

CHAPTER ONE

The blinking cursor on her computer screen mocked Astrid. With each second that passed, as it appeared then disappeared once more, it seemed to be winking and asking, *Why?* And again, *Why?* And once more, *Why?*

If she couldn't write the words that had been flowing so freely up until now, then why should she have special permission to use a computer in her conservative Amish community? And if she didn't need a computer, then she surely didn't need the solar panels her brother, Jesse, had installed in order to power the machine. If she had no more words, then those things were completely unnecessary.

And her pen name. That would have to go.

And the income. That would leave as well.

And then Astrid Kauffman, also known as Rachel Kauffman, onetime author of the Willow Bend Creek Amish romance series, would have to . . .

Bake. Or sew. Or heaven forbid, get a job at one of the restaurants in town, seeing as how she could neither bake nor sew.

For as long as she had been writing, each book started the same way. There wasn't hardly anything quite so intimidating as staring at a blank page, or computer screen, as it were, trying to make a story appear. Normally, she wrote a little bit on notebook paper in longhand, then transferred it over to the Word file that would eventually become a manuscript. She supposed that habit had come about since the first book she'd ever finished was written completely in longhand on that yellow paper that lawyers preferred.

Then, two books into her budding career as an author, she had gained special permission from the bishop of their small community of Paradise Hill. She took her first royalty check and bought herself a computer. A laptop, they called it, though she wasn't sure why. It wasn't like it sat on her lap. Most days it hid in the rolltop desk in the corner of the dining room. But on days like today when she was working—or trying to work—she placed it on top of the dining room table, sat in her customary chair where she normally ate, and instead typed out the words to make her Amish characters fall in love.

She heard the mutterings around town. She would have to be deaf not to. But the truth of the matter was *jah*, her uncle was the bishop. *Jah*, he had given her special permission. But if anyone else had asked for such permission to write, she felt confident that he would have given it to them as well. Her uncle was a generous man, and he was a fair bishop, and he knew just as well as she did—and just as well as everyone else in the community of Paradise Hill and its neighboring community, Paradise Springs—that Amish pens had been writing for *The Budget* and *Die Botschaft* for years.

Of course, it didn't hurt that she donated a great deal of the profit she made from her books to the community itself. If she had to give up her computer, her pen name, and writing, then those donations would stop as well.

Astrid sighed and pulled her thoughts away from such matters. Thinking about donations and special permissions and laptops would not help her to write this book. She needed to keep her mind on thoughts that would help her achieve her goal.

She raised her hands above the keyboard and wriggled her fingers a bit, as if warming them up for the task at hand. She wasn't a very good typist. She didn't know one Amish person who was, come to think of it. But she did okay. Over the years she had found her own way of typing. It was mostly successful.

When she had words.

Astrid kept fingers poised and ready, then closed her eyes.

Lord, please give me these words today. I know I ask for much. I know I'm not worthy. But I believe You gave me this talent. And I believe You did so for a reason. Now I ask, Lord, that You help me deliver this talent to my editor on time. Amen.

Heaven help her, she couldn't even get the words for prayers right these days.

Sarah Bauman. That was her heroine's name. And Sarah Bauman was . . .

Sarah Bauman was on her way to teach school on the first day of classes.

Not exactly the beginning to set the world on fire, but it was a beginning.

She had her lunch cooler in one hand and a stack of books cradled in the crook of her left arm. As she wal—

A knock sounded at the front door.

Astrid closed her eyes, but to gather her patience, not to pray this time. She had finally gotten started. She didn't need any interruptions or distractions.

As she walked toward the tiny one-room schoolhouse just off Dandelion Lane, three of her more rambunctious male students passed her. Not that she knew them. This was her first day as teacher.

Astrid stopped. That was dumb. She backspaced until she got to "Dandelion Lane" once again.

three rowdy boys sped passed on their scooters. She knew them from church. She had already been warned by last year's teacher, her friend Esther Yoder, that they could try the patience of Job. But she was ready for them.

How was she ready for them?

Astrid tapped one finger against her chin and tried to determine what she would do if she were the teacher of rowdy boys in a one-room schoolhouse.

But nothing came to mind. Just scratch teacher off her list of possible employment opportunities that she could pursue once her editor cut her loose from this contract for being unable to fulfill her obligations and write a book.

Never mind. She would figure that out in a second.

Sarah waved to Fat Dan.

The man who was so slender he would blow away if a strong wind kicked up cupped his hand around his mouth and called out to her. "Ready for the first day of school, Sarah?"

She gave him a thumbs-up and—

The knock sounded again, jarring Astrid out of the flow she'd gotten into. Okay, so *flow* was completely overstating it. But it was a trickle, and she needed it.

And she was *not* getting up to answer the door when she knew that it wasn't for her. "Jesse!"

She had heard her brother come into the house not too long ago. At the time she had suspected he was getting a snack or something to drink and that he would soon be headed back out to his workshop. But seeing as how whoever was knocking was at the door of the house, it stood to reason he was not in his workshop.

She listened for a moment, but Jesse didn't respond. Not that that was saying much. If he was in the kitchen scrounging around for something to eat, then perhaps his mouth was full of last night's ham.

Either way it wasn't her concern. Whoever was at the door wasn't there for her.

Astrid turned her attention back to Sarah and the first day of school. She couldn't let herself get distracted. But she supposed that was the problem with having a brother who had a workshop right out front. If no one answered the door to his shop, they came straight to the house. Yet with any luck they would turn around and head back to Jesse's shop. He really needed to get his sign up so people would stop doing that, coming to the house instead of stopping off at his workshop and not bothering her.

It's just when the words were hard . . .

In truth, starting any new book was hard. At first she hated everything she wrote, but by chapter eight or so, she usually found her rhythm with the stories. By then the characters would present themselves for who they were and what they wanted. But things had changed with the last novel she had turned in. She had written it out of habit, "autopilot" she heard it called. The idea hadn't excited her, her characters hadn't occupied her every thought, the story hadn't kept her up at night thinking about what was going to happen next. And now this book.

This book seemed especially trying. This was her third attempt to start chapter one this week. Which didn't sound so bad if she pointed out that it was Friday. It did, however, look devastating when she mentioned the fact that she had only started working on it on Wednesday. Every word she had written between then and now she had erased.

Making matters worse, Sarah was a schoolteacher. How many schoolteachers had she written about in her series? She couldn't remember, but more than three was at least two too many.

How was she supposed to compete in the *Englisch* market with the same old, same old ideas? How was she supposed to glorify God? How could she expect people to pay money for the same old book just with different names in place of the last?

No. This one would be different. She just had to be patient, be diligent, and keep writing.

That was right. She was writing and she wasn't answering—

The knock sounded yet again. Louder this time. With more urgency.

"Jesse!" She called even louder and with her own increased urgency. Jesse didn't answer. "For pity's sake."

Astrid hit the save icon on her computer screen, then stomped to the front door. Who knew where her brother was? But if she was going to get any peace in this house, she was going to have to grab it by the horns herself.

She wrenched open the door at the same time loudly saying "Hill and Valley Leather Works is across—" A woman stood on the opposite side of her threshold. "The drive," Astrid continued, in a more normal tone of voice.

Just because this guest was a woman, and just because she didn't have a broken harness or hitching in her hands didn't mean that she wasn't there to see Jesse about leather goods. But something told Astrid this woman had arrived at their doorstep for something else entirely.

"I'm here to see the matchmaker." The woman's voice was soft, bordering on timid, and decibels below even the plainness of her appearance.

Astrid wasn't trying to be unkind. The woman was simply . . . unremarkable. She had hazel eyes and flat brown hair. She was neither tall nor short, not fat nor slender. The most extraordinary thing about her was the spattering of freckles across the bridge of her nose.

"I beg your pardon," Astrid replied. For a moment she thought the woman had said "matchmaker." That just couldn't be. Maybe she had said "hatch maker." Was there something out of leather called the hatch?

Or "latch maker." Harnesses had latches, didn't they?

The woman leaned forward and looked from side to side as if their conversation could be overheard at any moment. "I'm here to see the matchmaker." She hadn't exactly raised her voice, more like she said each word slowly and succinctly. Either way there was no mistaking what she wanted.

A matchmaker.

Astrid shook her head. "I'm sorry. There is no matchmaker here."

"But . . ." The woman's brow wrinkled, and she leaned back as if checking the house numbers. "You're Astrid Kauffman?" It was more question than anything.

Astrid nodded. "That's right."

"I was told that you are a matchmaker."

Astrid propped one hand on her hip and cocked it to the side. "Me?" It wasn't disbelief as much as allowed disruption. She knew what she was doing, recognized it for what it was, though she allowed herself, for the time anyway, to have this distraction. Standing at the front door talking to . . . whoever this was wouldn't put words on the paper, but since words weren't being put on the paper in the first place . . .

The woman looked from side to side again, then leaned close once more. "Can we talk inside?"

On a normal day with normal words flowing, Astrid may have perhaps told the woman no. That she was mistaken. That she needed to be on her way. But today was not a normal day. Normal words were not flowing. And frankly she could use the intrigue. Maybe a little bit of subterfuge could boost her creativity once more.

Astrid stepped back so the woman could enter, then for good measure poked her head out the door and looked both ways. Then she shut the door behind her and motioned toward the sitting room. As they walked toward the space, Astrid caught sight of her computer sitting so mockingly on the dining room table, almost taunting her. Well, she knew how to fix that. She pulled the pocket door closed, then turned back to her guest.

"You have me in a disadvantage," she said.

The woman whirled around to face her. She was plain all right, as plain as they come, but there was a desperation about her that set her apart. Made her seem a little wild, almost unstable. Not in a mental capacity, but as in she might do something totally against her nature. Was that why she wanted to see the matchmaker?

"How's that?" the woman asked.

"You know my name, but I don't know yours."

"Imogene," she said. "Imogene Yoder."

Astrid smiled, hoping she might relax the woman a bit. The poor thing looked as if she'd been laundered with heavy starch. Extra-heavy starch. "It's nice to meet you, Imogene. Will you sit down?" She gestured toward one of the chairs gathered around the fireplace but didn't settle in one herself. "Can I get you something to drink?" she continued. "Water? Coffee? Tea?" *Something stiff the bishop would not approve of*?

Imogene shook her head. She was perched on the edge of the seat, as if at any moment it would become a large mouth and gobble her up.

Astrid decided against fetching something for herself and instead sat down opposite the poor woman. "I suppose you should start at the beginning."

Astrid felt a small stab of conscience that she invited the woman to continue when she truly wasn't a matchmaker. But she told herself that she had informed the woman of that when she first answered the door. She also tried to assuage her attack of morals by telling herself that allowing the woman to have her say might make her realize the folly in her request. A matchmaker was no solution for an Amish woman. Not even one as plain as Imogene Yoder. Love, Astrid had discovered early on in her career, was best left up to God.

"My . . . my husband died," Imogene started.

Astrid set up a little straighter in her seat. Not perhaps where she would've started the story, but it did garner her attention. "Not recently?" Astrid asked.

Imogene shook her head and picked at a spot on her apron. It wasn't a church apron by far, nor was it as worn as the everyday apron Astrid herself had donned that morning. So she was trying to put on a good impression. "About five years ago," Imogene said.

Astrid nodded but didn't speak. It seemed that Imogene had finally gained enough courage to tell her story, and she didn't want to stop her now.

"My boys," Imogene continued. "I have twin boys. They were about five at the time. And then—at the time—they accepted Abner's death. You know, the way we do."

Astrid murmured something that she hoped sounded encouraging and waited for Imogene to continue.

"But lately . . ." She trailed off and allowed her gaze to wander toward the window on her side of the fireplace. There wasn't much on that side of the house, just a large oak tree and a tire swing hanging from one of its lower branches. "Lately they've been asking questions, and when I don't have the answer they want, they've started acting out." She gave Astrid a weak smile. At least Astrid *thought* it was supposed to be a smile. It was truly more of a tremble of her lips that came and went in the blink of an eye.

"They need a firm hand," Astrid said.

Once again, Imogene nodded and picked at an invisible speck on her clothes. "That's right," she quietly agreed. She didn't need to continue for Astrid to realize that Imogene didn't have a firm hand for her twins.

"That's why I need you." Imogene raised those unremarkable hazel eyes to Astrid and pinned her on the spot.

"Me?" Astrid asked before remembering her ruse.

"A matchmaker." It seemed Imogene picked that moment to find her backbone. She stood and gestured grandly at herself. "Look at me," she commanded. "I haven't lived in this body for thirty-four years without knowing how average it is. I don't have good conversation skills. I'm bashful. I'm shy. How I ever got Abner to notice me to begin with I'll never know. I suppose that was all part of God's plan."

The problem was that the rest of God's plan included Abner dying and leaving Imogene to raise twin boys she couldn't handle. Suddenly a small attack of conscience rolled up in Astrid like a storm cloud.

She should tell her right now that she wasn't a matchmaker. She wasn't even married herself and never planned on it. Aside from her career as a romance writer, she was wholly unqualified to help anyone find a mate. Certainly being a romance author was by no means any training for such a feat. In actuality she had complete control over her characters and could direct them as to the right time to say the right thing to make it all fall into place.

Wait . . . that might come in handy.

"Did you have anyone in mind?" she asked Imogene.

The other woman shook her head. "But I need someone strong. Someone who can handle my boys."

"What about love?" Astrid asked.

Imogene Yoder turned a delicate shade of pink and once again lowered her gaze to the fascinating spot of nothing staining her apron. "Love isn't that important."

"Isn't impor—" Astrid pulled herself back. Shouting at the poor woman wouldn't help a thing. "Love is every-thing," she countered quietly.

"Maybe once," Imogene said. "But not any longer."

It was perhaps the saddest thing Astrid had ever heard. The wave of compunction she had felt earlier disappeared in that instant. She would help this woman. She had to help her. "But if you could get love . . ." Astrid prodded.

"We plain girls can't be too picky." Once again Imogene mumbled the words into her lap. "That's why I'm here."

Astrid smiled. "Don't you worry none," she said. "You came to the right place. And I know just the man."

CHAPTER TWO

"You do?" Imogene raised her gaze, those muddy green eyes filling with tears and hope. Mostly hope. But the tears got to Astrid all the same. She was right to do this. Completely and wholly right.

To call it anything other than giving in to distraction would be a terrible misstatement, but thankfully she was the only one calling it anything at all. So there was that.

"Of course." Astrid nodded and stood, silently prompting Imogene to do the same. Poor thing. She really was malleable, and Astrid was instantly glad that Imogene had picked her to serve as matchmaker.

Still, Astrid would like to know who had started such a rumor, but she was thankful, nonetheless. Why, the poor woman could have ended up at Marie Lapp's house instead. Who knew what Paradise Hill's resident busybody would have done with the sadness and despair that Astrid found herself presented with? Marie Lapp might be the wife of their district's preacher, but she conducted herself more like a news reporter, making it her sole purpose to spread whatever she heard to the far corners of their tiny little community.

Imogene smiled then, the first true smile Astrid had seen from her the entire time that she had been sitting in the parlor talking to her lap. "*Danki*," she said. She grabbed Astrid's hand and shook it vigorously. For a moment she looked almost . . . not plain. There was a sparkle in her eye. Maybe hope? "*Danki*, Astrid. I knew I made the right choice to come here."

"Of course," Astrid said, gently extracting her hand from Imogene's.

"Oh." The woman's expression fell. "What do we do now?"

Astrid motioned toward the door. "You go on home, but plan on coming back for church on Sunday. Wear your best church dress," she instructed. "I'll take care of everything else."

"Church?" she asked. "But church is . . . church."

Astrid nodded. Church was a sacred time, but it wasn't like they were going on a date. "I know, but you're just coming to meet him and the rest of the people here in Paradise Hill. It's nothing. So come," she added. "And wear your best church dress. Good impressions and all that."

"Best dress," Imogene parroted as she made her way to the front door with Astrid right behind. "Where's church on Sunday?" she asked, suddenly turning at the door to face Astrid once again.

"Never mind that. Be here at seven on the dot, got it?"

Imogene nodded. "Seven," she repeated.

Astrid opened the door for Imogene, who scuttled out into the bright Indian summer.

"*Danki*," she called again as she hoisted herself into her buggy and started the horse into motion. She waved.

Astrid raised one hand in return as her brother, Jesse, came out of his workshop.

He stared after the departing buggy, wiping his hands on a faded shop towel already stained with the dyes he used for his leathers. "Who was that?"

Astrid shook her head. "Never you mind," she replied. "She's about to be engaged."

Imogene tried to make herself as small as possible as she crossed the line that separated Paradise Hill and Paradise Springs. It was an invisible line usually, though around the time when the *Englisch* high school went back in the fall and let out for the summer, someone—most likely a student or two—painted it in. Sometimes it was blue and sometimes red, depending on which side was responsible, she supposed. No one had ever said for certain. But today it was merely a line on a map drawn by two brothers who both wanted sole control of the area.

It sounded like something from an *Englisch* fairy tale, but the dueling brothers had been Amish, both wanting to lay claim to their father's legacy and neither willing to step aside for the other, a rivalry that lived on to this day.

So it wouldn't do for anyone to notice that her buggy was coming from the side of Paradise Hill. She could always say she got turned around or she was visiting one of the businesses that sat near the border between the towns. But she didn't want to have to answer those questions. She didn't have it in her to lie. Not really, though she was about to tell a doozy.

Imogene kept her head down, her eyes focused on what little bit of the road she could see before her. Just a couple of blocks more and she would be free and clear.

But today's trip had been worth the stress. Already the knot of tension that had been lurking in her shoulders and neck eased. All she had to do now was show up for church in Paradise Hill on Sunday, and Astrid would do the rest.

That knot of tension returned and pulled even tighter than before.

Astrid was positive, self-assured, and firm in her beliefs, but now that Imogene was out of her presence, her own confidence had vanished.

But she could do this, she told herself. She *had* to do this. For the boys.

Matthew and Mahlon were more identical than two people ought to be, even twins born three and a half minutes apart. And they were a constant joy in her life. Until they got it in their heads that they didn't understand why their father had died.

Sometimes Imogene thought they might even blame her for Abner's death. It was an accident. Plain and simple. He had been fishing in the creek. Folks said it looked as if he was trying to cross in a low spot, where the jagged river rocks created a shallow bed. The authorities said it appeared that he had slipped on one of those mossy stones. He hit his head on one of the rocks when he fell and landed facedown, knocked out cold. There had been just enough cool water trickling by to drown him.

The whole town had shaken their heads in disbelief. When they looked at the chances of all the elements that made up his death, a person had to see that it was beyond nature. That it had to have been up to their higher power to save him or not. God's will.

Imogene accepted that. She had been raised to accept that. It didn't mean she liked it. It didn't mean that she mourned him any less. She just accepted that he was gone, leaving her two confused children to raise on her own.

At the time of Abner's death, Matthew and Mahlon had accepted what she had said. Their father was gone, but they would continue. They had nodded and cried and hugged her, and that had been that. But in the days, months, and years that followed, they had begun to ask more questions.

Then this past January, on their tenth birthday, everything went terribly sideways.

She had taken them out for their family supper to the Paradise Chinese Buffet, their favorite place to eat. But they quickly pointed out that they weren't a family since there was no *dat* sitting at their table. Ever since then, they had been almost more than Imogene could handle.

Which was why she hated lying to her aunt and telling her that she had a doctor's appointment and urgently needed someone to watch the boys. Otherwise . . . well, in the last nine, almost ten, months she had pretty much run through all her available sitters. The boys had ruined their chances of being cared for by most all of their immediate family members. Right now, her aunt was the last before Imogene would have to start in on the string of seconds cousins.

She pulled her buggy into the drive at her aunt's house. Kaye Schrock was her mother's sister and had been such a blessing to Imogene after Abner had passed. The best thing about Kaye . . . she had the patience of a saint. Another reason why Imogene had waited this long to bring the boys over for the day. Imogene needed that "ace in the hole," as the card players said. She had a little idea of what it meant in reality, but for her it meant someone to watch Matthew and Mahlon when an emergency came up. And today was an emergency. Just not in the way Imogene had led her aunt to believe.

She secured the reins to the hitching post near Kaye's porch and made her way up the steps to the front door. She pushed her way inside and stopped in her tracks.

What had happened here?

The cushions were off the couch. The quilt that her aunt normally kept tossed across the back of it was strung between the nearby armchair and the wooden rocker that sat next to the fireplace. Newspapers were scattered about. Or maybe it was simply one newspaper in many different pieces. A bowl of soggy cereal and milk peeked out from under the coffee table, and twin juice boxes sat in sticky-looking puddles next to the pottery bowl of nuts her aunt kept in the center of the coffee table. And the shells! Everywhere. The hulls and bitters had been sprinkled across the room as if someone had tossed them about like confetti. That was the only way to describe it.

She stopped. Sighed. She didn't need to ask what happened. Truthfully, she already knew.

But where were the boys? Where was her aunt? For all the mess scattered around, the house was strangely quiet.

Imogene resisted the urge to straighten up the mess and instead squared her shoulders and marched toward the kitchen. But there was no one in there either. Just another disaster that had Matthew and Mahlon written all over it. Dish towels on the floor and a puddle of water near the sink, but nowhere near the towels. Dishes were piled high on the counter, and a sludge of dirty gray water filled both sides of the double sink. Little bits of carrots and corn and something green floated around in the yucky-looking water along with something in dingy white that appeared to be some sort of fabric. Or perhaps paper.

"What in the world?" Imogene muttered to herself, not wanting to believe her eyes. *Jah*, the boys had been a handful for the last few months, but this . . . this was the worst she had seen yet!

She sidestepped the puddle, avoided the mound of dish towels, and headed toward the back door. The house was too quiet for them to be inside. Way too quiet. She could even hear the tick of her aunt's grandfather clock.

Out on the screened-in porch her aunt's washing machine squatted next to a stack of wood that was used to heat the water when necessary. Thankfully, nothing on the porch appeared to be in such chaos as the rest of the house. That small fact gave her a little bit of hope.

But only a bit.

Neither her aunt nor her sons were on the porch, but from there Imogene could hear them in the backyard. Not her aunt, just the boys, hollering like banshees. Just two more steps and she could see them through the screen-enclosed porch, still bellowing like something crazed and running around in a circle so small she couldn't tell who was chasing who. Each held a stick high in the air as they ran and whooped and hollered.

Kaye, bless her heart, was sitting underneath the large oak tree. She was propped up against the trunk, legs tucked underneath her. Poor thing! She looked absolutely exhausted. She must've been watching for Imogene, for the moment she saw her, Kaye was on her feet in an instant.

"Imogene!" The relief in her voice was so thick you could have cut it with a knife. An uncomfortable chuckle escaped Kaye as she dusted off her skirt. "You're here." From her tone, Imogene suspected that Kaye was beginning to believe she was never coming back.

Goodness! Had the boys been that bad? "I'm here," Imogene assured her.

When they heard her voice the boys stopped running in their circle and instead ran to her. "Mamm! Mamm! Mamm!" They jumped all around her talking at once about two different things, so she heard only words and no meaning. They held their sticks at their sides as they danced around her.

She tried to hug their squirming bodies but didn't succeed.

"Are they always so . . . spirited?" Kaye asked as she approached. "I don't remember them being this . . . active."

"Did you give them a lot of sugar?" Imogene asked. She hated the hopeful note in her voice. Sugar definitely wound them up. Or rather too much of it. "Or red drinks. I read this story in a magazine at the doctor's office that red drinks can make kids a little antsy." Though she hadn't tested that theory yet. It was on her list of things to see about.

"I gave them fruit punch," Kaye said. "I didn't know."

Imogene nearly wilted in relief. If she could blame the red drink and sugar for the boys' behavior, she might just get Kaye to babysit again. If she was going to start dating—if Astrid's efforts proved fruitful, and she prayed that they did—she would be needing a sitter some. At least more than she did now. "It's all right, Kaye." She smiled apologetically toward her aunt. "You didn't know, but," she said, shushing her boys, who remarkably responded by jumping a little less and being not quite as loud. "We cannot leave Kaye to clean up the mess you made in her house. So get yourself together and let's go take care of that."

"Aw," the boys said in unison. It was a little unnerving when they did things like that, but Imogene was becoming accustomed to it.

"Go on," Imogene said, silently praying that they would obey. It was always a surprise, the times they decided to do as she asked and the times when they didn't.

They dragged their feet and their sticks as they trudged toward the back door.

Imogene said a silent thanks, then turned her attention back to her aunt. "I'll go help them." Which was basically code for *I'll go do it while they stand around and tickle each other.* But she had got them to the house and that was something. Today was a good day.

"How was your doctor's appointment?" Kaye asked.

The women turned and started toward the house.

"Doctor—" Imogene stopped herself in time. "It was good. Just a sore throat, nothing more."

"I thought you were having problems with allergies," Kaye commented.

"Oh. Yes, that's right. Allergies. But the allergies were causing my sore throat."

Kaye nodded understandingly, and Imogene breathed a small sigh of relief. It would've been larger, but she didn't want to alert Kaye. And that knot of tension dug itself a little deeper.

Not surprisingly, the boys weren't cleaning up the mess in the kitchen. They were more like rearranging it. If she wasn't mistaken the puddle of water seemed to have grown to twice the size it had been when she stepped over it earlier.

The boys were on their knees, acting like the wadded-up paper towels in their hands were race cars, zooming through the puddle and barely soaking up any of the water as they whizzed by. They were laughing and giggling and crashing into each other.

"That is not how we do things," Imogene said using her most firm *mamm* voice.

"I'll just go—" Kaye said, and slipped past them and into the other room.

But Imogene had her attention trained on Matthew and Mahlon.

The boys straightened up a bit, but it still took Imogene a good fifteen minutes to clean up the mess they had made in the kitchen. Mainly because they kept remaking messes as quick as she could clean one up. She knew that it was a perfect opportunity to work with them on responsibility and minding, and she would have, if they'd been at home. Right now, she just wanted to get her kids out of the house before something disastrous happened.

Once the kitchen was clean, she turned the boys toward the living room and marched them out. One more mess and then everything would be taken care of.

But when they entered the living room, the mess had been cleared away.

"Kaye," Imogene started, "you didn't have to do that. The boys should have cleaned that up."

Kaye smiled gently, tiredly. "That's all right. There was more than enough to do in the kitchen."

Imogene was certain that was code for *I really need them to go home now.* It was disheartening to say the least.

She placed one hand on each of the boys' shoulders and gave them a small nudge. "Thank your aunt for taking care of you today while I went to the doctor."

"*Danki*, Kaye, for taking care of us while our *mamm* went to the doctor." There went that unison thing again.

"Now go get in the buggy," she told them.

They ran toward the doors as if the floor were made of hot coals and hurried out the door. It slammed behind them, and Kaye started a bit with the noise. Imogene had expected it and braced herself for its coming.

"I'm sor—" Imogene stopped herself from apologizing. She shouldn't do that. If she continued to apologize, every-one would know that something was wrong. "I mean, thank you for watching them today. I hope they weren't too much trouble. You know boys."

Her aunt smiled and nodded. "*Jah*." But that was all she said.

Imogene made her way out to her buggy, sucking in a fortifying breath with each step she took. The carriage was rocking on its axles, the boys no doubt engaged in some sort of horseplay. They were rowdy and growing rowdier by the day.

At least she had a plan.

The matchmaker of Paradise Hill would surely be able to solve the problem. Then once Imogene was married and had a husband to help with her boys, everything would be a whole lot better.

She hoped anyway.

CHAPTER THREE

And there he was.

Astrid peered over the paint cans perched on the shelf in front of her. She was just tall enough to see across the top of them to the handsome man behind the big wooden counter. Ira Oberholtzer.

And handsome he was. See, Astrid knew handsome. After all, she was a romance writer.

Jah . . . handsome. His neatly trimmed dark beard was just beginning to show signs of gray, as was his raven hair. What she could see of it anyway. It curled around his ears and under the brim of his straw hat. By romance author standards he appeared fit. No middle-age paunch stretching out the dark caramel-tinted fabric of his apron that protected his regular clothes—a sky-blue button-down shirt and midnight-colored pants. His beard couldn't hide the dimples that slashed down each cheek, and his blue, blue eyes sparkled as he talked to the customer he was helping.

Jah. He was perfect. For Imogene, of course. Astrid herself wasn't interested in getting married. This was for Imogene, and for Astrid's own career. All she had to do was plant a couple of seeds in Ira's mind, set him on course, and stand back while love worked its magic.

She waited until he finished with the customer before casually heading around the aisle with the paint cans.

He caught sight of her and smiled. "Can I help you?"

Handsome and kind. He was more perfect than she had originally thought. Not that looks were something to focus on solely. Everyone knew what was on the inside counted far more than looks, but it didn't hurt to have a pretty face to see every day. Everyone knew that as well.

"Uh, *jah*." Astrid returned his smile and searched her brain for what he could help her with. Why hadn't she come up with an excuse before she walked into the hardware store? "My brother and I recently moved into a new house," she started. "And I'm thinking about having a room built onto the back."

At least that part was true. She had been thinking about building some sort of enclosed porch where she could concentrate and write. Someplace better than the dining room table. "What do you think about that?"

He blinked at her and for a split second she wondered if he spoke English. Maybe she should switch to Dutch. Wait. He had spoken English just a moment before.

"I don't know much about building rooms," he finally said. "I'm more of a handyman, fix-it kind of guy."

There was a difference?

Astrid had no idea. She just wanted to strike up a conversation with the man and hopefully drop some hints about Imogene. "Oh. I see."

"You got a leaky sink," he started, "I can fix that. But building something brand-new . . . Well, I might do something like that for a friend or myself, but I wouldn't tackle it for someone else. You'll have to call a contractor for that."

"Oh. I see." Now she seemed simple. "Okay. Thank you." She turned and made her way down the main aisle to the exit doors of Hill Hardware.

"I have a few numbers of people if you want them," he called after her.

She turned before leaving and shot him the brightest smile she could muster. "I'll give it some thought." Then she waved and made her way into the still-bright, late-summer sun.

She had sounded so dumb. She'd thought she was prepared to come in and talk to Ira Oberholtzer. But she had been wrong. Very wrong.

Astrid untied her horse from the hitching post and climbed into her buggy. With the flick of her reins, she started for home.

So she hadn't actually introduced the idea of love or even Imogene Yoder to Ira. Nor had she got him to thinking about Imogene, but that didn't mean that today's scouting expedition was a total bust. She had found out some good information. Or so she told herself.

First of all, Ira was honest. He didn't try to smooth her over or wheedle his way into building a sunroom for her.

Some would say, *Of course he's honest. He should be. He is Amish, after all.* But not all Amish men were honest. Heaven knew, every nice and quiet Amish community had their share of rogues. Even Paradise Hill. But as far as Astrid was concerned, Ira Oberholtzer's honesty was definitely a plus.

And he was handy. Even if he wouldn't build a screened-in porch onto the back of her house, a porch that only in the last couple of days had started to be in her plans. And not just because of Ira Oberholtzer. She really could use the space to write. One place that was hers where she could go and clear her head, stop and think without distraction. Where maybe the ideas would return.

But until then she had a plot. A brand-new plot to take a young widow and a handsome business owner and make them fall in love. And for now that would have to be enough.

Ira dragged his feet a bit as he tromped up onto the porch and let himself into his house. He was tired, bone-tired, after a long day at work. In fact, it had been something of a week at work.

"Elam?" he called, shutting the door behind himself. "Elam?" He knew his son was home. His buggy was still parked outside.

A muffled voice floated in from somewhere upstairs, then Elam appeared on the landing. "Hey, Dat. You're home."

Ira chuckled. "I am." Home and tired. "Hey, why don't we go get some alfredo pizza tonight?"

All the meals that his daughter, Ruthie, had prepared before she moved out were long gone, and Ira was a little tired of coming home after a ten- or twelve-hour workday and cooking. Not that he really minded cooking. Tired was tired.

He got it now. Most widowers remarried in order to keep their houses running smoothly, but when his Ruthann died, Ira had Ruthie to step in and run things. Except now Ruthie was married and no doubt planning for a family of her own, which left Ira stuck with cooking. It was surely a chore he couldn't trust sixteen-year-old Elam to perform. Not if he wanted something edible.

Truthfully, pizza was way down low on his list of

favorite things to eat, but Elam loved it. Even the chicken alfredo style that Ira had to eat since he was allergic to tomatoes.

"I can't tonight," Elam replied. "A bunch of us are going over to get pizza and hang out."

Of course, Ira thought. It was a Friday night. Elam was sixteen and just beginning to start running around. Of course he had plans with his friends.

Perhaps Elam sensed something in Ira's demeanor for he paused. "I mean, I can go with you. If you really want me to."

That was when Ira noticed Elam had on his best shirt. His hair was freshly washed and the tiny nick on his chin still had a small scrap of toilet paper stuck to it to keep it from bleeding. Must be a girl involved. Or maybe it was enough to have merely the idea of girls.

Ira shook his head. "That's all right. You go on with your friends, son. Have a good time."

Elam grinned widely. "I will."

Ira waved him away and Elam disappeared back to his bedroom, no doubt to finish getting ready for his big night.

Ira walked into the living room and eased down into his favorite armchair. He removed his shoes, stretching his toes in tired satisfaction.

So no pizza with Elam tonight. Which meant Ira would have to go into the kitchen to find his own meal. He just wasn't sure what.

He sat his shoes to one side of his chair and stood, his knees popping a little with the motion. Then he made his way into the kitchen.

Supper, he thought, opening the refrigerator and peering inside. Nothing elaborate. Just something to fill the hole and get him through till breakfast tomorrow.

"Dat, I'm going," Elam called, but the door shut behind him before Ira could even respond.

"Bye," Ira said to the empty house.

He pulled the ham from the refrigerator. It was about the only thing he did know how to cook and only because Ruthann had taught him one day. He couldn't remember why, but she had. According to his late wife the best way to cook a ham was put it in a pot, pour a Coca-Cola over it, and let it bake. Simple and good. But honestly, he was growing tired of ham to the point that even pizza would've been a nice change.

Ira tried not to sigh as he grabbed the package of white bread from the top of the fridge, the mayonnaise and lettuce from inside it, and the salt and pepper off the kitchen table. A couple of his daughter's pickles on the side and he had himself a dinner.

Ira cleaned up his mess and carried his sandwich into the living room. Normally, he ate at the table and only at the table. But normally, he had a family to eat with. Now as the years were passing, his family members were disappearing on him. First Ruthann died, then Ruthie got married, now Elam was running around.

And Ira was alone.

He sat back down in his favorite chair, balancing the plate holding his sandwich on one of the large, cushioned arms. Thoughtfully he took a bite and chewed, amazed at how loud the action sounded. Or maybe it was just how quiet the house seemed. And the house was quiet.

It was September and though it was after seven and still light outside, Ira knew that wouldn't last for much longer. Soon fall would truly be upon them. After that, the short winter days.

The tick of the clock seemed to echo around him. The sound of him eating seemed to mock him.

Chew, chew, chew. Tick, tick, tick.

Had the house always been this quiet and he just hadn't noticed it before?

Had the quiet always been there under the noise, just waiting to resurface? For now there was no end in sight. Ruthie was gone and married. Elam would run around and get married himself, and the home that Ira and Ruthann had built would grow steadily quieter. It was not something he was looking forward to. Yet what choice did he have now but to accept it?

"Do we have to?" Matthew's voice was set to an annoying whine.

"*Jah*," Imogene said. She knelt down in front of the boys and started tucking their shirts into their waistbands and straightening their suspender straps.

"It's not fair." Mahlon joined his brother in the protest. "We just went to church last week."

"*Jah*," Imogene said. "But an extra dose of the Lord's word won't do you any harm." *With any luck it might do some good,* Imogene thought. But she didn't say the words out loud.

The truth was she couldn't find anyone to take care of the boys today. Most folks were out visiting, getting in those last family picnics and such before the weather started to cool too much. And with all this visiting, no one wanted to drag around her misbehaving boys. So they would just have to go to church.

"I've already explained it to you twice. We're going to church with my friend today."

"If it's your friend, why do we have to go?" Mahlon asked, not that Imogene had an answer beyond _because I said so_.

"It's not f—"

"A lot of things in life aren't fair," Imogene broke in before Matthew could finish taking up his brother's argument. "But you should be thankful for a beautiful day to go to church on."

The argument of weather was a moot one as far as the boys were concerned. Rain or shine they were out playing. It didn't matter to them. But after the rain yesterday Imogene was thankful for the sunshine.

She licked her thumb and rubbed at a spot on Matthew's cheek. The boys had just come from the bathroom after washing their faces. Yet they always seemed to need a little touch-up.

"Now," she said. "Go get on your shoes. It's almost time to leave."

Their protest rose anew, but Imogene shook her head and pointed in the direction of the living room, where she had set out their shoes earlier. "Go now or there will be no dessert for the rest of the week."

They stopped for a moment as if gauging whether she was serious or not. But this was dessert they were talking about, and both boys had a large sweet tooth. Unfortunately, it was about the only leverage that Imogene had. Once it was exhausted, getting them to do as she asked was almost impossible. Thankfully, this time they took her at her word and trudged into the living room to don their shoes.

With the boys set to their task, Imogene ducked into the downstairs bathroom, the only place in the house where she had a full-length mirror. It was on the back of the door, so she shut it, blocking any view of herself. Good thing, she didn't want them to see her staring critically at her reflection. They were only ten, but they asked questions. A lot of questions that had led them to where they currently were—them wanting to know more about their father and his death. More importantly, why he had died. And why he'd had to die when he did.

Imogene turned this way and that, looking at herself with new vision. She looked okay, she supposed, but not fantastic. She wanted to look fantastic, but when you were widowed, it was so easy to let things slide. She hadn't made a new dress for herself in months. Maybe even longer.

The light blue frock she wore was her best church dress. But in truth that wasn't saying a whole lot. She really needed to take a little time and make herself a new dress for church. Especially since . . . she peered down at the bottom of her apron. There was a tiny tear. She hadn't noticed it before. How had she not noticed it before?

Imogene sighed. It was too late to change now, though she was certain her green dress had a stain on it. She had dropped a pickled beet in her lap last service, and the purple smudge it left was proving impossible to remove.

Jah. This week. She needed to . . . somehow. Somehow between work and her home duties, between taking care of the boys, keeping them out of trouble, and keeping them clothed and fed and trying to start a new relationship, she needed to make herself a new dress. Somehow. She owed it to herself.

Until then, it was a tiny tear and surely no one would notice it.

She sighed again and focused her attention on her face.

It wasn't a bad face, but it wasn't a memorable face either. What would this new man think about her face?

She was under no illusion concerning her attractiveness to men. Her entire life she had been plain. She had never had any other suitor. Just Abner. Abner Yoder had been her one true love. The one man who loved her and knew her above all else. The one had she had mistakenly dreamed she would grow old with.

Truly, she wasn't looking forward to going out on dates. She wasn't even going to pretend she wanted to fall in love. She needed a man to help her with life's chores. She just hoped this man would accept her how she was.

"Mamm!" Mahlon called from the other room. "Mattie just picked his nose and wiped it on my pants."

Another sigh escaped her lips. "I'm coming," she called in return, pausing only long enough to grab a washrag and wet it.

All of them, she silently amended. She hoped this man accepted them for who they all were. Boogers and all.

"Where have you been?" Astrid rushed up to Imogene before she even got out of her buggy. They were already fifteen minutes late. It was impossible to make up time in a horse and carriage, especially on Sunday morning.

Imogene looked near tears, and Astrid immediately regretted her harsh tone. She didn't mean to be mean, just urgent.

"Mattie wiped something on Mahlon and he retaliated by elbowing Mattie in the nose and he started bleeding so we had to change his shirt." The three sentences came out on one long gush of air.

"Never mind all that," Astrid said with a quick flick of

her hand, then she swung herself into the buggy and patted the side. "Let's go."

They sat there for a moment more. Then Astrid slapped her hand against the side of the buggy once again. "Come on."

Imogene took up the reins and started the horse in motion.

"Turn left up here," Astrid directed. "At the end of the drive. Is that what you're wearing?"

The woman sitting next to her looked down at herself and back up to Astrid. "*Jah*, it's what I'm wearing."

Astrid shook her head but managed not to tsk.

Note to self: Have Imogene Yoder get a new dress.

It wasn't that her dress was *bad*. It just wasn't *good*. Astrid needed everything to be tip-top. This was an important day.

Of course, everything would be a whole lot better if they were on time. Astrid had wanted Imogene to meet Ira before church. That way he could have the entire service to look across at her and think about her. And God. It was church after all. But she wanted to get those seeds planted. The seeds she hadn't been able to plant on her trip to the hardware store. But at the rate they were going now, they would get there just in time to walk in the doors. Possibly even the last ones to enter the service.

"I'm nervous," Imogene said.

Astrid smiled confidently. It was a confidence she didn't quite feel. But she could make this happen. She was going to make this happen. Then she was going to write about it. "There's nothing to worry about," she lied. "Ira is just going to love you."

Imogene shushed her, then cut her eyes to the back of the buggy. "Not so loud."

Astrid turned her attention to the two boys sitting behind them, then looked back to Imogene. "They don't know?"

Imogene shook her head.

"Surely you need to tell them," Astrid replied.

"There's nothing to tell yet."

Astrid smiled once again with a confidence she pulled from thin air. "Not yet," she said. "But soon. Soon, there will be a lot to tell."

CHAPTER FOUR

"Don't leave me," Imogene whispered to Astrid, then clutched her hand so tight, Astrid thought her fingers might snap.

She patted Imogene on the hand and extracted her own from that tight grasp. "I'm not going to leave you."

But Imogene was already on to something else. She rushed ahead and grabbed both boys before they splashed in one of the nearby puddles. Yesterday's rain had left everything soaked, including the yard in front of the Lapps' barn, where church was to be held this morning.

"But, Mamm," one of the boys protested.

Suddenly it all became clear to Astrid. Why would two ten-year-old boys willingly go to church on a Sunday that wasn't their church Sunday? God's word might be golden, but sitting on a bench for three hours and listening to grown-ups talk was surely not on their agenda of the best ways to spend time.

"Ice cream," Imogene said, the words desperate. "I'll take you for ice cream tomorrow."

"Promise?" the second boy asked.

"Promise," Imogene said. "But you must be on your best behavior today. *Best*," she emphasized.

The boys nodded in unison, and Astrid had to wonder if that was an identical twin thing. Jesse was her twin, but they didn't seem to have near as much in common as these two rascals. And as cute as they were, Astrid could see the light of mischief in their eyes, there with the slash of pain and all the questions they held back.

She couldn't blame them for having those questions. She had her own share, and she wasn't nearly as young when her and Jesse's parents had been killed. They had been orphaned with one turn of the wheel. A horrible accident between a buggy and a truck. When those two meet, the truck always wins.

Imogene let go of the boys' arms, and they took off toward the door of the barn. Astrid figured they were just following the crowd, but they screeched to a halt before entering the large, wide doors. Instead of slipping inside, they waited for their *mamm* and Astrid to catch up to them.

"Do we have to sit with you?" one of them asked.

Surely, there was a way to tell them apart, though Astrid hadn't even been formally introduced to them. In fact, she wasn't even sure Imogene had mentioned their names. On the way over here, they had talked about nothing save Ira and what Imogene could expect from church.

"Who else do you know to sit with?" Imogene asked, stopping next to them.

"Does it matter?" one twin asked.

"It matters very much," Imogene said. "You need to sit with someone to help you pay attention in the service, and since you don't know anyone on the men's side, you may not sit there."

The boys looked as if they were about to wind back up to another fit, but before they could successfully launch it, Jesse came out of the barn.

"Astrid," he said. "It's about time you got here." He looked from his sister to Imogene. "Hey," he said before turning his attention back to Astrid. "What are you doing?"

Astrid gave him her best bland, *I know nothing* smile. "I'm going to church."

Jesse cut his eyes back toward Imogene and the twins. "No. What are you *doing*?"

"Imogene, this is my brother, Jesse."

Imogene nodded at him nervously. "I'm pleased to meet you. This is Mattie and Mahlon."

Jesse nodded toward the three of them. "It's a pleasure."

"We can sit with you," one of the boys said. Astrid thought it was Mahlon.

"No," Imogene said. But her voice wasn't very strong, and Astrid had a feeling what was coming next.

"Why not?" the same boy asked.

"Because I said so." But again her voice was weak. Or maybe just tired.

"You said we could sit with someone that we know on the men's side. We know Jesse now." Mattie, she thought the twin was. Short for Matthew? Probably.

"Astrid, we need to go in."

Astrid waved him away. She needed to get Imogene and the twins inside first. They couldn't very well stay outside the barn while church was being held and try to meet up with Ira later. No, she needed Imogene in the church service where Ira could see her. Even if Astrid hadn't been able to introduce them beforehand.

"You can't sit with Jesse," Imogene said. "You just met him."

"*Jah*," Mahlon said. "So now we know him."

"It's time to go inside," Imogene said. She gestured toward

the big barn doors, but Mattie and Mahlon seemed prepared to stay right where they were until they got their way.

"That's not fair," Mattie said.

This was taking way too long.

Astrid turned to Jesse. She didn't even have to say the words.

"Are you serious?" Jesse asked.

"Just for today," Astrid replied.

"I don't know if that's a good idea," Imogene interjected.

"I don't understand—" Jesse started.

But Astrid cut him off. "I'll explain everything later. Now will you just—" She nodded toward the boys.

"Are you sure they'll be okay?" Imogene asked.

"They'll be fine," Astrid assured her. And they would be. Jesse was a responsible man. He might not have children of his own, but all the kids loved him.

Jesse sighed and shot Astrid that *you owe me* look. Then he gestured toward the doors. "Let's go, boys."

"Awesome," they said in unison, then hustled into the barn.

"If you're sure," Imogene mumbled.

Jesse continued to stare at Astrid for a moment more before heading inside himself.

"Remember what I said," Imogene called behind the boys.

Astrid motioned for Imogene to head inside as well. "Now," she started, "Ira usually sits on the third row on the left-hand side."

"Ira?" Imogene said. "That's his name? Ira?"

"Ira Oberholtzer. I'll introduce you after church. If we had gotten here sooner . . ."

"I know," she said. "I'm sorry." Imogene ducked her

head as they slipped into two of the last spaces left on the women's side.

The whole row had to shuffle a bit to make room for them to sit together, but thankfully they made it in time. As the service started and they sang the first song, Astrid could see Imogene straining to get a good look at the man on the other side.

"That's him?" Imogene whispered.

Astrid glanced over. Not only was Ira Oberholtzer sitting in his normal spot; Jesse and the twins had settled down next to him. "*Jah.*"

"He's . . ." Imogene stuttered, and all at once Astrid was extremely pleased with herself. She had hit a home run with this one.

"Handsome?" Astrid supplied in a hushed whisper.

"Kind of old," Imogene whispered in return.

"What?" This time she'd forgotten to be quiet and drew looks from several ladies sitting around them. Astrid murmured an apology and tried to figure out what in the world Imogene was talking about. Ira Oberholtzer was not old.

But Benny Schrock was. As old as the hills. And he was sitting in third row on the right. Or his left.

"Our left," Astrid whispered. "Not his left."

"Oh," Imogene said, then shifted her attention to the left. "Oh," she said again, but this time the exclamation held a different tone. One of appreciation.

That made Astrid even more pleased with herself. Why hadn't she thought of this sooner? She spent so much time planning out her books, plotting each step from meeting to the end. It seemed so much simpler to introduce two people and let nature do the rest. All she had to do was record her findings. Which made her like some sort of love scientist.

"Ira Oberholtzer," Imogene whispered beside her.

Love scientist, Astrid repeated to herself. She liked that. She liked that a lot.

It might've been the longest three hours of her life, Imogene thought, but finally the last song was sung, the last prayer was given, and they were dismissed to set up for their meal.

It wasn't that she didn't enjoy the service, but it was hard to have her boys across from her with a man who was basically a stranger. And Mattie and Mahlon had been so unpredictable lately. They knew better than to act up during church, but what they knew and how they had been acting lately . . . well, she figured it was only a matter of time before that impertinence leaked out into every part of their lives. So she had spent the service worried about them and silently praying that they would behave themselves until the final prayer.

As a visitor, she wasn't expected to help set up and serve, but since she knew hardly anyone else in the district, she stood by Astrid, waiting for her time to go and meet Ira Oberholtzer. What a fine name that was.

It had been such a tense morning, forcing the boys to go to church on what they considered their off Sunday, then driving to town and hoping no one noticed she was riding around in her church clothes. If she'd had to stop somewhere in Paradise Springs, how would she have explained that?

But all that stress was about to pay off. She nibbled at a piece of bread smeared liberally with peanut butter spread and cup cheese. Her appetite had completely disappeared. She knew it was nerves. She also knew she didn't need to end up with a headache, so she did her best, even though her stomach felt like every bite was fluttering inside.

"Everything will go fine."

Imogene jumped as Astrid appeared beside her. "I . . . I know." Well, she wished she knew. But still, she was trying to be positive.

"Here's what we're going to do," Astrid said. "I'm going to take you around to meet some of the people who live here, then we're going to go up to Jesse. He's going to be talking to Ira, so I will introduce you then. That way it won't look suspicious and you get to meet him."

"Jesse is okay with this?" Imogene asked. She didn't know why she asked. It just seemed sort of presumptuous. Maybe Astrid had worked all this out with her brother beforehand. But considering the look on his face before they walked inside the barn this morning, she wasn't quite sure.

"Just follow my lead," Astrid said.

Which left Imogene no choice but to go along.

Ira was only half listening as Amon Zook told a story about a playhouse he was building for Harry Simonson, Mayor of Paradise Hill. Mayor Simonson, it seemed, had a granddaughter with an affinity for lavender. The entire house had been painted in varying shades of purple.

"I don't know what it was about that paint," Amon continued, "but I cannot get it off my fingernails." He held out his hands as if in proof.

The men standing around all laughed at the state of Amon's nails. Each one looked as if it had been painted by one of the girls who worked at In the Hills Nails and Spa, that fancy women's fixer-upper place off Main.

Ira chuckled as well, though his mind was on that woman. Astrid Kauffman. He never paid much attention to her before, and yet he had noticed her today. She'd been standing with another woman he didn't recognize, a woman he was pretty sure he had never seen before. A visitor from some other district, he presumed.

As far as he knew, Astrid had lived in Paradise Hill most of her life. He never thought about it much. He'd never thought about *her* much. Not until she had appeared in his hardware store, peering over the cans of paint and talking about building an enclosed porch onto the back of her house. Maybe that was the reason why he was thinking about her now.

There was something about her that drew his attention, and he couldn't figure out what it was. Just didn't make sense. Why would she think he would know how to build a sunroom onto her house? Why was he even thinking about doing it? He told her that he would do it for himself or a friend. She was neither. Well, of course she wasn't him, and he really couldn't say she was a friend. Not an enemy, but not a friend. Yet he found himself thinking about her back porch and how he would design it if he were to build it.

Maybe it was just because things had been slow at the hardware store these last couple of weeks. It always happened this time of the year. Everyone was winding up their summer stuff, so there were no more emergency lawn mower purchases or cutting tools for trees and bushes. Most all that had already been done. It wasn't quite time yet to gear up for fall and cover those tender bulbs to help them last through the Missouri cold. In these slow, in-between times when there were no customers in Hill Hardware, he found himself drawing a diagram of the perfect porch.

"Hey, Jesse," Amon said.

Ira looked up as Jesse Kauffman joined the group.

Jesse nodded in return greeting.

Funny how Ira had just been thinking about his sister and the man appeared.

"So I hear you're building a porch," Ira said.

Jesse blinked at him blankly. "I'm building a porch?" He gestured to himself as if to make sure of Ira's words.

"Not you," Ira amended. "But your sister. Astrid. She came into the hardware store and asked me about building some kind of sunporch or such onto the back of your house."

"That's the first time I've—" Jesse stopped. "Astrid's always into something," he said.

Ira wasn't sure what to make of that. He was fairly certain Jesse had no idea his sister was planning to build a porch. Now he just hoped he hadn't ruined some sort of surprise that she was planning to give her brother. But if the gift was a porch, it would have to be built, so it couldn't be a *huge* surprise. At any rate, Ira hoped he hadn't ruined it.

He chuckled in an attempt to make light of the situation. Instead it just sounded uncomfortable, so he nodded his head. "She seems like that."

Now, why had he said that?

Because you spent half the church service staring in her direction. Staring at her.

If it sounded unusual to anyone else in the circle, no one said. Instead Jesse turned to Chris Lapp, the owner of the property where they now stood.

Chris was perhaps one of the oldest people in their

district. Definitely the oldest who still lived on his own property. He and his wife had only had two children and they'd had them young. Both children had gone on to buy farms in the area, leaving Chris to farm his until the time when he got simply too old to do it. By then he was a widower. He still owned the farmland, but he leased it now and let the others do the work.

From time to time, though, Ira would come out and check on things, porch railings and such, just to make sure the old man was safe. He knew others did as well and his children came when they could, but their property was on the far side of Paradise Hills almost into the Springs. It was a good jog on any day and couldn't be made quickly.

"Me and Samuel Raber were talking," Jesse started, directing his words toward their host. "We're going to go this week and get a wagonload of dirt and come out here and fill in these holes."

Chris smacked his gums and looked around at the huge divots that cratered his front drive. There actually seemed to be more puddles than dry places to drive. It wasn't too bad when you were in a buggy, but it was harder to pick your way through if you were just walking around, which was exactly what the church district was doing. The holes probably should've been filled long ago, but since church was held at each house only about one time a year, if someone hadn't been out to the house, they wouldn't know. Chris wasn't the kind who came looking for help. It just wasn't his way.

"I would appreciate that," Chris said with a nod. He stroked his beard, his long, gnarled fingers smoothing the wiry gray strands. Chris was old-school, proven by the fact that his beard nearly reached to the third button on his shirt.

Ira wasn't certain he would get used to something like that if he allowed his own beard to grow. If his got too much past his chin, he got concerned that he would be walking around wearing his lunch. That alone was worth risking the bishop fussing at him about trimming it.

"If you need some help," Ira started. "I'd be happy to."

Jesse nodded. "We could always use a hand."

"I happen to have a couple of bags of dirt that I can add into the mix if you'd like. When they come in and bust open, it's hard to move them around in the store. We set them around back and wait for things like this."

"That would be great," Jesse said. He looked over Ira's shoulder as if waiting for something or looking for someone.

Ira returned and glanced in that direction. Astrid and the lady she'd been sitting with during the church service were approaching. As they drew nearer, Ira felt like the woman looked vaguely familiar. He and Elam used to sneak across into Paradise Springs every so often and eat at the Chinese food buffet there. It was about the only place he visited when in Paradise Springs, and he wondered if perhaps she worked there. A couple of Amish women did, though he had never paid them much mind. Or maybe he was just thinking she was familiar because he had seen her in church.

"There's Astrid," Jesse said unnecessarily.

Ira nodded.

Astrid arrived at their little group deftly jumping over a puddle and landing squarely in front of Ira. "Hi," she said by way of greeting. "I have someone I want you to meet." She gestured back to where the woman was doing her best to pick her way through the puddles of water standing on the drive.

She was just about to step over the largest one when a voice rang out.

"Mamm!" It must've been her child who called, for she turned around and in doing so slipped and fell face-first into the puddle.

CHAPTER FIVE

"Imogene, sweetheart, you need to stop crying."

Astrid had lost count of how many times she said those words on the trip from Chris Lapp's back to her farm, and frankly she was starting to get concerned. She didn't know this meeting had meant that much to Imogene.

After Imogene had literally fallen at Ira Oberholtzer's feet, Astrid and Jesse had helped her up and bustled her over to her carriage. Imogene had cried and cried while Jesse had rounded up the twins and stashed them in the back of his carriage. With Jesse driving the boys home, Astrid was left to drive Imogene's buggy and soothe the woman as best she could.

"It's ruined," Imogene responded. She used the back of one hand to wipe the tears still streaming down her face. But since her hand was dirty and her face was dirty, all she did was transfer mud from one spot to another. Poor thing! She really was a mess.

"At least it was memorable." She shot Imogene an apologetic smile. "Next time you see each other, he'll definitely know who you are."

Imogene's lower lip trembled, and Astrid was afraid she

was about to burst into sobbing tears once again. "There's not going to be a next time."

"Why not?"

"Are you serious?" Imogene wailed. "I go to meet him, and I fall in a mud puddle? What could be worse than that?"

Astrid shrugged one shoulder. "A lot of things."

"No," Imogene started, pulling herself together a bit more and only sniffing from time to time. "It's ruined now."

"Why, that's the silliest thing I've ever heard. You still think he's worthy, don't you?"

"*Jah*." Imogene sniffed again.

"I can tell you he's a good man," Astrid continued. "You can't just give up because the first time you tried wasn't successful. Life isn't like a romance novel."

"But I can," Imogene said. "And I am." The tone she used was forceful. For her, anyway. But Astrid wasn't giving up even if Imogene *thought* she was.

Astrid pulled Imogene's buggy into the drive at the house.

Jesse and the boys were already there, though Astrid couldn't see hide nor hair of them. She supposed they were in the barn brushing down old Judy, their ancient mare.

Astrid stopped behind her own carriage and turned toward Imogene, the reins still loose in her hands. "Are you going to be okay this afternoon?" she asked. "You can stay here for a while if you need to."

Imogene looked pitifully down on her mud-covered church dress. "I need to be getting home."

"Come by tomorrow," Astrid instructed. "We need to make plan B."

Imogene shook her head. "There's no need for a plan B."

"Try to come when the boys are in school," Astrid said. "That way we can talk."

"Did you hear me?" Imogene asked. "I just want to forget the whole thing."

"But you said you thought he was handsome."

"*Jah*," Imogene admitted.

Astrid could hear the reluctance in her voice, but no matter. *It ain't over till it's over.* "You still want a new husband?"

"*Jah*."

And I still need a plot for my next book. "It's settled then. Tomorrow, plan B."

Every wise woman buildeth her house: but the foolish plucketh it down with her hands.

The verse from Proverbs rang in Imogene's head as she lifted her hand to knock on Astrid's door the next day, though she couldn't bring her knuckles to touch wood.

She had to be out of her mind to be here. It was all some sort of ridiculousness. Yet here she was.

"Ouch! Mamm, Mattie pinched me."

"Matthew, leave your brother alone." She stared at the door, her hand still raised in the air.

"Ouch! Mamm, Mahlon hit me."

"Mahlon, leave your brother alone."

"He started it."

"Nuh-uh. You stepped on my foot."

Unable to take any more, Imogene whirled around. "Boys!" But as she turned back, the door in front of her was suddenly wrenched open. Her hand flew to her mouth, to stifle her surprised yelp. "Astrid," Imogene said. She pressed her hand to her chest. "You scared me."

"I can see that. What are you doing out here on the porch?"

"I came to see you. That's what you wanted, right?"

Astrid stood back so Imogene could make her way into the house.

She did so, with the boys following reluctantly behind. At least they had stopped torturing one another.

"I thought you were coming a little earlier." Astrid motioned for Imogene to go into the room where they had sat before during her previous visit.

"I had to work."

"Where do you work again?" Astrid asked.

Imogene settled down in the same chair as she had the day before. The boys made their way over to the small couch that sat under one window. They were being quiet and well behaved for the moment, but Imogene knew it wouldn't last. It never did.

"Paradise Amish Buffet," she replied.

"I thought I smelled something delicious," Astrid said.

Imogene raised a fluttering hand toward her hair and her prayer *kapp*. It seemed no matter how hard she scrubbed or how much dry shampoo she used between washings, she always smelled like fried chicken and gravy.

"How long are we gonna be here?" Mattie asked.

"Hush," Imogene said. "I probably shouldn't have come at all."

"Nonsense." Astrid fluttered a hand in the air as if to erase the words Imogene had just said.

How she wished she had such confidence. If she had the self-assurance that Astrid had, if she were that extraordinary, she wouldn't be worried. She would've found someone by now, but Imogene didn't have bright ideas or bright plans. She didn't have such confidence. She just simply *was*.

And her *was* was most certainly not like Astrid's was. That woman seemed to shine wherever she went.

"We just need a plan B," Astrid continued.

Imogene didn't have time to respond before one of the boys cut in. "How much longer?" Mahlon.

"Just a little bit," Imogene falsely assured them. She had no idea how long this would take, probably much longer than a little bit and most likely longer than the boys' patience would allow. She should've never come. She was crazy to believe she could hire a matchmaker to get her life back on track. Yet here she was.

They hadn't even talked about the price. She might not be able to even afford Astrid Kauffman's services.

"How much is this going to be?" Imogene said hesitantly.

"Mamm." Mattie stood to get her attention. "Mamm."

"Sit down, Mattie," she said without looking at him.

"I'm Mahlon," he complained.

"Sit down," Imogene said again, and miraculously he did as she asked. "How much?" she asked Astrid again.

Astrid shrugged in that nonchalant, so-confident way she had. "I don't know, dear. Love takes time."

"No," Imogene started, "money. How much money is this going to be?" This had her so flustered she couldn't even tell her children apart.

"Money?"

Astrid seemed confused by her request, so Imogene continued. "For the uh . . ." She wasn't sure how to say it, and she certainly didn't want to say it in front of her boys. "Never mind." She stood and pulled the strap of her handbag up onto her shoulder. "Thank you for your time."

The boys were on their feet in seconds.

"Ice cream, here we come," Mahlon said, his tone more

pleased than Imogene would've wanted it to be. She was a little ashamed that she had to bribe them with ice cream not once, but twice, in so many days in order to get them to behave.

"Where are you going?" Astrid followed them to the door.

Imogene hurried along, the boys skipping in front of her. "This was a mistake. I can see that now."

"If this is about money," Astrid said, "I'll do it for free."

Imogene stopped. Sighed. "It's not about money. It's just—" She closed her eyes. "Some things just aren't meant to be." She opened the door, and the boys happily ran outside.

Astrid followed them out onto the porch. "Everyone deserves love."

"Maybe. But 'deserve' and 'will end up with' are two very different things."

"Boys," Astrid called to Matthew and Mahlon as they started to get into the buggy. "Y'all play outside. Your mother and I have something to discuss."

"What about the ice cream?" Mattie asked.

"Maybe in a bit," Astrid said. Her tone brooked no argument and surprisingly enough she got none from either twin. "Now go play." She took a hold of Imogene's arm and dragged her back into the house.

Imogene wanted to protest, but she didn't have it in her anymore. The last couple of days had taken all her fight.

"Now sit," Astrid commanded, pointing toward the seat that Imogene had so recently vacated. "We've got work to do."

"But the boys," she halfheartedly protested as she sank back into the chair.

"They'll be fine. Now, here's what we need to do."

* * *

There was nothing like a move to put a body behind, Jesse Kauffman thought as he looked around his shop. Even though he knew the move was right for both him and his sister, it just took so much time to get everything back to rights.

He had orders to catch up on, new orders to fill, and a workshop that was twice the size of the one he had before. And it was a total mess. He still had boxes of leather to unpack, and boxes of finished product to unpack, and a sign to hang out front.

Expanding Hill and Valley Leather Works had been Jesse's dream for a long time now. Though his work had been stacking up on him and he felt like he worked from sunup to way past sundown, he was grateful.

Jesse looked around the shop trying to decide exactly how it should be organized. He needed to get at least a little merchandise displayed, but he hadn't decided on the layout yet. The leather key chains with the initials on them that he sold to the Amish and *Englisch* alike should go close to his work counter. Tooled leather belts with the person's name on the back just inside the doors. Now he just had to decide where to hang all the horse straps, the dog collars, the dog leashes, and cat collars. Perhaps he should allow a section for each animal. Then what to do with the Bible covers and bookmarks.

A large clatter sounded from outside.

He ignored it. He had work to do. Couldn't go check on every little noise. It was probably a stray racoon or possum, maybe a cat messing around the trash cans.

But then the sound came again.

He wasn't going to check and see what it was. He needed to keep his focus, but when raised voices that sounded like children joined in, he could take no more. He stalked to the door of the shop and out into the yard to see what was going on.

Matthew and Mahlon were standing near the big oak tree, scuffling over something he couldn't see. The clatter kept sounding as the tire swing, which currently had a metal garbage can lid attached to it, crashed into the tree. Where they had found the lid was anybody's guess. There were several abandoned pieces of discarded items scattered across the property when Jesse and Astrid had moved in.

"What is going on out here?" he demanded.

It took a moment, but the boys finally stopped trying to wrestle each other to the ground. They were breathless as they both started to explain at the same time.

Jesse couldn't understand what either of them was saying, but the accusatory tone was enough. He did pick up something about taking turns and something about being stingy and being a baby.

He held up his hands to put an end to their tirade. "Stop. Stop."

"He started it," Mattie said. At least, Jesse thought it was Mattie. The boys were so identical that unless they were standing side by side and *still*, it was difficult to tell them apart. Though they were standing side by side they were by no means being still. Even as he said the words, Mattie flung an arm out and hit his brother in the stomach.

Mahlon returned the gesture. "I did not. You started it."

"That's not true." Mattie shook his head.

"I don't care who started it," Jesse said. "I'm going to stop it."

Remarkably, the boys quit punching and shoving one another long enough to stare up at him questioningly.

"Mahlon, why are you here?" Jesse asked.

Mattie started to answer, but Jesse stopped him. "I asked Mahlon."

"Our *mamm* is here to see your sister."

"I figured that one out on my own," Jesse told him. "Why?"

Mahlon shrugged. "I don't know."

Jesse turned to Mattie. The boy shrugged, an identical gesture to his brother's. "Maybe you should go ask them."

He supposed he would have to if he wanted to get any answers. Jesse started toward the house, but Mahlon's words stopped him. "I wouldn't go in there if I were you. Mamm looked like she was about to start crying. I hate it when women cry."

Jesse bit back a snort at the boy's words. Truth be known Jesse himself hated when a woman cried too. He felt helpless. A man wasn't supposed to feel that way. He stopped and turned back toward the twins. "If I go back into my shop, are you two going to behave?"

They both nodded vigorously. A little too vigorously. Jesse had the feeling that if he turned his back on them for more than two minutes, they would be back at each other again. He surely couldn't get any work done if he had to keep coming out here to run interference between the two.

He pointed toward the shop. "Into the shop. Go."

They both blinked at him as if they were not sure what he actually said.

"Now."

The boys scrambled toward the workshop, somehow sensing that Jesse meant business.

Jesse grabbed the broom and dustpan kept by the door and handed it to the boy closest to him. He figured that if they were going to be underfoot, then they could be useful. "Here, Mattie, you can sweep."

"I'm Mahlon." He didn't reach for the broom handle.

Jesse shook his head. "Never try to kid a kidder. And never try to trick a twin. Now sweep."

The boy gave up his ruse and took the broom from Jesse.

"Just go around the boxes to get all these little scraps up. It doesn't have to be perfect, but it needs to be good."

"*Jah*," Mattie said. "Okay." Surprisingly enough he started to work.

"Come here, Mahlon."

The boy approached as if he had told him to go to the woodshed.

"See this board with the little holes in it? That's called a pegboard, and these are the pegs." He gestured toward the box of prongs sitting on a makeshift table made out of two sawhorses and a piece of decking. "I need you to put one of these in every other hole, then skip a line and do it again. Can you do that?"

Mahlon nodded, but slowly as if the words in the request were completely foreign to him.

"Can you do it?" Jesse asked.

"*Jah*. I can do that."

"Okay then," Jesse said with a dip of his chin. "Get to work." He watched for a moment to make sure the boys were sticking with their tasks, then he went over to the stack of boxes that still needed to be unpacked. They were all neatly labeled and organized. There just were so many of them.

He took the box key chains and pet collars over to where Mahlon worked.

"How long do I have to do this?" Mahlon asked.

"Are you getting tired already?"

Mahlon gave that loose shoulder shrug that mostly looked as if he had ants in his pants. "I don't know. I guess I'm just wondering."

Jesse went over to his workbench and grabbed a piece of chalk. He took it back to the pegboard and made a mark a little more than halfway down. "You can end here, okay?"

Mahlon nodded. "Okay."

"When do I get to quit?" Mattie asked.

"When you have your chore done," Jesse replied.

"That's not fair," Mattie said. "His chore's more fun than mine."

"There's a lot in life that's not fair," Jesse said. But he understood twin mentality. Even as a set of fraternal twins, he and Astrid always had to have things in balance. It was very hard for one of them to get something when the other one didn't. There were times when it happened. Then there were times like this when he could do something about it.

"*Jah*, we know," Mattie said.

"All right then," Jesse replied. "See the clock over there?"

They both turned to stare at the large-faced, black-and-white clock at one end of the workshop. "When ten minutes passes, you can switch, but no dillydallying or wasting time until the ten minutes is over, got it?"

Even on opposite sides of the room, their identical nods were in perfect unison. If he hadn't been a twin himself, he might have thought it creepy.

But they were good boys, he decided. A little rambunctious and perhaps even heartbroken. He and Astrid had lost their *dat* when they were older than these two, but still not old enough. Then again when was anyone old enough to lose the ones they loved? Unfortunately, loss was just part of life. It was something he knew so well.

That was another problem with the work he was doing, organizing and trying to get his shop put together. It gave him too much time to think. When he was designing something or working on a particularly hard item to craft, his mind was on the task at hand. But going through boxes, separating finished product from raw materials, and setting up displays allowed his mind to wander, most times to places he didn't want to go.

Amanda.

She was his one true love. The one God had meant for him. She'd been gone for many years now, thirteen to be precise, and he still missed her every day. As each day passed, he never missed her any less.

He had known practically his entire life that Amanda Byler would be his wife. They had grown up together, right next door. She had been his friend. Or perhaps he should say that he had been her friend first, the one who came over to play to keep her from being alone.

Even as a child, Amanda had been sickly. Born that way, her parents had always said. It was God's will that she couldn't run and play like the other children. On top of her limited physical abilities, she had also been plagued with asthma.

But Jesse had loved her desperately and as soon as they were able, he had married her. She had tried to protest that he needed to find someone healthy and strong. Someone to have his children. Someone to grow old with. But Jesse had brushed aside her pleas and swept her into marriage.

He had known from the start that she wouldn't be his for

long. But knowing didn't make it any easier. Just as missing her didn't change that she was gone.

She had been his for a time, and for that he was grateful. There was nothing else to ask for. Nothing more to move toward. He had had his love and he had lost his love, and that was all there was to say about it.

CHAPTER SIX

"I don't see how you talking to him is going to solve the problem," Imogene told Astrid. "I know you mean well, but he is never going to forget that I fell in the mud at his feet."

Astrid shook her head. "Men have short, short memories for such things."

Imogene wished she believed that. She wished she could believe all of what Astrid was saying about how everyone deserved love and there was somebody out there for everyone. What if she already had her someone?

It wasn't even a what-if. She *had* already had her someone. Abner. Was it arrogant to think that God had made another just for her?

Jah. It was. "Maybe we shouldn't worry so much about love and just maybe concentrate on mutual need. You know, like he needs somebody to cook and clean, and I need somebody to help with the boys. So we can help each other."

She hadn't even finished half of what she said before Astrid started shaking her head. "Everyone deserves love."

"Right now, I'd settle for companionship," Imogene admitted.

Astrid didn't respond. Imogene supposed she felt she

had already had her say. So the two of them sat there in a moment of silence.

Silence! Where were the boys? They were never silent unless there was trouble.

She was on her feet in a second. "I've got to check on the twins." Without a look back she rushed outside, her eyes scanning the yard and not finding anything. Or anyone.

She stepped out onto the porch, knowing Astrid was right behind her. "Where are they?" she breathed.

"Now, don't panic," Astrid said. "They've got to be around here somewhere."

That was a lie, and they both knew it. Anything could have happened to them while they were outside, and she had just allowed it. They could have been snatched up by a wayward *Englisch* traveler just driving around the countryside looking for little boys to kidnap.

Her heart started beating faster in her chest. It was just anxiety. She knew it. But somehow calling it by its name didn't make it any better. She sucked in a deep breath. Let it out slowly. Closed her eyes. Breathed again. Opened them and . . .

Nothing.

She turned to Astrid. "We've got to find them. Now," she said.

"I'll get Jesse." Astrid brushed past her and headed toward the large building that sat in front of the house, but off to the left.

Imogene had to keep it together. These days she felt so incompetent as a mother. Something like this surely didn't help.

She started off the porch, walking around the buggy as if that would give her some sort of clue as to where her boys had gotten off to.

*Lord, please just let them be around here somewhere.
Maybe playing hide-and-seek or even asleep in a field. But
safe. Lord, please let them be safe. Amen.*

"Imogene," Astrid called from the door of the shop.
"They're in here."

A tidal wave of relief washed over her. She was so
thankful she almost went completely limp. Her legs shook
like overcooked casserole noodles as she made her way
toward her newfound friend.

"What are they doing?" she asked as she peered inside.

"Hey, Mamm." Mahlon waved from the other end of the
shop. He had a broom in one hand and was pushing a pile
of leather scraps toward her, between the rows of boxes.

"We're helping Jesse." Mattie was perched on the
second rung of a stepladder, hanging leather belts on metal
prongs fitted into the wall.

The relief was almost too much. Her heart slowed as her
fingers started tingling. "I can see that."

"Are you ready to go now?" Mahlon asked. "I'm not
finished with my work."

Imogene blinked in surprise. Who were these boys and
what had they done with her rowdy twins?

"Nope," she told them. "I just wanted to check on you.
You finish up with what you're doing."

She turned to Jesse. "Is that okay?" she asked. "If they
help you?"

He smiled at her then, and Imogene could see in him
that same charisma his sister carried. Though they weren't
identical, they did favor each other. Imogene had seen fraternal twins who looked more alike. Sure they both had
honey-colored hair and clear green eyes. But it wasn't their
looks that made them similar. It was some kind of energy
that came off them, some sort of magnetism. A magnetism
that Imogene had never possessed.

"*Jah*," Jesse said. "I can always use a good hand around here."

"*Danki*," Astrid said.

Imogene got one last look at her boys happily helping Jesse in his workshop before Astrid snaked her arm around hers and led her back to the house.

"See?" Astrid said. "They're fine. Now let's go figure out how to make Ira Oberholtzer fall in love with you."

Make Ira Oberholtzer fall in love with you.

That seemed like such a monstrous task. One that was completely undoable. But Astrid was the matchmaker. She was the one who knew what she was doing. Imogene simply had to trust her.

The plan was simple. Astrid was going to drop by the hardware store as many times as she could in the coming week and drop hints about Imogene. Then when the next event happened in Paradise Hill, Imogene would attend, with the understanding that Astrid would get Ira to attend as well, and from there they were going to let nature take its course.

Imogene tried to explain to her that nature didn't have a course for plain girls, but Astrid waved away her protests.

She came across so confident, so sure that this was going to happen the way she said it was going to happen, that Imogene found herself going along. So half an hour later she let herself out of the matchmaker's house and made her way across to the shop where Jesse had her boys occupied. That in itself was a miracle. Imogene said a small prayer of thanks before rapping lightly on the door and letting herself in. She could hear the rustle behind her and figured Astrid had followed her out once more.

"Are you boys ready to go?" Imogene called.

"*Jah*," they said in unison. They immediately dropped what they were doing and started toward her.

"Hold up," Jesse said. "We need to put the broom up, and we need to close the box of belts and store it for safe-keeping. Go to it."

Imogene could hardly believe her eyes. Without one protest the boys did as Jesse commanded. Without any protest at all!

The boys made their way back over to the door where now all three adults stood.

"*Danki* for your help today," Jesse told them. The man reached into his back pocket and pulled out his wallet. He opened it and took out two five-dollar bills. He handed one to each of them.

Imogene watched as their eyes grew wide.

"What's this for?" Mattie asked.

"When a man does good work, a man gets paid," Jesse said with a small nod.

"Wow," Mahlon said. "This is awesome."

"What do you say?" Imogene asked.

"Do you want to go get ice cream with us?" Mattie asked.

Imogene chuckled uncomfortably. "Not exactly what I was looking for."

Mattie and Mahlon bounced up and down on their toes. "*Danki*," they said together. "*Danki, danki.*"

"It's me who should be thanking you," Jesse said to the kids. "Thank you for a job well done."

The boys beamed. She hadn't seen them look this happy since . . .

"Now, what about that ice cream?" Jesse asked. He turned those green eyes to Imogene.

"It's nothing really," she said with a small shake of her head. "I told them yesterday that we would go eat ice cream today, but they had to wait until after I visited with your sister. Not a big thing at all." She waved one hand in front of her as if that dismissed the invitation, but all she succeeded in doing was making a motion like a fish flopping out of the water.

"We want you to come," Mattie said.

"*Jah*," said Mahlon, backing up the invitation. "It would be great fun to have you come get ice cream with us."

"You don't have to, if you don't want to," Imogene said.

But the boys were having none of her objection. "Please." They said the word lending it many more syllables than normal.

Then to her surprise Jesse smiled. "I would love to. I love ice cream."

"Will you come too?" Imogene turned her attention to Astrid.

The woman shook her head. "I don't do good with too much milk," she explained. "Lactose intolerant."

"That's one thing we don't share as twins," Jesse said.

Mahlon's and Mattie's chins dropped.

"You're twins?" they asked.

"*Jah*," Jesse said. "Not all twins look just alike. Some are even one boy and one girl, instead of two boys or two girls."

"Wow," Mattie said.

Mahlon grinned. "That goes double for me. I've never heard of such a thing."

Jesse returned the boys' smiles. "Now you have."

Jesse pulled the horse to a stop and everyone clambered out of the carriage.

Zook's Paradise Hill Creamery sat far enough back that Astrid hadn't seen it coming until Jesse turned. That was when she noticed the sign—a large wooden sign painted cream with swirly brown letters.

"How did you know this was here?" she asked.

Jesse gave a tilt of his head that served as a shrug as he hitched the horse to the hitching post next to the others. A large pond sat off to the left, blocked from the road by a bank of trees. Ducks and geese and animals of all sorts waddled around picking up corn and other feed thrown by the visitors.

"You get a cup of feed with any double dip," Jesse told the twins.

"Two dips is my favorite," Mattie said.

Jesse laughed and Imogene enjoyed the sound. The stress of everything, even the stress of trying to meet and make Ira Oberholtzer fall in love with her or even notice her and decide that marriage would be a good thing, just melted away.

"Two scoops of what?" Jesse asked him.

"Two scoops of anything," Imogene supplied. "That boy loves his ice cream."

"Not Mahlon?"

"He's more of a pie guy," Imogene explained.

Jesse put one hand on Mahlon's shoulder. "Then I have the dessert for you."

He steered them all to the window where a young girl was taking orders. A black chalkboard hung to one side of the window and listed the ice cream flavors of the day.

They stood side by side reading the choices.

"I don't know," Imogene said. "It all sounds good. Mint chocolate chip, cherry vanilla, butter pecan."

Jesse smiled. "Butter pecan's my favorite."

"I thought you said I could have a special dessert," Mahlon said.

"What about a special dessert for me?" Mattie asked.

Jesse turned both boys to face him. "Mattie, would you like an ice cream cone or a special dessert?"

"Does this special dessert include ice cream?" Mattie asked.

Jesse nodded. "But there's no cone."

"No way. I like the cone. A waffle cone," he clarified.

Jesse looked at Imogene. "Did you make up your mind yet?"

She shook her head. "Just order for me. There's too many choices to decide."

"So one special dessert for Mahlon, one double cone for Mattie, and one double cone for Mamm. What kind of ice cream do you want, Mattie?"

"Birthday cake and chocolate peppermint patty."

"Got it," Jesse said. "Y'all go ahead and find us a table," he continued, then stepped up to the window to order their ice cream.

"Let me give you some money," Imogene said, taking her wallet out of her purse.

"I got this," he said. "Go ahead and sit down."

She paused for a moment. She didn't like feeling that she wasn't paying her own way.

But Jesse held firm. He nodded toward the seating area. "Go on."

"How are you going to carry three ice cream cones and a special dessert?"

"We'll help," Mahlon said.

Mattie nodded in agreement. "*Jah*."

What choice did she have?

There were several picnic tables covered by brightly colored umbrellas scattered around the lake. Several were available, though Imogene imagined many times in the heat of the summer the place would probably be filled to capacity. She chose a table and sat where she could still watch Jesse and her boys.

They moved to one side of the window, allowing someone else to order while they waited for their ice creams to be served up. The boys waited patiently next to Jesse, talking animatedly up at him. Jesse himself looked attentive, open, and interested. Watching the three of them brought a smile to Imogene's face.

Then that smile quickly disappeared. They needed a man in their lives, someone to look up to. For the last few days, maybe even the last few weeks, it had been all about discipline, about getting them to mind, about how they were going to grow up if they didn't have the proper influence. But this was something different. This was about love and caring and interest.

Their number must have been called for Jesse and the boys approached the window once more. Jesse handed Mattie his ice cream cone, which was almost as big as his face. Then he handed Mahlon a dish filled with something made with ice cream, she was sure, but from this distance she couldn't tell what it was. Then Jesse grabbed two ice cream cones and the three set off toward the table she had found.

It took all the boys had for them not to run across the grass to show her their treat. They walked extremely fast, that sort of run-walk she'd seen when they had waited too long to go to the bathroom and had to hurry lest they had an accident. Each boy wore a huge smile on his face, and they plopped down at the picnic table as soon as they could manage.

"Mamm, look!" Mahlon cried excitedly. "It's pie made

out of ice cream! Chocolate chip cookie dough ice cream pie!"

But she only had time to give the dish a cursory glance before Jesse arrived at the table.

He slid into the bench seat next to her. "For you." He handed her the largest ice cream cone she had ever seen.

"It's huge," she said with a laugh.

Each dip was as large as a softball and she was sure that it was a wonder of nature that they could stay stacked on top of one another like that. The cone itself was the biggest she had ever seen and obviously made in-store. She wondered how big their waffle iron was to produce such a product.

"Best ice cream you'll ever eat," he said, still smiling happily.

"What flavor?" she asked.

Jesse continued to grin at her. "Butter pecan and chocolate chip," he said. "Just like mine."

Just like his.

Remarkably the boys were quiet and still—mostly anyway. They were smacking their lips and swinging their legs as they ate.

"How did you say you knew about this place?" she asked.

"First," he started but only after two bites of his treat, "I live in this community. Everyone in Paradise Hill knows where to come to get the best ice cream. And second, the man who owns it is my uncle."

She smiled. "That's impressive."

Jesse nodded. "He's made good for himself."

They ate in silence for a moment, each one enjoying their smooth and creamy treat. Imogene took that time to get a better look at Mahlon's "special dessert." It was indeed a pie made of ice cream, and it looked so delicious Imogene made a mental note to order it the next time they came.

Her thoughts came to a screeching halt. There wouldn't be a next time. She might be making a few trips to Paradise Hill in the future, but it wasn't like she was going to be coming to get ice cream with Jesse each time. She was coming to meet Ira and get to know him better. He might not even like ice cream.

Suddenly the brightness of the day dimmed a bit. She was dreaming about ice cream when she needed to be paying attention to her real plans. Making Ira Oberholtzer fall in love with her. Or at the very least consider her a proper wife for him. That was what this was all about.

"You okay?" Jesse asked.

Imogene nodded, though it was far from the truth.

He paused for a moment studying her face, so she smiled to reassure him. She was okay. Or she would be as soon as she and Ira got together as a couple.

He studied her for a moment, then finally he seemed satisfied and turned back to the boys.

"I almost forgot," he said. He pulled four tokens from his pocket and laid them flat on the table. "You want to feed the ducks?"

The boys cheered.

"Okay," Jesse said with a laugh. "Let's let Mamm finish her ice cream, then we'll all go down to the pond."

The boys groaned in disappointment.

Imogene shook her head. "Y'all go on without me."

"You sure?" Jesse asked, but the boys were already clambering to their feet and taking off toward the pond.

"*Jah*," she replied.

Jesse stood, then called out to the boys. "Come back and get the trash and put it in the can."

Amazingly they came back without protest. They grabbed up their napkins, empty wrappers, and containers, then pitched it all into the trash can nearby.

Jesse gave her one last look before handing the coins over to the boys and explaining how to get the feed for the ducks. Then the three of them made their way toward the pond.

Imogene watched them thoughtfully while she continued eating the world's largest ice cream cone. She must have been going too slowly; it had begun to melt down her hand. It didn't pay to get thoughtful when eating ice cream during an Indian summer. But as she watched Jesse and her boys feed the ducks, geese, and swans that were clustered around the lake, she knew she was making the right decision. The boys needed a firm male hand, and watching them with Jesse proved that a male influence would benefit them more than any amount of discipline she could dish out. That was why it was so important that she recommitted herself to making Ira Oberholtzer her husband. The sooner the better.

CHAPTER SEVEN

By the time Friday rolled around, Astrid was extremely proud of herself. She had managed to find some excuse to go into the hardware store every day that week. Even Monday after her meeting with Imogene.

She and Jesse had come back from having ice cream, and Astrid couldn't help but notice how much they looked like a family, the four of them, riding up the drive in their buggy. As far as Astrid was concerned, that was proof positive that Imogene did need to remarry, and Astrid herself needed to double her efforts with Ira.

Truth be known she was even more committed by Thursday. She found out so much about him during the week. She had learned that he had loved his wife. He had never remarried after she died because he was so much in love with her. Ruthann Oberholtzer had simply gotten sick one winter and never recovered. The flu had turned into pneumonia and the pneumonia proved to be more than her lungs could take. She had always had fragile lungs, Ira had told her with a sadness that made her want to reach out and touch his cheek.

Ira had also told her about his daughter and how she had just gotten married. About his son and how he had recently turned sixteen. Astrid knew how to read between the lines of all that. She could hear the note of sadness in Ira's voice, a note of loneliness that came around with the reality of an empty house. He had a daughter who just moved out and a son who was running around. He might not realize it yet, but he needed to remarry. Of course, Astrid couldn't come right out and tell him that. She couldn't be that forward. So she had devised a plan.

It'd taken her most of the week to come up with a plan B. Not the plan B that she had shared with Imogene, but the plan B she was really going to put into place.

Astrid pulled to a stop in front of the hardware store. She got out of her buggy and tied up her horse before going inside. As she walked down the aisle toward the counter where she knew she would find Ira, she went over her plan in her head. She adjusted the strap of her handbag and smoothed her fingers down her apron. Plan B was about to be executed.

He looked up as she approached, and a smile dawned on his face. He really was a handsome man. And he was nice, too. That was one thing she had learned over the last week, one thing she felt she could pat herself on the back about. She was a good judge of character.

"Astrid," he greeted. "What brings you in today?"

She smiled in return and suddenly grew nervous. It was not a feeling she was comfortable with. She needed to be confident, collected, and on top of her game, as they said. She took in a deep breath, resisted the urge to run her fingers down her apron once more and smooth out any wayward wrinkles she had gotten on the drive over. Instead, she stepped closer. "You've been such a big help to me all week," she said. "I just wanted to come and invite you to a little get-together at my house tomorrow night."

A tiny frown wrinkled between his brows, but it disappeared almost as quickly as it had come. "A get-together?"

He might not be frowning anymore, but he wasn't smiling, either.

"It's just a small something." She waved one hand in the air as if dispelling its importance. "Just a few close friends. I thought you might enjoy it too."

He hesitated a moment. A moment too long as far as Astrid was concerned.

"I really would like for you to be there," she said. She used her most sincere and beguiling voice. Not too much. She wouldn't want him to think she was interested in him. But she did want him to believe that they were friends. A friend he could trust. Like if she told him she knew someone who would make him a good spouse. Not that she was going to be that forward. "My brother, Jesse, will be there."

"*Jah*?" Ira said. "Anyone else I might know?"

Astrid gave an offhand sort of laugh. "Of course."

He waited for her to continue.

She laughed again, though this one sounded a little more uncomfortable than offhand. "Just some people from church." She couldn't tell him the truth, that there was only one more person coming and that was Imogene Yoder. Technically her brother would be there, but Jesse wouldn't be a part of the party she had planned. Not if she had anything to say on the matter. Tomorrow night's party was a party for two.

Ira shook his head. "I don't know."

Astrid took a step closer to the counter. "Please tell me you'll think about it."

"Of course," he said. "I'll think about it. But I'm not a party kind of guy."

"Well, it's not a party-party," Astrid backpedaled. "Just a little get-together. Nothing too big. Just intimate friends."

"Intimate?"

Was she ever going to get this right? "You just helped me so much this week," she said. "Let me thank you by feeding you supper tomorrow night."

"So it's a dinner party?"

"Something like that, *jah*." She was messing this up so bad.

"I don't know," he said. "I'm not sure what Elam's got going on tomorrow night."

Astrid took another step closer, this time literally bumping into the counter before her. "Please say you'll think about it," she beseeched.

Ira nodded. "I'll think about it."

What a week, Ira thought as he pulled his buggy to a stop just outside his barn. He unhitched the horse and led the beast inside. He would give the gelding a good brush down, then he would check and see what Elam had going on for the night. The boy had been gone half the day. Though to where, Elam hadn't said. He had just stated that he needed Saturday off for some function with his buddy bunch. Strange as it was, even though they were both supposed to be at work today, Ira missed having Elam around. Now Ira was looking forward to an evening with just the two of them.

For some reason, Astrid Kauffman's invitation popped into his thoughts. He had wanted to tell her that he was looking forward to spending the evening with his teenage son. To him it sounded kind and fatherly, but he was fairly certain that if he had said the words out loud, it would have held a pathetic ring. Or maybe that was the loneliness inside him talking.

There. He admitted it. He was beginning to get a little

lonely. It was never a state that he would have thought he would find himself in, but that was life, right?

He directed the horse into the stall, then went to the tack room to get the brush. He no more had it in his hand when he heard the screen door slam at the house. "Dat! Don't put the horse away!"

The urgency in Elam's voice raised the hair on Ira's forearms. What was going on?

He came out of the tack room just as Elam rushed into the barn. "Don't put the horse away."

"What are you doing, son?" Ira gently asked, trying to appease his own fears. "What's going on? What's the problem?" It was time to remain calm. Whatever the emergency was, they would get through it together.

"I'm late."

Ira stood, brush in hand, as Elam rushed into the stall and pulled the gelding back out, leading him into the fading sunlight once more.

"Late for what?"

"I got a camping trip, remember?"

How had he forgotten Elam's first overnight camping trip? His boy had done nothing but talk about it nonstop for weeks. Yet somehow Ira had managed to put it out of his mind.

"I thought Daniel was coming to get you." Daniel was Elam's best friend, and they had joined the same youth group.

"He's got some kind of stomach virus and is puking everywhere. He can't come get me, so I need a ride over to the bishop's house. That's where we're all meeting before we leave. We've got to hurry; the car is supposed to be there in half an hour."

Ira pushed his weariness away. "Go down to the shanty

and call them. Let them know that we'll be there as soon as we can. I'll hitch up the horse again. Where's your gear in case I'm finished before you get back?"

Elam grinned looking so much like his mother Ira's heart squeezed. "Just inside the house," he said before turning away and jogging down the drive.

A little over an hour later, Ira returned to his dark and empty house. He put the horse away in the barn, put the buggy away in the carriage house, and trudged inside as the last rays of sunlight cast shadows over his farm.

Standing in his living room he could hear the clock ticking from all the way in the kitchen. That was how quiet his house was: He could hear the clock ticking from rooms away. For some reason the sound unnerved him. Was this what his life was going to be like for the next few years?

He wasn't complaining; he was alive, and God was good. God had blessed him. But it was so quiet. So very, very quiet. He hated the quiet. He had never realized it before. Maybe because before he hadn't been smothered by the quiet. Surely there were times when his kids were growing up that he wished they were not as loud as they were. And surely of those times he had wanted the quiet, perhaps even craved the quiet. But now it was more than he could handle.

Suddenly Astrid Kauffman's image invaded his thoughts.

"Think about it," she had said.

A dinner party. He told her he would think about it, so that wasn't really the truth. He had no intentions of going to a party. Not even a dinner party. He just wasn't a party kind of guy. He never had been. He married his wife young, craving nothing more from life than a marriage and a family, a successful store, and the happiest life God could afford him. To ask for more would be selfish, maybe even unkind to others.

He was sure his plans for life were a little bit old-fashioned, even for an Amish man. But he didn't care. That was what he'd wanted and that was what he'd had for a long time. He couldn't help thinking that the Bible said there was a time for everything. He supposed that the time for him having a family was over and now he was going into his widower days. He wasn't so sure that he liked them.

Tick-tick-tick. He could hear the clock ticking over the sink in the kitchen. The battery-operated clock that Ruthann had hung. It was just now seven thirty. Not too late. But he supposed late for an old fogey like him. He wondered what time Astrid was serving supper. He supposed if it had already been served that he might still make dessert.

Ira shook his head at himself. What was he thinking?

He was thinking that his life was catching up with him and the life he had always wanted wasn't quite his. Being a widower was never part of his plan.

Maybe now those plans should change. Maybe now he should start accepting invitations to dinner parties. What was wrong with that? Other than he was going to arrive more than "fashionably late," as he had heard it said.

No matter. He was sick of hearing the clock tick on the wall. He was tired of that heavy burden of loneliness. He was going to Astrid's. But just in case . . .

Ira grabbed a piece of cheese from the refrigerator and an unopened box of crackers, then headed outside to hitch the horse back to the carriage. He had a party to attend.

* * *

Astrid looked out the window and back toward the clock sitting on the mantel. It was seven thirty. Seven thirty-five to be exact, and no one had arrived. She supposed that no one coming was better than only one of them showing up. She could imagine how Imogene would feel if she came to a party and the only other person who was supposed to come had not arrived. To top it off, Astrid was certain that if Ira showed up without Imogene here, he would think she was playing some sort of trick on him.

This wasn't how the party was supposed to turn out. First, their meeting was thrown off. Then Astrid had spent the entire week trying to get to know Ira better and making him feel comfortable enough to come to her house for the "party." She paced back to the kitchen to check on the food she had prepared. It wasn't anything elaborate. The truth of it? She wasn't a very good cook. But she could make a mean pot of spaghetti and pretty much anything that came out of a box. So spaghetti it was. The meat sauce was simmering on the stove while the pasta sat to one side getting cold.

Jesse hadn't even come in to eat. Which she supposed was fine because she hadn't wanted him to come in and ruin her party. Normally, him coming in would be fine. The more the merrier and all that, but not tonight. He had told her that he was going to work in his shop all day and as long as he could into the evening. When he chose an extra-long workday, he usually grabbed a sandwich and went right back. So she had no doubt that was what he would do tonight, but he hadn't even done that.

Where was everybody?

Astrid stirred the spaghetti sauce one last time. She tapped the spoon against the side of the pan and laid it on the saucer next to the stove. Then she went back to the living room and stared out the window once more.

Almost as if she had wished it, a horse and carriage turned down the drive. But only one horse and carriage. Someone was coming. But who?

She rushed to the door and stopped herself from flinging it open and hurrying out onto the porch. She had to make this look normal, as if she had planned it this way. She smoothed her hands over her apron and pulled her sleeves down a bit. She brushed back the sides of her hair under the edge of her prayer *kapp*, then ever so gently opened the door.

"Imogene," she breathed. "Where have you been?" She allowed the urgency to seep back into her tone.

This had all been set up for Imogene, and Imogene was in on the setup. Okay, so not the part about there being only one guest, but she knew that the party was for her to get in touch with Ira. Yet she still hadn't come on time.

Astrid immediately regretted her tone when Imogene's lower lip started to tremble. "You're not going to cry, are you?"

Imogene shook her head. "I'm okay; I'm just nervous."
Aren't we all?

"What are you wearing?" Again Astrid regretted her stern tone.

Imogene looked down at herself. "A dress?" she asked.

"I can see that," Astrid said, this time tempering her tone a bit. "What color is it?"

"Green?" Again Imogene sounded completely unsure of herself.

"Are you sure about that?" Astrid shook her head. "Imogene, I think you are a wonderful person, but that is the ugliest color of green I've ever seen in my life."

Imogene frowned a bit. "It's my best dress. I don't wear it very often."

"I can see why," Astrid said. "Come on in. And hurry. We have got to do something about this."

"About what?" Imogene asked.

Astrid grabbed her by the arm and hauled her inside. She steered her through the living room and into the downstairs bathroom.

"About this," Astrid said. She shut the door behind them and turned Imogene to face her reflection. "We need to do something before Ira gets here."

Something drastic, Astrid silently added. This matchmaking business was no joke. Especially when she had such reluctant subjects.

"But I—"

Astrid shook her head, and Imogene fell silent.

"Just wait right here," Astrid commanded. "You wait here, and I'll be back in a jiffy."

She didn't pause to see if Imogene would agree with her. Astrid rushed out of the bathroom, back down the hall, and up into her room. She had to have something different that Imogene could wear. Something that wasn't that putrid shade of puke green. She didn't even know they made material that color! And they would have to do something about her hair and her shoes and . . . Astrid started grabbing up supplies, and when her arms were full she made her way back downstairs. There was no time to lose.

CHAPTER EIGHT

Imogene peered critically at her reflection staring back at her. Wasn't so bad, was it? She'd had a doozy of time trying to find something to wear tonight. Her nicest dresses were reserved for church, and she couldn't wear one of her church dresses because they looked . . . churchy to her, even though they might not look that way to someone else. Plus they were church dresses.

All of her day dresses were stained here or a grease spot there or smelled like chicken. Or some had all three. It seemed impossible to get the food scent out of her work clothes. Everything else she owned just didn't seem good enough.

The dress she wore now was the only one that didn't have a mark or small tear or the hem coming out or a number of other problems that she seemed to encounter on a daily basis and never got around to fixing because these days she was just so very tired. What had happened to all her clothes? Work and time, she supposed.

She supposed this dress had been spared all that because deep down she agreed with Astrid. It was a very ugly color. She wasn't even sure why she bought it. Come to think of it, she hadn't bought the material that made up this dress;

her mother-in-law had gifted it to her for some occasion or another.

Imogene had done her best to do right by Abner, but his mother never seemed to fully take to her. Not that Nancy ever said as much, but Imogene wasn't dumb; she knew an icy attitude when she saw it. Nancy Yoder had always believed—whether she said it out loud or not—that Imogene Miller was not good enough for her son.

Those days were long gone, all in the past. Nancy had gone to her reward just after Abner had died, leaving Imogene with one less family member to help with the twins.

She shook that thought away. It wasn't kind at all. Whether or not Nancy was kind to her was another matter altogether. When you were as plain as Imogene was, kindness might be all that you had.

She jumped back as Astrid came bursting into the bathroom. She held a load of various items in her arms—what looked like a dress and apron, a pair of shoes, and a bunch of bottles and spray cans that Imogene could not identify.

Astrid dumped the armful of items on the bathroom counter, then turned back to Imogene.

"Get that dress off now," Astrid barked. "We don't have much time before Ira gets here."

Imogene quickly started unpinning her dress. But she thought she heard Astrid mutter under her breath, "I hope." But surely she was mistaken.

"And your hair," Astrid continued.

Imogene's hands flew to her prayer *kapp*. "What's wrong with my hair?" She patted all around the top of her head trying to discern what was wrong by feel alone.

"Never mind that," Astrid continued. "Dress first, hair later."

To her surprise, Astrid took hold of the bottom of her dress and pulled it over her head. Imogene had only a moment to feel any sort of modesty or embarrassment before Astrid shoved her head and arms into a new dress. This one was purple. A beautiful dark color, rich and vibrant.

"I can't wear your dress," she said. "It's too big." Actually, it fit pretty well, all things considered. It was a bit long in the hem and the sleeves, but not so much so that she couldn't make do since she wouldn't be leaving the house in it.

And it was such a pretty color. So much better than the green, she thought.

Astrid knelt down and took out a box of safety pins and folded up the hem, pinning it until it was a proper length.

"Now," Astrid said, popping back to her feet. "Your hair."

The woman became a flurry of action and talk, most of which went straight over Imogene's head. Mainly because she was so shocked at the whole situation.

Where were all the people who were supposed to be there? There had been only one buggy parked in the drive and that one belonged to Astrid. Imogene had recognized the little heart-shaped sticker her new friend/matchmaker had stuck in the middle of the orange slow-moving vehicle triangle.

If only Astrid's buggy was outside, that meant Ira wasn't here yet. No one else was there either. And she had been worried about showing up late.

She'd had a terrible time trying to get ready and then another hard time getting the boys to comply with her wishes. Like she hadn't seen that coming. But still.

"Why is no one else here? Is he coming?" she asked. She thought about what Astrid told her about the evening. A dinner party, with Ira Oberholtzer.

"*Jah*," Astrid said, then she continued. "I hope so, anyway."

"You hope so?" She closed her eyes, trying her best to pull all of her emotions together. Once again she doubted the prudence of hiring a matchmaker. Even one who worked for free.

"He'll be here." There went that confidence again. If Imogene only had a smidge of it.

"Ow!" Imogene's eyes flew open as Astrid pinched her cheek. Her hand flew to the spot and covered it, but Astrid was quick and got the other side before the sting even quit. "Ow again! What are you doing?"

"I'm putting some color in your cheeks."

"That hurt," she grumbled, still rubbing the spot. Though now she had two places that were stinging.

"Beauty is pain, isn't that what the *Englisch* say?"

"In case you haven't noticed, we're Amish," Imogene complained.

"That doesn't mean you don't need to look your best. Now come on." Astrid grabbed a bunch of the bottles and hooked her arm around Imogene's, dragging her into the kitchen. "Sit here." She pointed to a seat at the end of the table.

Like an obedient puppy, Imogene dropped into the chair, and Astrid immediately began removing the pins from her bob. "What are you doing now?" Her hands flew to her hair, but Astrid immediately pushed them back onto the tabletop.

"Now sit still," she said.

Imogene did as she was told. She closed her eyes when Astrid told her to close her eyes and allowed her to spread whatever it was on her hair. She'd never put anything in her hair except for shampoo and baby lotion. "What's that for?" she finally asked in a small voice.

"It'll make it look shiny, and when you roll the sides you should pick up a bit more. It makes it look thicker."

"If you say so."

"I say so," Astrid replied. Then she brushed out Imogene's hair, twisted the sides and pinned them back, then pulled the whole thing into a ponytail at the base of her skull.

"Okay now," Astrid said. "Head down." She shoved Imogene's head to the table. She hadn't had her hair done like this since she was six. Come to think of it, no one had done her hair for her until now.

"Can I see?" Imogene asked.

"Just a minute," Astrid said. She placed the prayer *kapp* in the precise spot on Imogene's head and pinned it into place. "There," she said, and took a step back.

Imogene grabbed up the handheld mirror and peered at her reflection. She wasn't about to go win one of those *Englisch* beauty pageants, but interestingly enough she did look better somehow. Her hair looked a little more vibrant and her eyes a little greener than the muddy color they usually appeared.

"Almost forgot," Astrid said. She squatted down on the floor and grabbed up one of Imogene's feet. With dizzying speed, she removed her shoes.

"What now?"

Astrid tsked. "You can't go on a date in your walking shoes."

"You can't?" Imogene asked bewilderingly. "I thought—"

"You shouldn't," Astrid corrected herself. "So you're wearing these." She slipped Imogene's feet into a pair of black flat shoes with no straps or ties or buttons. "Slipped" was a very generous word. It was more like she stuffed her feet into them.

"I think they're too small," Imogene said with a wince.

"It's just for a couple of hours."

Imogene shook her head. "Aren't we eating dinner? Won't I just be sitting at the dinner table? Will he even see my feet?"

"It's not worth taking a chance." Astrid stood. "And one more thing . . ."

"How many *one more things* are there?" Imogene asked. She didn't want to appear ungrateful, but she had been nervous enough to start with. Now she was wearing a strange dress, she had all kinds of goop in her hair, and she was wearing shoes that were at least a half a size too small. She was about to her limit of *one more things*.

Astrid reached into the waistband of her apron and pulled out a tube of lip balm. It looked like an ordinary tube of the stuff, but Imogene's lips weren't chapped. She was about to say as much when Astrid popped the cap off the tube. It was a bright pink.

"Is that lipstick?"

Astrid shot her a look. "Of course not; it's colored lip balm."

Imogene shook her head. "I do not want that on my mouth."

"It's just lip balm. There's nothing in the *Ordnung* against lip balm."

Imogene was still shaking her head in disbelief. "Maybe not, but that's probably because the bishop hasn't found out about it yet. That colored stuff anyway."

"The bishop can only get mad if he finds out about it, and the only people who can tell them about it would be me, you, or Ira. Besides, he's my uncle."

"Ira's your uncle?"

Astrid laughed and grabbed Imogene's chin before she could protest further. She generously applied the balm to Imogene's lips. It felt slick and slippery. "The bishop. It's all going to be okay because the bishop is my uncle."

Astrid pulled Imogene to her feet, then cocked her head to one side. "Did you hear that?"

Imogene shook her head. "What?"

"A buggy!" Astrid bounced in place like a schoolgirl. "He's here."

"How do you know it's him? Couldn't it be another of the guests?"

Astrid gave her an almost apologetic smile, but it held too much of that confidence to be anything but all Astrid. "He's the only guest that's coming."

"Are you kidding me?" Imogene squeaked.

Astrid took her by the shoulders and stared deep into those unremarkable hazel eyes of hers. The purple in the dress did make them appear a little bit greener, and Astrid was pleased with that part of the evening. She had done what she could to help Imogene draw Ira's attention. "You've got this," Astrid said. "It's just dinner, remember? You stay here. I'm going to go let him in."

Imogene nodded dumbly and Astrid turned loose of her shoulders and made her way to the door. She was there the heartbeat before he knocked. She swung the door open wide.

"Ira." She added as much warmth and welcome as she could to the one word. "I'm so glad you're here." She stood to one side and motioned him into the house.

"I thought that there would be more buggies," he said. He jerked a thumb over his shoulder in the direction of the drive.

Astrid shut the door behind him and gave what she hoped was a reassuring laugh. "You know how people are

these days. They say they're going to come and then . . ."
She trailed off. "But Imogene is here."

"Imogene?" he asked. A small frown of confusion
wrinkled his brow.

Astrid swept him from the foyer into the dining room.
"You remember Imogene," she said. "You met her at
church this week. She's from Paradise Springs."

He nodded in remembrance. "*Jah*, the woman who fell
in the m—"

"That's right." Astrid cut him off before he could finish.
"And I made spaghetti."

Ira shuffled a box of crackers from one hand to the
other, then handed it to Astrid. "I brought these. I wasn't
sure if there would be snacks or . . ." He cleared his throat.
"I was afraid I'd already missed dinner."

Astrid shot him a beaming, reassuring smile. "No,
you're just in time. Go ahead and sit down. I'll be right
back." She took the box of crackers and made her way into
the kitchen. She set the crackers down, then turned to Imogene. "Are you ready?"

Imogene sucked in a deep breath. She closed her eyes
and Astrid could almost see her pulling herself together.
Then she opened her eyes once more. "I guess I'm as ready
as I'll ever be."

Astrid reached up and pinched both of Imogene's
cheeks at the same time.

"Ow," Imogene cried, though hopefully not loud enough
for Ira to hear.

"Now you're ready," Astrid said. "Let's go."

Astrid had to all but drag Imogene into the dining room.
She was walking way too slow, mincing along as if her
feet were in casts instead of slightly too-small shoes.

As instructed, Ira had already taken a seat. Astrid directed
Imogene to sit in place opposite him. Honestly, what choice

did she have? There were only two places set at a dining table large enough to seat eight.

"Is this chair okay?" Ira asked. Then he looked up and saw Imogene and stood. "Hey, Imogene," he said. "It's good to see you again."

Imogene shot him a bashful smile. Her cheeks were bright pink, and Astrid hoped that she hadn't pinched her too hard. Probably not. Imogene seemed like the kind of woman who would blush.

"It's perfect," Astrid said. "Imogene, go ahead and sit down, and I'll bring in the food."

Naturally, Imogene did as Astrid instructed.

Then Astrid waved a fluttering hand in the air. "Go ahead and talk and stuff. I'll be back."

She bustled out of the dining room and back into the kitchen.

But she nearly bumped into her brother, who was coming into the dining room with a plate piled high with spaghetti.

"Hey," Jesse protested. "You almost made me spill my food all over my shirt."

"Tell me you're not thinking about going into the dining room," she demanded.

He took a bite of his food. "*Jah,* I was. I was about to eat dinner. I like to do that in the dining room."

"Not tonight you're not." Astrid crossed her arms emphatically.

"Where am I supposed to eat then?"

"In the kitchen," she said.

"What if I don't want to eat in the kitchen?" He gave her a pointed look and then took another bite of the spaghetti. "I live here too, you know."

Astrid shook her head, then spun her brother around and guided him toward the table that sat in the middle of the kitchen. It was a small dinette set with just four chairs and barely enough room to have that many people gather around it. But it was enough for him to sit and eat his supper while she tried to work magic on the couple in the dining room.

"If you can eat standing up, you can eat in the kitchen." Astrid grabbed up the plate sitting on the counter and took it to the stovetop. There had been two sitting there until someone—not to be naming names, but Jesse—snatched one up for himself. She filled the plate with spaghetti and took a second one down from the cupboard and filled it as well.

"What's going on in the dining room?" her brother asked.

She grabbed a couple of pieces of garlic bread and set them to the side. "Nothing you need to worry about."

"Where's the Parmesan cheese?" Jesse asked.

"In the dining room," she replied.

"Then I'm worried about it."

She picked up the two plates and started for that very destination.

"Why do you have two plates?"

"Why do you ask so many questions?" She turned around and backed through the swinging door into the dining room. It was so quiet you could hear a mouse faint. "Now, who's hungry?" Astrid asked. Her voice was too bright and too cheerful.

And too loud.

Had they been sitting there in silence the whole time?

She placed one of the plates in front of Imogene and the other in front of Ira. He looked down at it, then back up to her. "I guess I should have said something," he started.

"What's the matter?" Astrid asked.

"I'm allergic to tomatoes." He made an apologetic face,

but Astrid still wanted to walk up to the nearest wall and bang her head against it.

Was it too much to ask for one evening to go according to plan? But if he had told her in advance, what would she have made? Her culinary skills began at instant potatoes and ended with spaghetti, which everyone knew was the hardest dish on the planet to mess up. Now her Romeo was telling her that he was allergic to tomatoes?

She wasn't sure the evening could get any worse.

Just then Jesse pushed from the kitchen into the dining room. "Cheese? Parmesan cheese?"

Astrid closed her eyes and quickly pulled herself together. She opened them once again and smiled at the three people staring at her in wonder. Like they were wondering what she was up to.

She snatched the small ceramic bowl of cheese off the table and came around the other side. She thrusted it toward her brother. "Here."

He looked down at the white porcelain glass that held the store-bought, pre-grated Parmesan cheese. "This is it?"

"That's it," she said. She might not be a good cook, but she knew how to set a pretty table.

Jesse picked that time to notice that they had guests. He looked at Ira then to Imogene. "Hey." He might have been a little slow on the uptake, but it didn't take him long to notice the elaborately set table with only two people sitting around it before he got the hint. "Oh. Got it. I guess I'll see you later." He turned on his heel and disappeared back into the kitchen.

Astrid grabbed Ira's plate from in front of him. "I'll just take this . . ." She cleared her throat. "I'm sure I can find something. . . ."

Ira shook his head and stood. "Don't go to any extra trouble for me," he said. He pushed his chair back up to the table and nodded toward Imogene. "It was good to see you again, Imogene."

To her credit, she smiled in return, though Astrid caught the slight tremble of her lips. "It was good to see you again too, Ira."

"*Danki* for the invitation," Ira said to Astrid. "I'll see myself out."

"Good night," Astrid said. She wanted to run after him, beg him to stay, but what good would it do? The evening was a total bust.

Imogene stayed in her seat until they heard the front door shut behind Ira. Then she jumped up from her chair, knocking it backward as she ran for the downstairs bathroom.

CHAPTER NINE

"What was that racket?" Jesse picked that time to come out of the kitchen.

Astrid threw up her hands in frustration. "Ira left, no thanks to you," she said. "Imogene locked herself in the bathroom. Everything is ruined."

"How is Ira leaving my fault?" Jesse had the nerve to ask.

In truth, it wasn't Jesse's fault. He didn't have anything to do with Ira leaving at all, but Astrid needed somebody to blame and her brother was as good a somebody as any. "Maybe it is, maybe it isn't," she said. "I'm going to check the phone messages."

"At this time of day?" Jesse asked. He looked to the clock sitting on the sideboard. "Night?"

"Of course," Astrid said as if it was completely normal to check phone messages at eight o'clock on Saturday evening. She was hoping against hope that perhaps she'd heard from her editor and that she had loved the new idea Astrid had submitted. That idea Astrid had painstakingly pieced together before she got the idea to match Ira and Imogene and write their story. The original idea was nowhere near as good as the idea of matchmaking two people who belonged together even if they didn't know at the beginning that they did.

But since the Imogene-Ira angle was proving to be harder than she had anticipated, she was back to Square One. Or Idea One, as it would be.

She started toward the door.

"What about Imogene?" Jesse asked.

She really should go see about her friend, but frankly, she wasn't in a very consoling mood. It felt quite selfish to walk out, but she'd only be gone a minute. She just needed a little time to regroup and think. Walking out to check messages that were most likely not there would give her the time she needed to collect herself.

"She'll be okay for a bit," she said. "I'll be back in less than five."

Jesse watched his sister as she turned and made her way toward the front door. The phone was in the workshop, and her assurances of being back in less than five minutes were most likely spot-on. But he still couldn't believe she had walked out on her guest. Something was going on with his sister and normally he knew exactly what it was. After all, they were twins. Lately, though, she'd been acting downright squirrely. Then to abandon Imogene . . .

He shook his head and straightened the chair that Imogene had obviously knocked over in her haste to get away from everything. The thought struck him. Maybe Imogene needed the alone time as much as Astrid did.

He'd learned a couple of things in his thirty-plus years on this planet and one was to never get between two women, especially not when it concerned a man. He had a feeling that Ira had it out for himself, even if he didn't know it.

Jesse pushed through the swinging door back into the kitchen, where his spaghetti was all too quickly getting colder and colder. He had worked nonstop since breakfast trying to get his shop organized and get caught up on orders. He had almost succeeded. After all that work, was it too much to ask to have a decent dinner and have it be warm?

He sat down at his plate and took another bite. Spaghetti wasn't nearly as tasty at room temperature as it was when it was hot, but he was hungry. So he took another bite and continued on. But the thought of Imogene locked in their downstairs bathroom bothered him. He wasn't sure why. She was Astrid's friend more than his, but something in him was worried for her.

She'd been sweet and kind when they had gone out for ice cream at the beginning of the week. Jesse had to admit that sharing an ice cream with her little family and watching the boys feed the ducks at the pond on his uncle's farm had been a great start to his week. That made it even harder to sit and eat cold spaghetti while she was locked away.

Jesse stood, wiped his mouth on a paper towel, then made his way out of the kitchen and down the hall to the downstairs bathroom.

He stopped at the door to listen. Muffled sniffles filtered out to him, faint, but there all the same. He raised his hand to knock but stopped. It seemed too intimate to beat on the door while she cried behind it. Too personal. He turned as if to go back to the kitchen, but his feet wouldn't take him there. Only one thing to do.

He rapped lightly on the wooden door. "Imogene?" They were friends, right? Surely a friend could check on another without it seeming inappropriate. That was his justification, and he was going with it. For the time being anyway.

"I'll be out in a minute." Her voice sounded full of tears, and his heart broke a little for her. He wasn't sure what was going on between Imogene and Ira. And Astrid. But he imagined it was some sort of quarrel. Hadn't his sister told him that Imogene was engaged?

That was what Astrid had told him, but he hadn't heard any more about it since that first day she had come to the house. Not that he kept his finger on the grapevine in Paradise Hill or anything. He pretty much kept to himself.

Still, a man couldn't help but hear talk while in line at the grocery store and such, and he hadn't heard anything about Ira Oberholtzer becoming engaged.

"Are you okay?"

A sound, half chuckle–half sob, came next. "Of course," she returned. "Never better."

A bigger lie he was sure he'd never heard. "I mean, if you need to talk . . ." he started.

What was he thinking? The last thing he needed was Imogene crying on his shoulder. Hadn't he just said he wasn't going to get involved in matters of the heart that didn't pertain to him? Yet here he was.

The door to the bathroom slowly creaked open, and there she was. Her eyes were just a little puffy from crying and her nose a little red. Her lashes were thick and dark, clumped together by tears. She gave him a watery smile. "*Danki*," she said. "But I'm all right."

He frowned and wanted to ask more, but she brushed past him, walking barefoot down the hall and back toward the dining room.

"Where's Astrid?"

So that was how they would play this. Like nothing ever happened. "She went to check the voice mail messages."

Imogene frowned. "At the phone shanty?"

He shook his head. "I have a phone in my workshop. So she's just outside."

Imogene nodded and returned to her place at the table. She looked down at her food and reached for her glass of water. She drank it all in three big gulps.

He hoped the liquid wasn't meant to refuel her tears. He really hated it when women cried. It gave him such a defeated, helpless feeling, one he avoided as much as possible.

"I guess I'll just go . . ." He pointed toward the kitchen, where his cold spaghetti waited.

"You can join me here, if you'd like."

Jesse didn't have to think about it long. "*Jah*, sure. Let me get my plate."

The words had barely left his mouth when Astrid came rushing into the house. She practically slid into the dining room, her face flushed red.

"Get your things. We've got to go. Your boys are at the hospital."

"I should've never left them alone," Imogene wailed.

Astrid turned from her place in the front seat of the buggy and reached back to grasp Imogene's hand in her own.

As soon as she had heard the voice mail message, she had rushed back into the house to get Imogene. Her friend was so upset already that news of her boys suffering an injury left her nearly immobilized. So it was Jesse who had hopped behind the reins of Imogene's buggy and was now driving them over to the Paradise Springs Emergency Clinic.

"You didn't leave them alone," Astrid assured her. "You left them with Sylvie and Vern."

"I should've never left them with Sylvie and Vern," Imogene corrected.

"Honey, it was an accident," Astrid reminded her. "It could have happened wherever they had been and with whoever was watching them."

"But they're at the hospital."

"They're at the emergency clinic. I didn't mean to scare you. I'm sure they're fine." This is just what she didn't need. She would never be able to get Ira and Imogene together and they were never going to be able to spend any time alone. Time alone would never happen if Imogene felt like she couldn't leave her boys in someone else's care.

It wouldn't be good for Imogene herself, either. That sort of worry for another person, a child, was once removed from Astrid. She understood the need, but she had never experienced it herself. She had no nieces or nephews or children of her own, and she was certain her assurances were falling on deaf ears. Aside from the fact that Imogene was worried sick about her children, if she ever stopped to consider the source, Astrid was sure she would toss her suggestions right out the window.

But Imogene had stopped listening. Not because Astrid had no children of her own and was not able to give good advice on the subject, but because she was praying.

Imogene had closed her eyes; her lips were slowly moving though no sound came out. Astrid squeezed her fingers in a gesture of support and turned back around to face the front.

"Can't you go any faster?" she asked her brother.

Jesse shot her a look. "I'm pretty sure this old mare has never won any races, and she's not about to start now. I'm doing the best I can."

"Well, do better," she said. Astrid was pretty certain from that point on Jesse simply ignored her.

It seemed to take absolutely forever to get from Paradise Hill to Paradise Springs. It wasn't a trip that she made often, and that fact coupled with the urgency and the darkness that surrounded them made the trip seem to take even longer than normal. She supposed they could have called a driver, but by the time they found one and the driver made it to the house, they could have had the horse and carriage halfway to their destination. But finally, *finally*, they pulled up in front of the emergency clinic. Imogene didn't wait for either one of them to get out of the buggy; she simply crawled over Astrid and ran inside.

"Where are her shoes?" Astrid asked.

"I don't know." Jesse shrugged. "She came out of the bathroom like that."

Astrid supposed in their haste to get to the hospital Imogene had forgotten to put her shoes back on. Then she remembered that she'd made Imogene wear a pair of her own. A pair that was a little small. She shouldn't have done that. She was just trying to make her as pretty as possible. Everyone deserved to feel pretty from time to time, even if pretty wasn't something a person should overly focus on.

With a sigh Astrid climbed out of the buggy.

"Don't mind me," Jesse called. "I'll just wait right here."

She waved a hand at her brother without turning around and made her way inside the Paradise Springs Emergency Clinic. Even though it was after nine on a Saturday night the place was buzzing. Or maybe because it was after nine on a Saturday night the place was buzzing. Astrid truly didn't know how things worked.

Several injured people were scattered about the waiting room along with their companions. There was a man who looked like perhaps he had broken his arm and a woman with a bloody nose and another poor soul who held a small trash can at the ready.

Imogene was standing at the counter. Yep, barefoot.

"I'm their mother," Imogene was saying.

The woman behind the counter was dressed in one of the aqua-blue pajama-looking outfits that medical professionals seemed to prefer. Her blond hair was pulled back in a stubby ponytail, the strands that had pulled free tucked behind her ears. She paused for just a moment as if trying to assess the truth in Imogene's words, then decided the information she was giving out was acceptable.

"They were treated and released," the woman said. "That's all I can tell you."

"They're not here anymore?" Astrid said as she came up behind Imogene.

"It looks like they were discharged about ten minutes ago," the nurse said.

"I'm sure they went back to the B&B," Imogene said. "I hope."

Astrid cocked her head toward the door. "Then let's go."

In record time and yet what seemed like an eternity, Jesse parked their mare to one side of the Paradise B&B. Once again Imogene scrambled out without one look at Astrid or Jesse. Good thing Astrid decided to ride in the back for the short trip. Riding behind sure beat being climbed over.

Jesse tied the horse's reins to the hitching post as Astrid followed Imogene into the B&B.

"Mamm! Mamm! Mamm!" The boys rushed to Imogene, jumping excitedly around her.

Astrid held back as Imogene did her best to hug their

squirming bodies. Behind her Jesse came in, closing the door quietly after himself.

"Are you okay?" Imogene asked, her voice once again thick with tears. Astrid hoped at least that these were the happy kind. "Let me look at you."

Miraculously, the boys remained still enough for Imogene to inspect the mirrored cuts on their foreheads.

Sylvie Yoder, owner of the Paradise B&B, came up behind the boys as Imogene tried to assess their injuries. "I'm so sorry, Imogene," she said. "They were just running around having a good time and the next thing we know there's blood everywhere."

Vern King, Sylvie's intended, stood next to her, nodding in support. "They were just being boys."

"I'm so glad you're okay," Imogene said, rubbing a hand down the side of each one of their faces. She had that one instant to comfort them before they spun away and started demonstrating what happened.

Vern immediately stepped between the boys. "We'll have none of that again," he told them. "One trip to the hospital a night is enough."

"Aw," the boys complained, then began using wild hand gestures to explain.

They really were cute boys, Astrid thought. But definitely a handful. No wonder Imogene wanted to get married again. She was outnumbered.

"We hope this won't keep you from allowing us to look after them again," Sylvie said.

Imogene stopped and stared at them, the look on her face unreadable. "You want to babysit them again?"

Vern grinned. "They're a lot of fun. And until our little Linda Beth gets big enough to run around, it gives us something to do."

"Who's Linda Beth?" Astrid wanted to know.

A bright light sparkled in both Vern's and Sylvie's eyes. "Linda Beth is my niece's little girl," Sylvie explained.

"And my soon-to-be great-granddaughter," Vern added.

"How sweet," Astrid said. And it was.

The boys continued to animatedly explain their injuries and what they had done all evening and how fun it was to come and play with Vern and Sylvie.

"Speaking of sweet," Vern said with a nudge at Sylvie. "How about some of that pie?"

Mahlon jumped up and down excitedly. "I love pie."

"A whoopie pie?" Imogene asked.

That was oddly specific, Astrid thought. But she didn't have time to comment as Imogene turned to explain.

"Sylvie makes the best whoopie pies in the county."

"No," Sylvie said. "It's just a regular pie. I lost my title this spring."

Astrid remembered now. The big Whoopie Pie Festival that was held in Paradise Springs. That was why Sylvie's name seemed so familiar when Imogene had told her who she had gotten to keep the twins. Sylvie Yoder was something of a legend in Paradise Valley. She'd been the longest reigning Whoopie Pie Queen they'd had ever had. But she had lost the title this past spring to a newcomer, Sadie Yoder.

Astrid didn't know Sadie, or anything about her, really. Sadie hadn't been in these parts long enough for the gossip to seep across the dividing line between Hill and Springs.

"I wouldn't mind a piece of pie," Jesse said. "My dinner's still sitting on the kitchen table."

Imogene turned toward him, her mouth open in astonishment. "Jesse. I'm so sorry."

He waved away her apology. "It's not necessary. Especially not if I can get pie. I'd rather have Sylvie's pie than Astrid's cooking any day of the week."

Everyone laughed but Astrid. She poked her brother in the side but couldn't dispute his comments about her culinary skills.

"Come on in and get comfortable," Sylvie said, pointing them toward the downstairs common room. "I'll go get everyone a little snack."

"So how was your dinner?" Vern asked after Sylvie had disappeared into the kitchen.

The boys settled down at a small table with two chairs that sat next to the window. A checkers board had been set up and looked to be in mid-game. Astrid supposed that was what the boys had been doing when they had decided to crash into each other for whatever reason boys have for crashing into each other.

Imogene gave a rueful smile. "Not so well."

"I'm so sorry," Astrid said. "We're not giving up."

"Giving up what?" Jesse and Vern asked at the same time.

Astrid immediately wished she could take those words back. She just hadn't been thinking.

Imogene shot her a helpless look.

"I'm sorry," Astrid said again. It was all she could do. The cat was out of the bag so to speak. She had spoken first and not given a thought to what her words would mean to the other people in the room.

"What?" Jesse asked again.

"I agreed to help Imogene find a new husband."

Jesse paused for a moment, then laughed a bit. Astrid couldn't tell if he thought it was funny or if he simply couldn't believe the words she had said. "Ira Oberholtzer?"

"What's wrong with Ira Oberholtzer?" Imogene demanded.

"Nothing," Jesse said quickly. "Nothing." Jesse paused. "Except he's at least a decade older than you are."

"Eight years," Astrid corrected. "Not hardly a decade."

Imogene chewed her lower lip. "But other than that he's okay? I mean, he would make a good husband for me . . . someone."

"Of course he would—will," Astrid said. "I've been talking to him all week. Ira Oberholtzer is a fine, upstanding man and any woman would be lucky to be his bride."

"Bride?" The twins were on their feet in a moment. They rushed toward their mother, their expressions unreadable and identical.

"Who's getting married?" Mahlon demanded. At least Astrid thought it was Mahlon. She wasn't quite sure how to tell the boys apart yet. If they were lucky, their cuts would scar over and a body would be able to tell one from the other.

"Nobody's getting married," Imogene said.

At the same time Astrid replied, "Your mother and Ira Oberholtzer."

Those unreadable expressions turned to obvious annoyance. Maybe even downright anger. "You can't marry this Ira person," the other twin, possibly Mattie, said.

"If you marry him, he'll be our *dat*," Possibly Mahlon interjected.

"We don't want him to be our *dat*," Possibly Mattie cried. "We want Jesse."

"*Jah*," Possibly Mahlon said. "If you marry anybody, you need to marry Jesse."

CHAPTER TEN

Jesse felt the heat rise into his cheeks, but one glance in Imogene's direction and he could tell the poor woman was mortified.

"Promise! Promise!" the boys chanted, intermittently jumping up and down with each word spoken. "Promise us you'll marry Jesse."

"I . . . I can't promise you anything of the sort," Imogene finally managed. "There's more to marriage than just deciding you're going to marry someone."

Jesse was glad she said those words out loud, and he hoped that she heeded them before his sister got her into all kinds of circumstances she might not be able to get out of.

He loved his sister, but she had a bunch of cockamamie ideas and had a tendency to go off without fully thinking the situation through. Now she had got it in her head that she was going to make two people whom she barely knew fall in love.

It was times like this when he hated being the youngest. He might be younger by only a few minutes, but she always twisted it around and used it against him.

Who was he trying to kid? It didn't matter who was born first, Astrid was headstrong and at times a little too offbeat for her own good.

"Who wants pie?" Sylvie came back into the common room carrying a large tray with a slice of pie for all of them.

She set the tray on the sideboard next to the window and started doling out the sweet treats.

She was one smart lady, Jesse decided. She hadn't been in the room for more than a few seconds, and she could tell something had happened in her absence.

"What's going on?" She pinned Vern with a knowing look.

"It seems Astrid here has promised Imogene that she can marry Ira Oberholtzer and the boys think she should marry Jesse."

Astrid shifted uncomfortably in her seat. But Jesse noticed that Imogene was purple with mortification.

"That's not exactly how it happened or what I said," Astrid argued. "Imogene came to me as a matchmaker and asked me to find her match. So I did. Ira."

The boys were shaking their heads vigorously. So vigorously that they were almost falling down. Jesse stood and put a hand on each one of their shoulders. They instantly calmed.

"That's not how we want it to go," Mattie said. "We like Jesse."

"*Jah*," Imogene said, somehow managing to get herself together enough to respond. "We all like Jesse. But that doesn't mean I can marry him. Now, let's talk about something else." Pure Imogene. She was a rule follower through and through and talking about marriage in such mixed company—males and females, family and acquaintances— was not how things were traditionally done.

Mahlon turned his face toward Jesse, craning his head back to look up at him. "Why? Are you married, Jesse? You're not married, are you?"

"I'm not married," Jesse admitted. "But," he said before

either boy could respond. "Your mother gets to choose who she marries."

"I thought we had agreed to talk about something else," Imogene tried again.

"We don't have a say?" Mahlon said. "That stinks."

Jesse bit back a laugh. These boys really were something else. Any man would be lucky to be their *dat*. "I'm sure your mother will take your feelings into consideration. But if she is thinking about courting someone like Ira, maybe you should give him a chance."

The boys looked skeptical, but there was pie waiting on them and neither one wanted to fuss about adult things too much longer. He could almost tell the instant when they decided to let it go and eat instead. But he had a feeling it wasn't over.

"I do believe this is the best pie I've ever tasted," Astrid said.

Sylvie beamed in pride. "*Danki*," she said. "I know it's a little early for pumpkin, but fall is coming."

And with it, the annual Fall Festival in Paradise Hill.

"You should enter this in the baking contest in the festival."

Sylvie shook her head. "My baking contest days are over."

Vern shot her a disbelieving look. "Since when?"

Sylvie set up a little straighter in her seat and sliced off a bite of pie with the side of her fork. "Since now."

"Since Sadie Yoder took the whoopie pie title," Vern muttered under his breath.

Jesse couldn't tell if Sylvie actually heard him or not. But he was fairly certain she had decided to ignore the comment and instead enjoy her own slice of pie.

She swallowed that bite and turned her attention to Astrid. "So you're matchmaking?"

Vern grinned. "We know a little about that, don't we, Sylvie?"

"You do?" Astrid asked.

By the way, when had she decided she was a matchmaker? The last time he checked, his sister was a romance author who was running out of time to turn her book in before the deadline. Shouldn't she be working instead of trying to get two people she barely knew to fall in love?

"Is it against God's will?" Jesse asked. He hadn't meant to say the words out loud. They just flitted through his head and popped out of his mouth of their own accord.

"Of course not," Astrid said. "I'm actually helping God's will along."

"If you say so," Jesse muttered, then he turned his attention to his own pie. Sometimes there was no winning with his sister. Most times it wasn't even worth the effort to try. When she set her mind on something, it was pretty much impossible to get her off it. So if she had set her mind on making sure Ira Oberholtzer and Imogene Yoder got married, then she would move mountains to make it happen.

"I think helping love along is a fine idea," Sylvie said.

"Hear! Hear!" Vern raised his fork in toast.

They all took a bite of pie.

Mahlon looked around the room to make sure all the adults were busy chewing before saying, "Fine. Just as long as Mamm marries Jesse."

He hadn't thought it possible, but Imogene turned an even deeper shade of pink.

She stood. "I think it's time we get home."

"We only brought the one buggy," Astrid pointed out.

They had been in such a hurry, they had jumped in the only buggy hitched up—it just so happened that it was Imogene's—and hustled over to the emergency clinic. But now that everything had settled down that decision was proving to be inconvenient.

"Whose buggy is it?" Sylvie asked. "Whose buggy did you bring?"

"Mine," Imogene said.

"I'll tell you what," Vern said. "Imogene can take her buggy and the boys on to her house, and I'll run you folks home."

"All the way to Paradise Hill?" Astrid asked.

"It ain't nothing," Vern said. "Besides, my horse needs to get out more these days. The run will do him some good."

"That's mighty kind of you," Jesse said.

Vern waved away his words. "That's what friends are for."

Imogene could take no more. Her emotions were frayed. All of them. Because she had used them all this evening. She had been so incredibly nervous just thinking about spending time with Ira Oberholtzer, then she'd been humiliated when he had left without even eating dinner. She had been half scared out of her mind when she had learned that the boys had had an accident and had to go to the emergency clinic. Then she had been flooded with relief and happiness to find out they were fine and safe. Now she was embarrassed beyond belief. Yes, it was time to go home.

She stood. "Okay, boys, eat your pie and take your plates into the kitchen. It's time to go."

"Why do we have to?" Mahlon asked.

Mattie shoved his last bite of pie into his mouth. "*Jah*, do we have to?"

"Yes," Imogene said. "We have to. And don't talk with your mouth full." Behind her she heard Vern chuckle.

"Don't you worry," Vern said. "You'll be coming over plenty to visit. Right, Imogene?"

Imogene took a second to get her mind wrapped around what she was hearing. "You'll really babysit for me again?" She had family members who had vowed never to babysit the boys again.

"They're great fun," Vern said.

"*Jah*," Sylvie said in agreement. "We had a lot of fun tonight. Until they got hurt. We are so sorry about that."

"No, it's all right," Imogene said. Their injuries were not severe. The emergency clinic had put a butterfly bandage over the cuts and sent them home. They would be fine tomorrow, having forgotten all about their crash, as they got into something new. She just couldn't believe that her friends were willing to care for them again. There came that relief again.

"I really appreciate that," Imogene said.

"Did you hear your *mamm* say to take your plates to the kitchen?" Jesse asked.

Imogene appreciated the backup. She felt like she stayed on the boys constantly. She barely had time to tell them that she loved them, she was so busy making sure they did what they were supposed to do. It was exhausting and she really appreciated any help she could get.

"Just set them on the tray there," Sylvie said. "I'll take everybody's dishes to the kitchen."

The boys stood obediently and carried their plates to the tray Sylvie indicated.

"I should help clean up first," Imogene said.

"No," Sylvie said. "Go on and get those boys to bed. I'm sure they'll have headaches as soon as they slow down enough for the pain to catch up with them. I'll see to the dishes."

"I'll help," Astrid said.

But Sylvie was shaking her head at that offer as well.

"Just a few plates ain't nothing," Sylvie said. "Everybody go on and get home. It's been quite an evening."

That was the truth, Imogene thought.

Everyone said good night and Imogene bustled the boys back into their buggy.

"You're really not going to marry Ira Oberholtzer. Are you, Mamm?" Mattie's voice came from behind her as she pulled her buggy out onto the street.

They weren't too far from home, but she didn't like driving after dark. There were times when it was necessary, and she supposed tonight was one. But she kept her eyes on the road as she answered him. "Ira is a good man, Matthew."

"So's Jesse," Mahlon interjected. "I like Jesse."

"Me too," Mattie added.

"I like Jesse too," Imogene said.

"See? Then you should marry him. It's un-animous. We all like him."

"Unanimous," Imogene said, correcting his pronunciation of the word. Still it brought a smile to her face. "I bet you boys will like Ira even more," she continued, though she didn't know that for a fact. He was a lot older than her, and his kids were both practically grown. He might not have one thing in common with her rowdy twins. He was a good man, and a matchmaker was setting them up. She could hardly ask for more than that.

"Matchmaking can be great fun," Vern said as they drove along. Jesse was sitting in the front next to him while Astrid rode in the back. She was all right with that placement. She needed the dark and quiet of the near solitude to get her thoughts in order. Tonight had not gone as planned on many, many levels.

Note to self: Before serving a dinner with the intent to get two people romantically involved, find out all food allergies of the guests.

But hopefully, she wouldn't have to be doing this again. Hopefully, her creative side would kick back into gear, make an appearance once again, and help her get this book done. Until then she would just have to remember that Ira was allergic to tomatoes.

"Of course, I'm not a pro like you," Vern tossed over his shoulder.

"She's not a professional matchmaker," Jesse said.

Astrid wanted to pinch her brother like she used to when they were kids. She managed to refrain. "You could say that I am. I get people together and make them fall in love all the time."

Jesse leaned a little closer to Vern as if revealing a great secret. "Astrid is really a romance writer."

Vern turned back to look at her. "You don't say."

Actually, she hadn't. Jesse had. "That's right."

"Wait; the bishop doesn't kick up a fuss?"

"Amish people have been writing for newspapers for years, decades even," she said.

"The bishop is our uncle," Jesse interjected.

"Will you be quiet?" Astrid said to her brother. Really. She didn't need him dragging this conversation out. She had more important things to think about at the moment, like how she was going to get Ira and Imogene together again.

Matchmaking in books was easy. Matchmaking in real life was hard. "That's not why he gave me permission to publish," she continued. "My books are chaste, and about the Amish. I help people understand our ways and bring a little joy into the world. Plus, most of the money I make on them—above what we need to pay our bills—I donate to the community fund. I give back."

She hated the defensive note in her voice. That was the exact reason why she didn't tell people that she was an author. Even *Englisch* people had a preconceived notion of authors and the books they wrote and the lives they lived. It was even worse when you were Amish. People made way too many assumptions concerning romance novels. Most thought they were all of the secular variety and had no idea there was a whole subgenre of clean books where people fell in love.

"Now that is something else," Vern said. "I'm going to look up your books and read one for myself."

"Her pen name is Rachel Kauffman."

"Not Astrid?" Vern asked.

"Her publisher thought it didn't sound Amish enough." Jesse was being so helpful tonight.

"Rachel's my middle name," Astrid said. "And, *jah*, I suppose it does sound a little more Amish than Astrid."

"Our mother loved flowers," Jesse said.

"I guess it's a good thing she had at least one girl then," Vern said. "Or you might've ended up being named Rose." He laughed at his own joke and of course Jesse laughed with him.

"She also loved books," Astrid said. "She told me once that between the flower and the books she read when she was a young girl, she'd always wanted to have a daughter and name her Astrid."

Astrid loved her name except that it was a little unusual. She just wished she could remember the title of the book that her *mamm* said she got her name from. Astrid had searched and searched. Perhaps that was why Astrid loved books so much. And she did love books. She always had.

"Ira Oberholtzer will make a fine husband for Imogene

and those boys," Astrid said. The conversation in the front of the buggy had lulled and she hadn't meant to say the words out loud. But it was done now.

"I don't know the man myself," Vern said. "When I need what he sells, I go to Paradise Hardware. It's closer, you know."

"He's a good man," Jesse said. "I've got nothing against him." She heard something in her brother's voice she'd never quite heard before. She wasn't sure exactly what it was, but it sounded a little like jealousy. But why would Jesse be jealous of Ira Oberholtzer?

Perhaps it was that Jesse was envious of Ira's decision to move on after being widowed. Jesse had been married once before for a brief, brief time. So brief, in fact, his wife, Amanda, had died before their first anniversary.

Still she wondered if she was trying to convince Jesse, or her own self.

It was true, Imogene needed a husband like Ira. That had been Astrid's plan from the beginning. It's just that before she decided that Ira would make a good husband for Imogene, she'd never thought much about Ira as a potential husband. She hadn't really thought too much about how handsome he was or what a good worker or a good father or a good and godly man he was. Now that she was thinking about it . . .

Actually, Astrid couldn't say for certain that he would make a good husband, but from the outside looking in, it certainly appeared that way. Astrid herself had never been married. The truth was, she had always been something of a bookworm, losing herself in the pages of a novel, or the Bible, or the back of the cereal box. When she got older, she started losing herself in the pages of the books that she was writing. But the sad truth of it all? She continued to prefer fiction to real life. Now there was Ira Oberholtzer, looking like he stepped out of the pages of one of her novels in his work apron and straw hat. She shouldn't be interested in him at all like that. She couldn't be. She was supposed to be making him fall in love with Imogene. Imogene was depending on it. Astrid's book depended on it. She had promised. And that was all there was to that.

CHAPTER ELEVEN

Sunday morning dawned, and so did Astrid's renewed sense of duty. She *would* make Ira Oberholtzer fall in love with Imogene. She would somehow get Imogene's boys to fall in love with Ira Oberholtzer, and they would all live happily ever after. Even her editor. She would be ecstatic that Astrid had managed to find a new storyline for her series.

But this Sunday was a church Sunday for Imogene. Astrid wished she'd thought about that the day before. She could've talked Ira into going to church in Paradise Springs, but hindsight and all that.

She put on her Sunday, stay-around-the-house clothes and bustled downstairs to cook breakfast. Technically, she was not allowed to work on Sundays, but she didn't have full control on when ideas came to her. Ideas came when they came. Today she would like to make a few notes concerning Imogene and Ira's romance.

She opened the fridge and pulled out a carton of eggs. She would scramble them today. That was Jesse's favorite. She hated to admit that she didn't like to make scrambled eggs because it dirtied up another fork and another bowl that was completely unnecessary, but it was the truth all the same. She liked her eggs fried so she could get them eaten with one less bowl and piece of flatware left to wash. But for Jesse she would do this, especially after everything she put him through the night before. Of course, she was still a little miffed at him for the way he talked to Vern King on the way home. Like they were buddies from way back.

She was just cracking the eggs into the bowl—the unnecessary one if you eat fried eggs—when Jesse came into the kitchen. He was freshly shaved wearing his crisp white church shirt along with the black vest he wore on Sundays.

"Where are you going all dressed up? Did you get your Sundays confused?" She continued happily cracking open the eggs.

"Church," he replied as if she somehow had taken leave of her senses.

"We don't have church today."

"No," he said. "I'm going over to Paradise Springs this morning. Mattie and Mahlon invited me to come."

"But you are going to eat breakfast."

"I got a long trip across town, so I was thinking I would just take a peanut butter and jelly sandwich and eat it as I drove."

Astrid looked down in the bowl of eggs. Five yolks stared back at her. "I wish I would've known that before I cracked all these eggs." Truthfully, she was doubly mad at him. "How am I going to get Imogene's boys to fall in love with Ira if you keep accepting invitations from them?"

Jesse got down the bread and the peanut butter and started making his sandwich as if he hadn't a care in the world.

Make that triply mad at him.

"First of all, it's church."

"I know it's church." She knew she sounded like the worst Amish woman ever, but this was love they were talking about. Love and her romance novel that might never come to be if Jesse didn't stop interfering.

"Secondly, I only accepted one invitation from them, and third of all, how can I turn down two little boys?" He got out the jelly and started applying that to the second slice of bread.

"Easy," Astrid said. Though she knew that wasn't the truth. Matthew and Mahlon might be a handful, but they were pretty adorable.

"You try looking into those big blue eyes and telling them you can't come to church today." Jesse smashed the two sides of the sandwich together and wrapped it in a napkin.

"You should be ashamed of yourself, eating on your way to church on the Lord's day."

"I'm going to church on my off Sunday; I don't think the good Lord will mind." He put everything away, then grabbed the milk from the fridge. "Now I got to go before I'm late." He poured a thermos full, then stashed the milk back in the fridge.

"Aren't you going to clean up the rest of this mess?"

"What mess?" Jesse asked.

Astrid gestured toward the counter. "All these crumbs and stuff."

Jesse shot her a look, then sat his stuff on the kitchen table and used one hand to wipe the crumbs into the palm of the other. Then he dusted his hands over the sink and shot her an *Anything else?* look.

"Bye, sis," he said, then he grabbed his food and left.

He actually left.

She could hear the rattle of the harness and heavy clomp of the horse's hooves against their driveway as he pulled away.

She looked down at the bowl full of eggs that no one

was going to eat. At least she wasn't going to eat them.
There was no way she could eat five eggs for breakfast.
She found a piece of plastic wrap and covered the bowl,
then placed it in the fridge. Maybe she would make a pie
later.

Thinking about that pie made her think about the pie
they had eaten last night at the B&B. Sylvie Yoder might
not be making whoopie pies these days, but she was a very
good regular pie baker as well. Astrid made a mental note
to get her pumpkin pie recipe the next time she saw the
woman. With fall settling in, it might be good to have a
new recipe in her recipe box.

In fact she wished she had some of that pumpkin pie
right now for breakfast. Yum!

Instead, she grabbed two slices of bread and butter, then
stuck them in the oven to toast. She would rather have that
than eggs anyway.

Once her toast was ready she poured herself a fresh cup
of coffee, grabbed a notebook and a pen, then sat down at
the table. She didn't bother to move into the dining room.
She'd cleaned up the mess last night after Vern had
dropped them off, but she knew for a fact there were still
some bad memories rattling around in there.

She opened her notebook to the first blank page and
across the top wrote *how to make Ira and Imogene fall in
love*. Then under that she wrote *fun things for Ira and
Imogene to do*.

Of course, they could go to church with each other. But
she wasn't going to add that to the list. Church was . . .
church. It was a sacred part of their lives. They would naturally go to church together, but since their botched first
meeting, Astrid hadn't wanted to push that line.

Plus church was an ongoing prospect. She needed more
event-type stuff, the type of stuff where they could get to

know each other. The first thing coming up, that she could remember anyway, was the Fall Festival.

Paradise Springs might have the Whoopie Pie Festival in the spring, but the Fall Festival was better than that. It was more like a state fair with agricultural groups showing their animals and a prize given for the biggest pumpkin. There were all sorts of canning and cooking competitions, a quilt show, an art show—for the *Englisch* people—and rows and rows of trucks selling junk food. It was four whole days of rides and cotton candy and all sorts of other good things. It was the perfect time to get Ira and Imogene together.

Somehow every year when the Fall Festival started, it seemed as if the good Lord would send a chill to the air to make everyone realize that it was indeed fall. Was there anything more romantic than smelling wood burning in the cool crisp air of late September? Not hardly. It didn't always stay as cool after that first little break in the weather, but that first break in the weather created hope and hope created love. Right?

Jah. It did. That was her story, and she was sticking to it.

Astrid wrote *Fall Festival* at the top of the page. She took another bite of toast and thoughtfully chewed it while tapping her pen against her chin.

What else? What else?

But nothing came to mind.

See? This was why people needed to get married when they were young. The young people had it all figured out. They went to singings and had camping trips and bowling leagues and—

A bowling league. It was perfect. She and Jesse could join too; that way the pressure would be off the two of them. They wouldn't feel so isolated, and they would get to know each other better. Plus, Sylvie and Vern had promised to take care of the boys whenever Imogene needed a babysitter.

Jah! That was the perfect idea. Astrid got up and went to the kitchen cabinet. She pulled open the third drawer next to the fridge. It was the one they called the junk drawer and contained exactly that. But she thought . . .

She rummaged around until she finally found it. She'd picked it up in town a couple of weeks ago. A brochure from Paradise Pins.

She smacked it against her open palm and with a smile on her face she sat back down. Bowling was perfect. She opened the brochure and scanned down to see the times and dates for the bowling leagues. Even more perfect there was one starting now. Though the deadline was fast approaching. She wrote *bowling league* under *Fall Festival*.

Bowling.

Paradise Pins was the perfect place for a woman from Paradise Springs to fall in love with a man from Paradise Hill. Why? Paradise Pins sat on the boundary line between Paradise Hills and Paradise Springs. In fact, there was even a line that ran across the lanes showing where the boundary was. Technically, you got to sit in Paradise Hill while you knocked the pins over in Paradise Springs. Someone had told her once that the line was something of a joke, though it did sit in the proper place. They had also told her that there was a movie a long time ago about a little country watering hole that sat on the state line, half in one state and half in the other. Of course, she had never seen it. She could write books, but she surely wasn't pushing it by watching the movie. She would just have to take their word for it. It was all in good fun. Paradise Pins had to be the most neutral ground in all of Paradise Valley. *Jah*, it was the perfect place to make Imogene and Ira fall in love.

* * *

Jesse hadn't realized exactly how far it was to Paradise Springs until he pulled his buggy to a stop just outside of Uriah Lehman's house. That was the site of church today in Paradise Springs. Jesse had met Uriah before, somewhere or another. He owned Paradise Lumber, not that Jesse shopped there or anything. He bought his lumber from Hill Lumber. Mainly because it was closer. He stopped and wondered how much of that location situation kept the rivalry between the two towns going.

He gave his horse over to one of the boys who were responsible for setting them out to pasture, and made his way toward the house.

"He's here! He's here!"

He heard them before he saw them, then all the sudden Mattie and Mahlon came flying toward him. They hugged him quickly, then jumped around him in excitement. "You made it!"

"I told you he would." Mattie lightly pushed Mahlon.

"No, *I* told *you* he would." Mahlon pushed back.

"Now, there shouldn't be any shoving on the Lord's day," Jesse said, and the boys immediately stopped their scuffle. "How are your heads feeling?"

They beamed up at him.

"Mamm said it would probably scar," Mattie said as if it was the best news he had heard all day.

"I cannot believe you drove all the way over here from Paradise Hill." Imogene finally caught up with her boys.

"Good morning to you, too," Jesse said.

Imogene's cheeks filled with color. The rose color that he thought she wore so well. And speaking of wearing . . .

"You look nice today," he said.

She looked down at herself and laughed self-consciously. "*Danki,*" she said.

It was kind of sweet how she was so unassuming and unsure. Or maybe it was just refreshing because he lived with Astrid. His sister was something else, that was certain. He loved her with all his heart. But if he had to be married to her—or someone like her—he would probably do something drastic. *Jah*, he knew firsthand exactly why she wasn't married.

He couldn't help it, but he remembered Astrid this morning, fussing because he was allowing Imogene's boys to spend more and more time with him. How she was trying to get Imogene and Ira together. He supposed paying Imogene compliments would send his sister through the roof. He couldn't help himself. She did look lovely.

He had learned with Amanda that sometimes a woman needed a compliment or two. What did it hurt to say nice words to someone? It didn't hurt at all. Though he never said those words to anyone other than Amanda. He wasn't sure of the significance of that and instead concentrated on each step they took to the door of Uriah's barn. They were late, so they all walked in together.

Imogene steered the boys toward the women's side of the service, but they dug in their heels.

"I don't want to sit with the girls," Mahlon said.

"*Jah*, we want to sit with Jesse." Mattie tugged at his mother's hand.

Imogene opened her mouth to correct them, Jesse was certain, but he didn't mind and there was no sense in all the fuss. "They can sit with me," he said.

The relief in her eyes was clearly visible. "You don't mind?"

"Not at all," he said. "Men should stick together."

Mattie and Mahlon both beamed at having been called a man.

Imogene looked as if she were about to protest, then she finally nodded. "*Jah*. Okay. But you must be on your best behavior."

The boys nodded enthusiastically.

Imogene turned away, then spun around to face Jesse once again. She took a step closer. "Do me one favor please," she said. "Don't tell anyone that I've been visiting over in Paradise Hill. I don't want to get any rumors started."

What kind of rumors? That she and Ira Oberholtzer were going to start courting? Why did that need to be a secret? But Jesse didn't say that; he just nodded in return. "Of course."

She shot him a relieved smile, then turned to make her way to the women's benches.

Together the three of them—Jesse, Mahlon, and Mattie—made their way over to the church benches on the men's side. Thankfully, they managed to find a spot where they could all three sit together without disturbing those already in place.

His two church guests drew a couple of stares and a little bit of attention from both sides of the barn, but church was about to begin so no one asked him outright.

Just who in Paradise Springs did Imogene think he would tell about her coming over to the Hill? She knew all the people in Paradise Springs, and definitely many more of them than he did. But she wanted to keep her plans a secret and he would honor that.

As church began and the service commenced Jesse found himself having trouble concentrating. Somehow he had managed to seat himself directly across from Imogene Yoder. All he had to do was let his gaze drift away from the preacher and it landed smack dab on her every time. Like a magnet pulling iron fillings. He wasn't sure what it was about her that drew his interest. She surely didn't seem like the kind who would seek out a man's company. Not in the forward way that it seemed that she had.

Not that he was casting stones or anything. It just came across as odd to him. She always seemed quiet and demure when he talked to her. Not so open and forward.

But perhaps there was more behind her placid demeanor. As he sat there, he dissected her face as if that would give him some idea. Her nose was okay. It wasn't too big or too small. Her eyes were fine, hazel-colored, almost brown from this distance. Her hair was a true brown, not too dark, not too light. She didn't stand taller than anyone else in the community and she wasn't the shortest one there either. Somehow all of it mashed together to make the person she was and . . . *jah*, he wanted to get to know that person. That was the truth in it all. But if he were to tell that to Astrid, she would hit the roof. Mainly because she wouldn't understand. It wasn't that he wanted to be romantically involved with Imogene Yoder. He didn't want to be romantically involved with anyone. He'd had that pain and he wasn't about to open himself up to it again.

He and Amanda may have only spent a few months as man and wife, but it had been the sweetest time in his life. Somehow they had managed to not wait for the other shoe to drop on her health. They had found ways to enjoy the now, love in the moment, and not look too hard at the future.

Amanda had been his love, the one God made for him. To expect that sort of affection and adoration twice in a lifetime was arrogant. So he moved on and yet stayed in the same place.

He shook his head at himself, but still it plagued him. What would make a woman like that chase after a man like Ira? Or any man for that matter. It wasn't the Amish way. He knew that, Imogene knew that, even Astrid knew that.

But he'd had a thought. And that thought was that Astrid had more than matchmaking up her sleeve. His sister was nothing if not crafty.

CHAPTER TWELVE

Ira sat at the kitchen table, sipping coffee and flipping through the Sunday paper. He could hardly even say what he was looking at, and he surely couldn't read it. A man couldn't read when he could hardly think, and Ira could hardly think over the sound of the kitchen clock that ticked away on the wall.

When had the clock gotten so loud?

Had it always been this loud and he only noticed now?

He sighed. *Jah*, his house was way too quiet. The only thing he could do about it would be to add more people in. The only way he could do that was if he got married again.

He had talked a lot with Astrid Kauffman this week and somehow those conversations, though they weren't directly about it, had made him realize that he was alone in the world now. Ruthann was gone. Ruthie was married. And Elam would be in the house for only a few more years. But since he had turned sixteen and started running around, Ira had seen him less and less. That time would grow gradually less as the days and weeks went on.

It was the circle of life or some such he had heard people say. You have children knowing somewhere in your mind that eventually they would leave. But that was the way. They would grow up, find spouses, get married, have children of their own, find a job, some even moved out of state.

He wondered how Astrid felt about that. He'd thought a lot about what Astrid thought about things all week. But she had never been married. Not that she had said anyway. Maybe she had and her husband was gone too.

But with her coming in every day this past week, part of him thought, perhaps even hoped, that she had been making those trips to the hardware store with all these ridiculous requests for items that he had no idea what she was going to do with was just a way to put herself in front of him.

But somehow that thought felt arrogant. Vain, even. Yet without arrogance or vanity he could say that he was an eligible enough bachelor. Probably even a decent catch. He owned his own business. His kids were practically grown. He had all his own teeth, and his hair was just starting to gray. He was fit and healthy according to the doctor. Did women even care about such things? How was he supposed to know?

He shut the paper and pushed it aside. The activity was doing nothing more than getting newsprint on his fingers.

On the wall his clock still ticked away.

He needed to get out of the house.

He stood and pushed his chair back up to the table and made his way out the back door. It was a beautiful day, a beautiful Sunday. Normally, he would go visit with Ruthie, but she was out with her husband. They had invited Ira, but he turned them down. Somehow when he went to Lloyd's parents' house, he felt like an intrusion. Not that they ever did anything to make him feel that way; it was just

Ira wasn't part of that circle, and Ruthie was. It would've been different had Ruthann been by his side.

He walked around the side of the house, with no particular destination in mind. At least out here the birds were singing, chirping back and forth at each other in whatever language birds spoke, and the clock wasn't ticking.

Ira started off down the road just walking, almost forcing himself to enjoy the day. Which was ridiculous. It was too beautiful of a day not to enjoy.

He walked and hummed under his breath, letting his feet take him where they would. He just needed to be out.

Ira walked down to the stop sign at the end of the lane, then turned and started back. The phone shanty that he shared with his neighbors was coming up, and Ira thought perhaps that was a fine thing to do. He could stop and check the messages, see if he had anything, not that he was expecting any calls. Most people when they needed to talk to him called the hardware store, during business hours. But he stopped anyway.

He went inside and sat on the bench, picked up the receiver, and dialed the numbers that would get him the phone's voice mail. There was a message for old Benny Schrock, who lived on the other side of Ira. Seemed Benny was selling his smoker, and perhaps for a good price, seeing as how he had three people who called about it.

Ira carefully jotted down the numbers and the messages, then erased what was on the phone. He tacked the paper up on the wall of the shanty where Benny would find it next time he came. That was when Ira saw a message pinned up there for him.

Ira—
  Astrid Kauffman called
  bowling Wednesday
  will call Monday with details

Ira wasn't sure what to make of that. He grabbed the bottom of the paper and pulled it from the wall. Bowling? Why in the world would he want to go bowling?

He kept the paper in his hand as he walked back to his house. He looked at it two or three times on the way there, even though the walk wasn't far. He wondered who took the message. If it was Benny Schrock . . . well, the man was elderly. Perhaps he'd gotten a message wrong. Perhaps the message was about something else? What would sound like bowling over the telephone to a ninety plus-year-old man?

Ira had no idea, but it surely didn't involve bowling.

Ira supposed he could call her back, but he wasn't in the mood to play phone tag via phone shanty. He would just wait for Astrid's call tomorrow at work and find out what she really wanted. In the meantime . . .

He let himself back into the house. The clock on the wall immediately sounding like thunder. Not only was it loud, it was slow. Time was creeping by.

Back when his kids were little, time seemed to fly. When he had Ruthann at his side time whizzed by, almost whooshing in its speed. But lately, but there didn't seem to be enough activity to fill the hours that stretched before him. Only at work did time seem to behave in a normal fashion.

When you have time on your hands, read your Bible.

If he had a nickel for every time his mother had told him that, he would be a very wealthy man right now. He wished he had listened to her more back then when she was alive. But for now . . .

He went to the small occasional table that sat by the door and picked up his Bible. He kept it there so he always knew where it was. It was always in plain sight when he needed it. Now perhaps he needed it more than he had in a long time.

He did his best to ignore the loud, slow clock and sat down in his armchair next to the window. He would do as his *mamm* said. He had time on his hands so he would read his Bible.

He opened it to a random spot.

The soul of the lazy man desires, and has nothing; but the soul of the diligent shall be made rich. Proverbs 13:4.

Maybe not so random.

He shut it again and went into the kitchen to get a drink. He stared out over the backyard through the window above the sink. It was Sunday. There wasn't really much he could do.

What would he be doing if Ruthann was still alive?

Probably visiting. If not with Ruthie, then with someone else in the family. Why hadn't he gone visiting today? He supposed he hadn't thought about it. He hadn't thought about being all alone today and he was all alone.

Weeks, days, he'd been all alone. The truth was, he didn't like it.

Suddenly a thought occurred to him. Astrid. Amish women weren't as forward as he had heard some *Englisch* women could be, but now he had figured it out. That was why she had been coming into the hardware store. She was interested in him as a husband. It was so obvious now, and the idea was kind of appealing once he let it settle around him.

Astrid was a handsome woman, maybe a little energetic and bright, and not just the smart kind of bright. She just sort of shined wherever she went. Like a little light was following her around. He supposed it wasn't a bad thing perhaps, maybe even a good thing. *Jah.*

Now it all made sense. She probably had called about going bowling. He supposed he could think about it. Perhaps she was as tired of being alone as he was. *Jah*. Maybe he would go bowling after all.

Ira jumped every time the store phone rang on Monday. He hadn't thought it possible, but for the first time since he had lost Ruthann, he was thinking about marriage again. He supposed it had something to do with his Sunday with too much time on his hands and then figuring out Astrid's plan, why she'd been coming into the hardware store so often. *Jah*, maybe it was time to get married again.

This went beyond cooking and cleaning. He would get married again because he needed someone to be with, a companion. The Bible even told them that a man shouldn't be alone. That was why God had created Eve to begin with. For a time Ira had been alone, but with his children keeping him company. He hadn't noticed so much until they had grown up and gone out on their own.

The idea of marrying Astrid Kauffman gave him a warm feeling inside. Sure, he knew he was looking way too far into the future, but the dream of the idea gave him hope. A hope he hadn't realized he needed. Funny how that works.

The phone rang and he snatched it up before it even went silent the first time. "Hill Hardware, Ira speaking."

"Ira, just the person I was hoping to talk to."

Ira grinned in spite of himself. "Hey, Astrid."

"Did you get my message? I left one up in the phone shanty."

He nodded, standing there grinning like a fool. "I did. I

did. At first I thought maybe Benny had written it down wrong."

"I'm not sure what Benny wrote down," Astrid said. "But Jesse and I are thinking about joining a bowling league and wondered if you wanted to join us."

"A league?" He was a little stunned and a lot taken aback. "I don't know if I'm good enough to join a league."

She laughed and he decided he liked that sound. "You don't have to be good. It's a beginner's league."

"Won't that be like children?"

She laughed again. "You're funny," she said.

He was?

"Say you'll do it," she prodded. "We need one more."

"Who's the fourth?" he asked even though he had already made up his mind.

"Just a friend of ours." She said the words in that flippant way she had.

"When?" Ira asked.

"The first night is Wednesday. So you'll do it?"

"Wednesday?" He chuckled in spite of himself. "Okay," he said. "I'll do it."

"Bowling?" Imogene squeaked. "We're joining a bowling league?"

When she'd taken the time to stop work and take a break to call Astrid back from the restaurant's phone, this was pretty much the last thing she would have expected Astrid was going to tell her.

"It's all been set up," Astrid said. "All you have to do is show up Wednesday at six."

"This Wednesday?" Imogene did her best to make her voice normal, but it sounded like she'd been sucking on a helium balloon. She couldn't believe what she was hearing.

"Stop it. If you two are going to get together, you have to spend time with each other."

Every time they had tried, something disastrous had happened. Imogene was ready to give up on the whole thing. "About that," she started.

Astrid's demeanor immediately changed. "About what?" The words were firmly spoken and clearly conveyed that she'd better not dislike what Imogene was about to say.

"It's just that . . ." Imogene pulled at a loose thread on her apron. "It's just that I think I should probably abandon this idea."

"No," Astrid said. Imogene could almost see her shaking her head on the other side of town. "No. We're in it this far. We need to keep on with it."

"He doesn't like me," she finally said. And why should he? Ira was a handsome, successful man. She was a widow with rowdy boys and a job that barely paid the bills. She had nothing to offer the man. Nothing.

"He is just like all the men I've ever met," Astrid started. "He doesn't know what he likes. That's why we have to tell them."

Abundant confidence. Imogene was beginning to think that Astrid got her confidence and Imogene's as well. "I don't know," Imogene said.

"Well, I do," Astrid replied. "And I'm telling you he likes you just fine."

Imogene chewed one fingernail and looked out the one-way window at the manager's office there at the Paradise Amish Buffet. Callie, the hostess, just seated someone in her section. Break time was over. "What if I can't get a sitter?"

"I'll call over to the B&B. I'm sure Sylvie and Vern would be more than happy to babysit the boys for you."

Hadn't they said they wanted to keep the twins whenever she needed their help? "I don't know," Imogene said again.

"Then quit thinking about it," Astrid said. "Wednesday night. You, me, Jesse, and Ira are joining a bowling league. It's going to be all kinds of fun."

Imogene didn't have the chance to say anything back. Astrid hung up as Callie seated another group in her section. No doubt about it. Break time was over.

Paradise Pins was bustling with people on Wednesday evening. It seemed that the beginner's league was a popular thing, and Astrid was lucky to have gotten them the last team slot.

"They're beginners?" Jesse asked with a nod toward the four little old ladies who were seated at the lanes with them. They all wore matching pink shirts with a black bowling ball knocking down three white pins embroidered in the back.

Astrid shrugged. "Maybe. You can be a beginner and still have style."

"I wonder if we could wear matching shirts too?" Jesse asked just as Imogene rushed in. Her cheeks were pink and she was breathless from the exertion.

"Are you okay?" Astrid asked.

"I had to come over here from the B&B," she said.

"In your buggy, right?" Astrid asked.

Imogene shook her head. "One of my wheels got messed up while I was at the B&B and I knew I wouldn't be able to make it if I didn't run. So I ran. Now here I am." She sucked in a deep breath.

"Is Vern going to fix the wheel for you?" Jesse asked.

"He said he could. I hope so anyway." She shook her head. "I owe them so much."

Astrid was concerned for Imogene. She looked like she was about to slide down that slippery slope that led to self-pity and self-loathing. "Chin up. If Vern King said he can fix it, he can fix it. One of us will take you back to the B&B tonight so you don't have to walk."

"Fix what?" a male voice asked.

Astrid spun around as Ira came up behind her. "Imogene's wheel. She's had a problem today."

"Vern's going to fix it for her," Jesse said.

"But you can take her back to the B&B tonight to pick it up from Vern," Astrid said. "Can't you?"

Ira stopped for a moment, seemed to think about it, then nodded. "Of course I can."

"*Danki*," Imogene said. "I do really appreciate your help."

Ira gave her a sweet smile, and Astrid got a funny feeling in the pit of her stomach. Odd, but she never felt pride in her stomach before, but that had to be what it was. Her plan to get Ira and Imogene together was working. She should be feeling proud. And she needed to remember that this sort of pride wasn't a sin.

"I guess we should go get our shoes," Jesse said.

Astrid waved him away. "Get all of us a pair," she said. "We'll pick out our balls while you're gone."

"All right then," Jesse said. "What size does everyone need?"

They all rattled off their shoe sizes with Jesse repeating them to remember, then Astrid turned to the rack of bowling balls just behind their seats.

"I think the lighter ones are on top," she said. "Unless they got mixed up. I'm not sure how often they straighten that sort of thing." She waited until Ira started toward a rack before pointing Imogene in the same direction. "How about that blue swirly ball right there, Imogene? Why don't you give that one a try?"

"I guess," Imogene said, going to stand next to Ira.

She tried to pick up the ball, but evidently it was much heavier than it looked. Much, much heavier. Astrid could tell by the way Imogene nearly staggered under its weight.

"Here," Ira said. "Let me." He took the ball from her and placed it back on the rack. "Maybe this one would be more to your liking." He picked up another ball and handed it to Imogene.

"I don't know," Imogene said. "It's still pretty heavy."

Astrid watched them, that weird pride burning at the pit of her stomach, as Ira chose another one of the balls closer to the top. "Try this one," he said.

He handed it to Imogene and she tested the weight in her hands.

"Much better," Imogene said. She smiled at Ira.

Astrid watched, taking mental notes. She could have a scene like this in her book where the couples go bowling. That was a perfect idea. Everyone loved bowling. And she would write it up just like this. With the handsome hero helping the timid heroine find a ball for their new bowling league. Sweet. And perfect.

After helping Imogene find a ball, Ira turned back and found himself one in seconds.

Jesse picked that moment to come back, toting the four pairs of multicolored shoes.

"Okay, is everybody ready?" Jesse asked, handing out their shoes.

"I've still got to find a ball," Astrid admitted.

Jesse looked at her and frowned. "I was gone forever. There were three people in front of me," he said. "What have you been doing this whole time?"

CHAPTER THIRTEEN

"No, no, no, no, no, no." Imogene twisted her body this way and that as if by sheer will she could make the bowling ball change direction. No such luck. The marbled green ball that Ira had helped her pick out clunked as it fell into the gutter and rolled the rest of the way down the aisle. The automatic arm rose and pulled in the pins that she hadn't knocked down back to wherever they went to begin again.

"You twist your hand," Astrid said. "Right before you let go. That's what's making it turn back the other way."

Imogene shrugged. "Maybe," she said. But honestly she was having such a good time she didn't care if she knocked down any of the pins at all.

In fact, she had had more gutter balls than the four little old ladies they were bowling with. She hadn't realized that she needed a break so badly until she put on those crazy-colored bowling shoes and tossed that first ball. It was such a relief to be able to go out and not have to worry about her boys. She knew Sylvie and Vern would take care of them and it was a blessing beyond measure.

"Break time," Jesse said. "Are y'all coming?"

Ira stood. "I am."

The four white-haired ladies in their matching pink shirts

also filed past on their way to get a refill on their sodas and go to the bathroom or whatever.

Imogene sat down next to Astrid. "Do you need to go to the restroom?"

Astrid shook her head. "I went a few minutes ago. Snuck away while the pink ladies were up."

Imogene picked up a flyer that someone had left on their bench and fanned herself with it. "I've forgotten how hot you can get when you're bowling." She switched the position of the flyer and started fanning the back of her neck.

"Get yourself a drink," Astrid said, nodding toward the holders where their drinks sat, each printed with their names.

Imogene smiled at Astrid. "Good idea. Can you hand me my—"

Astrid was already reaching for the foam cup bearing Imogene's name. "It's almost completely full," Astrid said as she handed it to her. "No wonder you don't have to go to the bathroom."

The ladies chuckled and Imogene sucked down a large drink of the cool water.

"What do you think?" Astrid asked.

"About what?" Imogene returned.

"About Ira," Astrid said. "This has been a success, don't you think? So what do you think about it?"

Imogene had been so wrapped up in having a good time, that she hadn't even realized she was having a good time *with Ira.*

"He's okay," she said. Then she realized the words sounded mediocre at best. "He's nice," she started again. "He's kind and thoughtful. Plus, he seems to be a godly man." Though she couldn't tell for sure at a bowling alley. A person could only learn something like that over time.

"Can you see yourself married to him?"

Astrid's question shouldn't have taken her off guard, but somehow it did. "*Jah* . . . I guess . . . I mean, he seems like a very good man."

"But I'm rushing you." Astrid nodded at her own observation.

"I guess that's it," Imogene said. "I'm just not comfortable talking about marriage and things like that, I suppose."

"You're not talking about it with just anyone. I'm your matchmaker, remember?"

"*Jah*," Imogene said. "I remember." She stopped, turned her head to a different angle where she could study Astrid. Or maybe she wanted to see her full response. "What about you? Have you never thought about getting married?"

Astrid laughed. "Me?" she asked. "Why would I think about getting married?"

"It doesn't bother you to write books about people falling love with each other and not have that love for yourself?"

Astrid scoffed. "Not at all. I never even thought once about getting married." She stopped and seemed to think about it a minute. "That's not true. Every time I need something out of the attic, I think about getting married because Jesse's always busy. So there's no one there to climb the ladder but me."

"You're saying that if you had a husband, he would get into the attic for you?" Imogene guessed.

"Exactly," Astrid said.

"But husbands do more than climb ladders." Imogene could feel the heat steal back into her cheeks. She had blushed more the last week or so than she had in the rest of her thirtysomething years. "What about companionship and things like that?" It was the closest she could come to anything more. It just wasn't in her nature to talk about such an intimate thing.

"I don't think I'll ever get married," Astrid said. "I'm perfectly content with my life just the way it is. Adding in anything else would simply ruin it."

"Ruin it?" Imogene asked. Those were strong words.

"My job is a little different than most," Astrid started. "See, sometimes I'm in the mood to write and sometimes I'm not and sometimes I have to write even when I'm not in the mood to write. If I were to have a husband wanting this and that or the other during my writing time, well, that doesn't work. Not when I've got a really good idea going . . . no, I don't think I would like the intrusion. I get to do what I want, when I want to do it. If I want to have cereal for supper, I have cereal for supper. There's a lot of freedom to being single."

"I guess," Imogene murmured. She supposed that was the difference between her and Astrid. She had boys who needed to be taken care of and a job where she had to leave the house each day and return at different times. She needed the help of a spouse to make a family run smoothly.

"Don't get me wrong," Astrid said. "I think love is grand. It's just not for me."

Ira stopped just behind the steps that led down to the area where they were bowling. After he finished in the restroom, Jesse had said he was going over to get a slice of pizza and Ira headed back to the lanes. But he stopped when he heard Astrid say, "I don't think I'll ever get married."

She didn't think she would get married?

Ira's shoes felt glued to the floor. That . . . that totally busted up his theory. It had seemed strange enough when he had come up with it, that Astrid was trying to find a way to court him without courting him, a way to get him to notice her without coming right out and saying she was interested in him, but this . . .

Until now he hadn't been sure if Astrid was just using Imogene as a chaperone and that she was incredibly forward in her advances. Well, for an Amish woman at least. He had wondered if she thought that maybe she was in love with him. Maybe not in love, but definitely interested. That was the right word. He had thought Astrid was interested in him. As a life mate. As a husband or spouse, but if she thought she would never get married, then that idea would hold less water than a leaky bucket.

If Astrid wasn't interested in him as a husband, why had she been coming into the store all this time? Why had she invited him to bowling tonight? Why was she continually tossing around things that they could do, like going to the Fall Festival coming up next week? The only explanation he had now was that it was a coincidence. One of those funny things that happened when everything linked together even if they weren't linked any other way.

He supposed he would have to take what she said to Imogene as the truth. What reason would she have to lie?

He supposed he would file that away with all the other things she did that he didn't understand. One woman, one man, and too many whys.

Ira still didn't have any answers, not that evening, not the next morning, and certainly not the next day when Astrid came strolling into the hardware store once again. "Did you see the flyer last night?" she asked him.

"Flyer?" He didn't look up from the lawn mower blade he was sharpening. Frankly, he was afraid that his suspicions about her feelings for him would show in his eyes, and she would know that he thought she was interested in him. He didn't want her to know. He felt six ways an idiot for even allowing it into his own thoughts.

"It was hanging up there behind the desk where the guy was handing out the bowling shoes."

"The flyer about the Fall Festival, you mean?" He looked up and managed a blank stare.

Astrid blinked at him, then once again.

He could see that she had registered the change in his demeanor, but she had a strong personality and wasn't about to be put off easily.

"*Jah*," she said. "We've just got less than a week before it starts."

A big part of him wanted to shut down the conversation; that same part of him thought that perhaps she was playing games with him. But he needed to allow himself to talk to her. Perhaps that would give him some clue as to her motives.

Or maybe he was just being overly suspicious thinking that she had motives at all. Maybe she was like him, living in a too quiet house.

But she had Jesse, her brother. That wasn't the same as a spouse, but at least her house wasn't truly empty.

Her words from the night before came back about how she liked to have time of her own to develop her books and her ideas for stories. So it seemed an empty house was not the reason for her coming in this week and talking to him, or inviting him bowling, or any of the other times she had managed to put herself in front of him. "*Jah*," he finally said. "Less than a week. Do you have something entered in one of the competitions?"

She shook her head with a smile. "Jesse's entered the barbecue cook-off, but I've got too much work to do for that right now."

There were many, many competitions in the Paradise

Hill Fall Festival. Everything from a pumpkin cooking contest to a pumpkin decorating contest, a corn on the cob eating contest, and there were even events that only the *Englischers* entered, like a photograph contest.

"What exactly do you do?" Ira said. He couldn't recall anyone saying. "For a living, I mean."

"I'm a writer."

"A writer? Like for the newspaper?" He had no idea. But she shook her head.

Being a writer was perhaps the last thing Ira had thought she would say. He did his best to fit that information into what he already knew about her, and if that had any bearing on her inviting him places. That little detail still perplexed him.

"I write books," she finally admitted.

That really piqued his interest. "What kind of books?"

She pulled back just a bit. Not physically, but mentally. Maybe even emotionally. He could see it in her expressive green eyes. Then their color deepened once more. "Romance novels. About the Amish."

He had seen a few of those Amish books floating around here and there. There had probably even been a few at the house when Ruthann was still alive and before Ruthie moved out.

"The bishop's okay with this?"

"*Jah*." She gave a small shrug. More than anything it was a muscle spasm in one shoulder. "Plus he's my uncle."

In the short span of this conversation the potential for vanity and being a writer flitted through his mind. But until that moment he hadn't realized that the bishop was Astrid's uncle. Of course he would turn a blind eye to that sort of expression. Then again, how many *Ordnung*s out there had provisions for something such as that? But honestly, why shouldn't she be allowed to create words for others to enjoy?

"That's something else," Ira said in awe.

"That my uncle is the bishop?" Astrid asked.

Ira chuckled. "No, that you're a writer. A romance writer."

Jah, it had to be the lighting. He couldn't imagine someone like Astrid Kauffman blushing. At least not to the deep crimson color she appeared to be at that moment.

"I'm not the only one," she said. "There are other Amish women and even men who write all sorts of things."

"I guess I never thought about it." Ira nodded. "So you're not going to the Fall Festival because you'll be working?"

"No," she said. "I'm going to the festival. Plus I have a booth there on Friday," she told him. "Signing books and such. What about you?" she asked.

"Nah." He waved the idea away. "But it's extra special that you're signing books. Do a lot of people come out for something like that?"

She tilted her head from side to side. "Sometimes. Sometimes not. But it is good to get out and see people and let everyone know what you're doing."

"I'll have to come by and have you sign one for my daughter."

"I would like that," she told him.

He hadn't given it much thought until now, but her being a writer explained a lot. Like how she was able to run around all over town during the day and at all different times. He supposed she could write books any time of the day and that she probably didn't have a set schedule like someone like him who had a job in a store that he had to take care of. But it didn't explain why she kept inviting him all these places.

There was one sure way he could find out the truth. Or at least have a chance to. And that was to ask her outright. "Astrid, why do you keep inviting me places?"

His heart pounded as he waited for her to answer.

"Don't you think Imogene Yoder would make a good wife?"

"*Jah*," he said. "Sure she would." Then her words sunk in. His eyes widened. "You mean for me?"

She nodded. "For whom else?"

Ira sputtered looking for an answer, but he had none.

"You never thought about getting married again?" Astrid asked.

"Course I have." But not seriously.

"And now?" she prodded.

He nodded a bit in spite of himself. "Maybe."

"The house is getting too quiet," Astrid said in a low, almost soothing tone.

It was the truth, but how did she know that? "So you're . . . Me and . . . Me and Imogene?"

She sucked in a deep breath as if gearing up for something big. Ira had only a split second to wonder if he was ready for it. "Imogene is in the market for a husband, and you seem to be in the market for a wife."

Was he?

"Why not give it a try?"

Why not?

Astrid swung up into her buggy, going over the conversation she just had with Ira. She hadn't planned on being so forward with her intentions and her job, as it were, as a matchmaker between him and Imogene. But the man had asked her outright. She felt it was time to be completely honest. Jesse would've said that time had long passed, but she told Ira the truth. She had stood back and watched as a myriad of emotions had flowed through his eyes, the last one a dawning light of understanding.

He hadn't pulled away, he hadn't immediately shaken his head and told her how impossible the idea was. He simply let it flow over him, absorbed the idea on the surface, and she was certain he would take it out later and examine it closer. When he did that, he would see that what she said was true. Then the next time they met up with Imogene he would look at her with different eyes, eyes that had the intention of seeing a potential spouse.

Imogene might be a little on the plain side, and she was definitely on the timid side, but she was a good woman. She worked hard, she loved her family, and she deserved more from life than struggling. That was one of the main reasons Astrid wanted to help her.

Well, that and her book. It wasn't exactly coming out the way Astrid had thought. This watching two people fall in love was not what she had expected. First had been the mud fiasco, then the spaghetti fiasco, but now that she had let Ira in on her plans, perhaps things would go a bit more smoothly. Then she could get some good ideas for her book. Not that she had written anything at all. She was still taking notes, still waiting for this matchmaker plot to fall into place.

The last thing she had expected to do was tell Ira that she was a romance author, and yet she had. In fact, she was a little nervous about having a booth at the Fall Festival this year. It would be the first time she'd done such a thing. Even though there had been rumors floating around the district concerning her status as a writer and now matchmaker, she never bothered with the rest. Friday's booth would do that in spades. At least the part about her being a writer.

Honestly, the thought of all that backlash was a little off-putting. But there was no way around it now.

She turned her horse toward home and lightly flicked the reins to get the old mare started.

The look in Ira's eyes when she told him she was a writer. A little bit of amazement, a little bit of interest, and a whole lot of admiration. And she had basked in that even though she knew it was wrong. That was another benefit to having a pen name for her novels. It was a little harder to claim the glory for herself, if people didn't know she was Rachel Kauffman as well as Astrid Kauffman. And that left the glory to God. More of it anyway. That was the point, now, wasn't it? But she had enjoyed seeing his face light up in appreciation.

Truth was, she'd been thinking a lot more about Ira these days, but she wasn't the one in the market for a husband. She had told Imogene the truth when they were at the bowling alley on Wednesday. She never thought she would get married. She wasn't one of those little girls who talked about getting married from the time they could tie their own shoes until the day it actually happened. She never talked about what would happen when she got married, or what it would be like to have a husband or all the other things that little girls talked about.

Astrid was always more interested in books and what she might read next. Reading was an adventure, and it could take her anyplace she wanted to go. She could visit there anytime she wanted. If she wanted to know more about marriage, she read about it. If she wanted to know more about the ocean, she could do that, too. Plus reading about it meant she didn't have to worry about her husband's supper while she explored between the pages of a book. She had freedom. So why was she even thinking about Ira in a romantic way? It should have felt wrong on many levels. Yet somehow it didn't.

And for that she was expressly ashamed of herself.

Take heed that ye do not your alms before men, to be seen of them: otherwise ye have no reward of your Father which is in heaven.

Matthew 6:1. It was a verse she knew well and one she best not forget. Especially when two other hearts were at stake.

CHAPTER FOURTEEN

Imogene hated working the evening shift at the Paradise Amish Buffet. She hoped the boys weren't being too much trouble for her *aenti*. But she needed the extra shift. One of the other girls asked her to cover for her, and Imogene really had a hard time telling people no. Plus, the money would always come in handy with two growing boys.

She stopped for a moment, to rest, catch her breath, and wipe a tired forearm against her brow. Doing dishes at home and doing dishes in the restaurant were two completely different things. Even the quantity aside. Sometimes the speed was the hardest part. People kept eating, people kept coming in, people kept needing a clean plate. It was the bane of a buffet, she was certain. Normally she wouldn't be anywhere near the dishwasher machine, but the dishwasher person had needed time off and asked one of the waitresses to cover for him. Then the waitress needed off and asked Imogene to cover for her. So now she was washing dishes.

But hopefully there would come a time soon when she wouldn't have to pick up extra shifts washing dishes. And that time would be when she had Ira as her husband.

That was the other thing about washing dishes; it left a lot of time for the mind to wander and daydream.

With Ira as her husband she might even be able to go down to part-time or quit altogether. Then she would be cooking for her husband and her family and at the end of the day he would come in and take off his hat and . . .

That was where the daydream went a little sideways. It was Jesse standing there. Not Ira.

That was the boys' doing, she told herself. She pulled the tray of clean dishes out of the industrial washer and over to the side to cool while she pushed the other tray in, the one holding the dirty dishes.

She had to rouse herself out of a perfectly good daydream because it starred the wrong man. And all because her boys thought she should marry Jesse instead of Ira.

Not that there was anything wrong with Jesse. He was handsome and good with her boys and seemed to be an all-around, even-tempered, kind, and even godly man. But Astrid had made the connection, and Ira was her match.

The boys just didn't know Ira, that was all. In fact, they had barely crossed paths. But soon things would change. Maybe even as early as Sunday. As she was headed back over to Paradise Hill for church. She would talk her boys into going as well. By the time this courtship was over, she would've spent a small fortune on ice cream, the way it was going anyway.

Until then maybe it wasn't so smart to get too wrapped up in the daydream that might not come true.

She shook her head at herself and once again swiped the back of her arm against her forehead.

For now, she needed to be positive. Like Astrid. She needed a goal to look forward to. She needed a happy family, a role model for her sons, a husband and a companion for herself. And she would have it. Maybe even by Christmas. How would that be?

Perfect. That would be absolutely perfect. But the more

she daydreamed, the harder it became to replace Jesse's face with Ira's, a phenomenon she had no idea how to explain.

Astrid smiled when she saw the familiar buggy turn down the lane. She was here! Imogene had shown up again. But then another buggy turned into the drive behind Imogene. It took a moment for Astrid to realize it was Vern and Sylvie from Paradise Springs who'd come to visit as well. The more the merrier, she always said. It was church after all. Who couldn't use an extra dose of the Lord's word every now and then?

Astrid waved at Sylvie and Vern and waited for Imogene to pull her buggy to a stop. "Jesse's already gone, are you ready?"

Imogene nodded. "As I'll ever be."

Astrid swung her handbag into the buggy and chased it inside. Then she motioned for Sylvie and Vern to follow and they headed off toward Lloyd and Ruthie Stoll's.

"Is this as fast as you can go?" Astrid asked as they pulled out onto the road and started for their destination.

"I don't like to go much faster," Imogene said. "We aren't late, are we?" She looked to the tiny digital clock stuck to the dashboard. "I came right when you said."

"I guess I'm just a little impatient," Astrid replied.

Imogene sighed. "I guess I am a little bit impatient myself." But there was something she wasn't saying, Astrid could tell.

"What's wrong?"

Imogene shook her head. "Nothing."

Astrid decided not to push. Whatever was on Imogene's mind she would find out eventually. She always did.

"Where's the service today?" Imogene asked.

"Lloyd and Ruthie Stoll's house."

"Why do I feel like I should know them?"

Astrid did her best to make her shrug look offhand, to make it look like she wasn't hiding anything.

"Because Ruthie is Ira's daughter."

"What?" Imogene screeched. "You could have warned me!"

"Are you serious?" Astrid asked. "And give you the perfect excuse for not going to church today?"

"It's not even my church Sunday," Imogene complained.

"But we get ice cream for attending," Mahlon said from the back. At least Astrid thought it was Mahlon. The boys had been occupied playing some sort of a game, wrapping a string around their fingers and making shapes.

"That's awesome," Astrid said with a smile, then she lowered her voice in hopes that the boys might not hear. "You bribed them with ice cream?"

"My best babysitter wanted to come to church today too," Imogene said with a jerk over her shoulder. Astrid knew she meant Vern and Sylvie.

Astrid didn't say anything. She really couldn't cast stones on this one. She didn't have any children, she'd never had to find a sitter, and she certainly never had twin boys who missed their father to try to appease. But in her silence Imogene must have read some consternation. "I feel ice cream is a small price to pay for an extra dose of the Lord's word."

"I suppose so," Astrid said. "I told Ira."

Imogene turned toward her slowly. "You told Ira what?"

"I told him that you would make him a good wife."

She still held the reins in her hands, but Imogene's fingers went slack. She closed her eyes and sat that way for a moment or two. A moment too long as far as Astrid was concerned.

She shook her friend's shoulder. "Are you all right?"

Imogene slowly opened her eyes and pulled the veering buggy back straight. "How could you do that?"

"I'm playing your matchmaker, remember?"

"Yes, and you're supposed to get us together, not scare him off."

Astrid grinned happily, at least she tried to. "That's where you're wrong; he seemed quite smitten with the idea."

"He did?" Imogene seemed satisfied with that, then she crumpled once again. "Astrid, at his daughter's house? What if she hates me?"

"No one could hate you," Astrid said. "There's just too much to love."

They chatted about other things the rest of the way to the Stolls' house. When they pulled in, they did their normal before-church rituals, unhooking the buggy and milling around until the time they were called to enter the service.

Ruthie and Lloyd had a nice property with a large house, but no bonus room as of yet. Astrid wondered if they would build one out back to house the church service. A lot of folks did. Using the space for other things the rest of the year—storage, a playroom for the children, even a workshop for things like home canning and other projects. But for now the house was open for all those to enter. Beginning with the men.

They had barely said two words to Ira before the men were called inside. But Astrid knew there would be time after the service for milling around and chatting. In fact, she was counting on it.

"Well, looka here," a woman said, coming up to stand next to them in a somewhat triumphant manner.

"Hello, Marie."

Marie Lapp was perhaps the busiest of the busybodies there in Paradise Hill. Astrid knew it wasn't charitable to not like someone, so all she would say was that she defi-

nitely kept her time spent around Marie Lapp to as minimal
as possible. Marie was married to Elmer Lapp, the preacher
for their district, though Marie felt that he should have been
chosen as bishop. Astrid supposed it didn't matter that the
church elders were chosen by lot and therefore deemed to
be granted the position by God, and she wondered if Marie
thought God had made a mistake or if Elmer had messed
up grabbing the wrong Bible when the lots were chosen.

"It looks like we've got some visitors again today,"
Marie said. Her brown eyes were sharp and snapping, never
missing a thing.

Astrid made introductions all around, thankful at least
that Vern had gone inside already. But she could tell Marie
hadn't come over because Vern and Sylvie had come visiting. No, Marie was there because Imogene was and she
wanted to know what Imogene's business was attending
church in Paradise Hill two church Sundays in a row.

"That's so good of y'all to attend services in both districts," Marie said.

She said *y'all*, but she was looking straight at Imogene.

That meant one thing: Marie was suspicious. Astrid
could tell. But she couldn't do anything about it. Except
perhaps ignore the woman. Or . . .

"Perhaps you would like to join us over in Paradise
Springs next week?" Imogene said.

Astrid could have pitched Imogene for the invitation.
She might have too, if she weren't a peaceable woman. But
as it was, she had to remain still, and smiling, and enthusi-
astic about the idea, lest Marie get more suspicious at any
objection she held.

Marie turned that sharp gaze of hers around the circle
they created—Astrid, Imogene, Sylvie. Then she gave that
smile that looked a little too much like a crocodile about to
attack. "I just might at that."

* * *

"Trust me on this," Astrid was saying after church. "The last person you want to have visit you is Marie Lapp."

Jesse agreed, but he kept that comment to himself.

"There's always one in every church district," Vern said.

"Malinda Beachy," the three residents of Paradise Springs said at the same time, then they all laughed.

"So do you really think she's heading over there on Sunday?" Jesse asked.

Astrid shot him a look. But he was immune to those visual daggers she liked to throw. He had been fending them off for thirtysomething years.

"Say, Ira," Vern started. "I was wondering if maybe you wanted to come over to one of our senior meetings."

Ira chuckled, but even to Jesse the sound seemed a bit uncomfortable. "Not that it doesn't sound like fun," Ira started, "but I'm not quite a senior yet."

"Mah," Vern said. "We don't stand a lot of ceremony. I just thought you might like to come over and visit some folks. You know, get out of the house for a bit."

So it wasn't just Jesse's imagination. There was something about Ira that seemed a little . . . sad. Maybe "sad" was too strong a word. Melancholy, that might be it. Jesse wasn't a hundred percent sure; his sister was the one who dealt in words. He'd always had trouble expressing himself. Perhaps that was why he created things out of leather. It seemed to be a more tangible way to express what he felt inside. And much easier to work with than words.

"It's such a pretty day," Astrid started. "We should go over to the park and walk around."

Sylvie shook her head. "I've got to be getting back to my side of the line," she said with a chuckle. "I have guests checking in this afternoon and Millie and Henry are over visiting her parents today."

"That's too bad," Astrid said. "Maybe another time?"

Vern nodded. "I'll count on it." Then he turned to Ira. "That invitation stands."

Ira nodded. "I'll think about it."

"Good man," Vern said, and the two of them walked away to get their horse and carriage to head back to Paradise Springs.

"It looks like it's just the four of us," Astrid said.

"Six," Jesse corrected her. "Don't forget the twins."

"I've got an idea," Astrid said. She did her best to make her tone sound like it was something that had just occurred to her, but Jesse knew that tone and he knew his sister. "Why don't the two of you go on and Jesse and I will take the twins back to our house for a while."

Ira seemed able to handle his sister's bossiness and took it all in stride, but Imogene turned that sweet pink color again. His sister had embarrassed her. Astrid put her on the spot, even. But he was having none of it.

He grabbed Astrid by the arm and smiled at Ira and Imogene. "Just a second, y'all."

"What are you—" Astrid started, but he was not to be deterred. He wrapped a hand around her arm and dragged her away from the rest of the milling churchgoers and closer toward the barn.

"What are you doing?" Astrid said, snatching her arm free.

"What am I doing?" Jesse asked in return. "What am I doing? You've got to stop this, Astrid."

She brushed off her church apron and straightened her sleeves as if he had done a great disservice to her outfit. "There's nothing to stop."

"You're telling me that you're not trying to get the two of them together? You're not trying to play matchmaker?"

"Imogene asked me to."

He felt as if a large fist had squeezed his heart. "She asked you to make Ira Oberholtzer fall in love with her?"

Astrid lifted her chin and sniffed in a way that said she was above all this. "If you must know, she came to me thinking I was a matchmaker. Asking me to find a man for her to fall in love with."

"I'm not sure I believe all that." He looked back to where Ira and Imogene stood. They were staring back at them. He turned his attention to his sister once again. "He's not good for her." There. He'd said it. At least part of it.

"Ira Oberholtzer is a good man. He's a good father. He adored his wife. He's a perfect match for Imogene. Never mind the fact that he's handsome."

"'For man looketh on the outward appearance, but the Lord looketh on the heart,'" Jesse quoted.

Astrid crossed her arms. "You know what I mean."

He hated bickering with her like this. It was like they were five and not thirty-five. "He's not good for her." This time Jesse managed to keep his tone quiet and his voice steady. "He's a good man, and I like him, but he'll not make a good at husband for Imogene. He'll run all over her and not even mean to."

"Just what is that supposed to mean?" Astrid asked.

But Jesse had said his piece. He stormed away.

"Honestly," Astrid muttered. Her brother was impossible. *And* he didn't know the first thing about love.

She checked that thought. He did actually know something about love. But the one time he had had the love of someone other than family, she had died. Truthfully, Astrid never expected him to marry again. Amanda had been sweet, but frail, and Jesse had loved her with all his heart. When you love someone like that . . .

It doesn't go away overnight.

That was exactly how she wanted Ira and Imogene to feel about each other. Or the very closest to it they could come. Each one had loved someone in their past. Each one had lost that person. They had plenty of things to bond over.

She watched her brother stalk off, then turned back to her project, or the people in her project. Actually, Imogene and Ira. She pasted on the brightest smile she could and made her way back over to them. "Jesse's not feeling well," she said. Now that wasn't exactly a lie. Because he surely wasn't feeling like himself right now. "Why don't y'all go ahead and walk in the park. We'll catch up later."

"How will you get home?" Imogene said.

That was something Astrid hadn't thought through. "I'm going to try and catch Jesse." That would be a joy. "Or maybe Sylvie and Vern can give me a ride." Surely they hadn't struck out already. If Astrid hurried, she just might catch them.

"Have fun," she said with a wave, and hurried off to find a ride home.

CHAPTER FIFTEEN

Since Ira knew the way, Imogene and the boys followed behind to the city park. Unlike the park in Paradise Springs, the Paradise Hill park sat off to the side, not in the middle of town. It was long and narrow, stretching down one whole side of the town. There was a walking trail, bike path, and various pieces of playground equipment situated in a line like a children's version of an obstacle course.

Mattie and Mahlon ran ahead, sliding down the first set of slides before going on to the monkey bars. They seemed content in their play, though every so often they cast suspicious looks in Ira's direction.

He supposed they might have a few questions. First their mother started visiting Astrid and now, all the sudden, Ira seemed to be wherever they were. Not that either boy had said anything. At least not to him. Ira was fairly certain they never would. Yet they would still have questions. He would do his best to assure them that he would take care of them and their *mamm*.

They walked in silence, at least silence between the two of them. The park was teeming with people, children climbing on the playground equipment, dogs barking at one another, birds singing in the trees. Astrid was right. It was a beautiful day. He should be thankful for this time to get to know Imogene better. But she didn't seem to be in a very talkative mood.

What did one say in a situation such as this? He supposed they could call this a date. What had he and Ruthann talked about when they were dating?

Even if he could remember, he wasn't sure it would pertain. They'd been in their late teens at the time. About to click over to their twenties. They had talked about frivolous matters, he was certain. What they'd had for dinner, who was dating whom, and all that sort of stuff that took up the minds of the young people in their community.

Though he had told Vern that he wasn't a senior, and he wasn't, he still wasn't part of the youth in their community.

Middle age. He really didn't like that term, but what else could he call it? So what did middle-aged people talk about when they were on a date? He had no idea.

The twins climbed off the merry-go-round and sped after them. Instead of running along at the park side they came up on the asphalt trail where he and Imogene were strolling along. They got in front of them and stopped, facing them, arms akimbo.

"Is something wrong?" Imogene asked.

But they turned their attention to Ira. "We want Mamm to marry Jesse."

Ira blinked at them, trying to assess their meaning.

"Boys," Imogene started sternly, "you take that back immediately."

"But it's true," one of them said.

Aside from the cuts on their foreheads that appeared to be a mirror of each other, they were completely identical. Ira wasn't certain but he thought even their freckles were in the same place.

"True or not, that does not give you the right to be rude," Imogene said.

"How can it be rude if it's true?" Twin One asked.

Twin Two nodded.

Imogene sputtered, trying to find the words to reprimand her boys and somehow save face. It didn't take some kind of genius to see that poor woman was mortified by her children's behavior, any more than it would take a genius to see that her boys were just trying to protect their *mamm* and love her the way they knew how.

Yet the truth of the matter was he needed to win them over before this went much further.

"Tell me something," Ira started. He looked from one boy to the other. After he smoothed the situation over, he was going to have to learn to tell them apart. "What are we doing today here in the park?"

One of them shrugged. "We're playing on the swings and stuff."

"That's right," Ira said. "But your mother and I, what are we doing?"

"Walking around?" the other twin said. He seemed unsure of the answer, if it was going to be correct, and his stance lost a little of its starch.

"Right again," Ira said. "Now what about them?" He pointed to a couple who were also walking, two women with weights in their hands and headbands to keep the sweat from their eyes. "What are they doing?"

"They're walking around too," Twin One answered.

"But do they look like they're getting married to each other?"

"No, they're exercising," Twin One replied again.

"Now them." Ira pointed toward a mother and son walking side by side. The boy looked to be about four years old. "Do you think they're gonna get married?"

Neither twin could answer they were laughing so hard.

Finally Twin Two collected himself enough to say, "That's silly. She's his *mamm*."

"What about the two of you?"

"Definitely not," Twin One said.

"I get it," Twin Two said with a nod. "Just because people are out here walking doesn't mean they're getting married."

"Right."

Twin One looked as if he might say something else, but Imogene cut in. "Okay, that's enough. Go play."

The swings must've been more compelling than their worry over their *mamm* and who she might marry, and the boys raced off.

Imogene turned toward him. "I am so sorry. I don't know where they get some of these ideas."

"It's okay," Ira assured her.

"No, it's not. Not really. They were rude and—"

"They're boys. And they love their mother," Ira said. Then he waited a heartbeat before adding, "Astrid told me."

All the color drained from Imogene's face. "Astrid told you what?"

"Astrid told me that she was trying to set the two of us up."

"Oh my." The words were barely a whisper.

"It's okay," he told her. And it was. He hadn't thought about getting married again until Astrid had brought it up. But the truth was, his house was lonely. Though he wasn't quite willing to share that fact with Imogene just yet. Besides, she looked simply mortified standing there in the middle of the walking path in the middle of the park, just after the middle of the day.

She covered her face with her hands. "I'm so embarrassed," she said. That was what he thought she said, anyway. Her voice was so muffled he could barely understand her at all.

He gently plucked her hands away from her face and allowed them to drop to her sides. "It's okay. And even if Astrid is trying, that doesn't mean we have to do what she says."

He said the words, then realized what they sounded like. It sounded like he didn't like her.

"That's not what I meant to say. I mean, we can take some time and get to know each other. See where things happen from there, okay?"

She swallowed hard and nodded. "Okay."

He gestured toward the path before them. "Shall we?" he asked.

She nodded, then turned and continued down the way. He waited a moment more before joining her. He hadn't meant to sound like he didn't like her and he hoped she didn't take it to heart. But the biggest question he had was if she even liked him at all. She seemed much more comfortable with Jesse.

"I told you so," Astrid said as she slipped into the seat next to Jesse. Jesse bit his tongue to keep from replying. It was Wednesday night bowling league, and Jesse was certain that joining the league might be the worst decision he had ever made.

Because he hated bowling? Not exactly. Bowling was a fine sport and a lot of fun, but watching Ira teach Imogene how to bowl properly and actually knock down pins was setting his teeth on edge.

Imogene looked half-scared as Ira showed her the proper way to toss the ball on the lane. They were having a practice session before they actually got started. Several other people were bowling near them, but the four ladies who bowled in their group, the ladies with the matching pink bowling shirts, had not arrived yet.

"You're one stubborn man, Jesse Kauffman," his sister continued.

That much was true, but he'd always tried to use his stubbornness to his advantage. Like now, by refusing to reply to his sister. He was tired of bickering over everyday things with her. He loved his sister, but they didn't always see eye to eye.

"It's almost time," Jesse called to Ira and Imogene.

Ira turned and waved, acknowledging what Jesse had said. "One last ball," Imogene replied in return.

Jesse nodded, then watched as she did her best to execute the form Ira had been trying to teach her.

He didn't have anything against Ira, Jesse said to himself. Not one thing. He knew Astrid was right in her assessment of him. Ira seemed to be a kind and godly man. He was clean and he owned his own business. But he was too much to be paired with someone like Imogene.

No, that wasn't quite right either. He was too old.

Well, maybe a little.

Okay, so Jesse couldn't come up with exactly the words to express how he felt about Imogene and Ira together, but he did know one thing for certain: It was all wrong.

"They got our names wrong," Astrid said, looking up at the electronic scoreboard above them.

Jesse wasn't sure what he would find. "Imogene" wasn't that hard to spell and "Ira" surely wasn't. Had they put an *I* in Jesse's name, or totally butchered "Astrid"? He glanced up at the board, but there were no spelling errors. It was a matter of pairing. He and Astrid had been paired the first go-round and now Jesse was paired with Imogene. At the end of the night pairs scores would be combined for a grand prize to be given away at the end of the season.

"It's okay," Jesse said. "Where we sit doesn't matter."

Astrid thoughtfully tapped her chin. "Maybe it's not too late to change it. . . ."

She started to turn away to go to the office and see, no doubt, but Jesse grabbed her arm. "We're here to bowl," he said.

She gave him the stink-eye but relented. "Okay, but no flirting."

Jesse rolled his eyes at his sister, then returned his attention to the couple now coming off the lanes.

"Now everybody's here," Imogene said. "I've got something for us all."

She reached into the duffel bag she carried in earlier. Jesse had noticed it but hadn't thought twice about what she might have. For all he knew, she had gone out and bought her own bowling ball.

But it wasn't a bowling ball or even bowling shoes she pulled from the depths of that bag, but two matching shirts in a beautiful color of purple. Along with two matching purple dresses.

"Did you make these?" Ira asked.

Imogene blushed and nodded humbly. "I figure if we can't have matching shirts like the pink ladies next to us, we can at least come in matching attire."

"We probably could get matching shirts," Astrid said. "But I like this so much better."

Ira smiled. "Me too. Think we have time to change before everything gets underway?"

Everyone nodded and grabbed their new clothes and headed for the restrooms to change. When they came back out, Jesse couldn't help but grin. How did Imogene get the sizes right? Not only was Astrid's dress a perfect fit, his and Ira's shirts were as well.

"You're a very talented seamstress," Jesse said, knowing the praise would turn her cheeks a rosy pink.

"I'll say." Ira brushed one hand down the sleeve of his shirt. "I'm very impressed."

Her color deepened.

"*Danki*," Astrid said. "That was very thoughtful of you."

Imogene grinned and wiggled her head in a way that said it was no matter. It was almost a nod, almost a shake, and might've been considered a shrug. "You're welcome. I was happy to."

"I don't know how much you enjoy the work at the buffet restaurant," Astrid said. "But you could sure make a living as a seamstress."

"You think so?" Imogene said. "I mean, all women sew."

Jesse laughed. "Not hardly."

"I meant, Amish women," Imogene said as they went back to the pit that surrounded their designated lanes. "I thought so anyway."

"So did I," Jesse said. "Then Astrid tried to sew once and—"

His sister glared at him. "You don't have to tell everything on me now," she said, then she pressed her lips together as if trying to scare him into compliance.

"If she hangs out with you much longer, she'll learn without me saying a word," Jesse said.

"Not everybody has the same talents," Imogene said.

Astrid turned to her. Gave her a quick nod. "Thank you." She turned back to her brother and stuck out her tongue.

Jesse just laughed, and Ira joined in. So much for acting thirty-five.

* * *

Imogene was still floating by the time they got through their league's three games. Her arm hurt from throwing so many balls. Her face hurt from smiling so much. And her stomach hurt from laughing so long and hard. All in all it was the best evening she'd spent in a long, long time. Best of all, everyone loved their new bowling uniforms.

"Are you going to the festival tomorrow?" Astrid asked as everyone started pulling off their shoes and getting ready to leave.

"I'm planning to," Ira said. "I've got the store handled. Plus, the first day is so much fun."

"Have you entered anything?" Jesse asked.

"Not any of the big competitions," Ira replied. "But I thought I might see if there's anything interesting to do when I get there. Are you entering anything besides the barbecue competition?"

Jesse looked up from tying his boots. "How did you know—forget it. Astrid told you, right?"

Ira chuckled. "*Jah*. I can't wait to taste what you're cooking. Are you entering anything?" He switched his attention to Astrid, but it was Jesse who answered.

"Trust me, you do not want to eat her cooking."

Astrid shot him a mean look, but Imogene had figured out by now that she didn't mean it with the sternness in which it was delivered. Astrid and Jesse were typical brother and sister, maybe even more so considering that they got to the earth on the same day. They laughed and joked and teased each other more than any two people she had ever seen, and suddenly she wished she had a brother or sister to share life's little moments with. Just another reason to get married again. She would never have another brother or sister. But she could have another husband.

"You don't cook?" Imogene asked. "I thought you made dinner the other night."

"*Jah*. I made the spaghetti," Astrid said. She propped her hands on her hips and dared anyone to contradict her. "Not everybody has to be a good cook. Some people have other talents."

"*Jah*," Jesse said. "Though some people have yet to find theirs."

"I'm going to pretend like you didn't say that." Astrid lifted her chin and dared him to say otherwise.

"I'm entering the pumpkin cooking contest," Imogene finally admitted. All three of them turned and looked at her at the same time. Suddenly she felt like some kind of specimen germ under a scientist's microscope.

"I didn't know you baked," Astrid said.

Imogene gave a small shrug. "I bake some. But there's only so many baking things you can do with pumpkin," she said. "I wanted to go with something a little different."

"Like what?" Ira asked.

"It's a secret," she said. She wasn't sure exactly why it was a secret, but it was so hard to put yourself out there and leave your heart open for people to peck at it like chickens pecking the ground. They didn't mean to, just like the chickens. It was just what they did. She wasn't ready to share this yet. Not till after the judging had begun.

It wasn't that she thought she would win. What she had prepared was something completely different from the pumpkin muffin, pumpkin pies, and pumpkin cakes she was certain would be entered. She couldn't have these three people, these three people who meant more to her than almost anyone else, tell her that she had made a mistake. For that reason as well, she had to keep her entry a secret. For now anyway.

"I guess we'll find out tomorrow then," Astrid said.

"I guess," Jesse murmured.

Imogene smiled at him, loving that light of pride she saw in his eyes. That light in his smile bolstered her confidence a little bit more. Who cared if she actually won tomorrow or not? She had tried, and that was a lot more than some could say.

CHAPTER SIXTEEN

They all decided to meet in front of the hardware store and together walk over to the festival. The park that Astrid had sent Imogene and Ira to walk in on Sunday had now been transformed into a charming midway filled with games, a few rides, booths for vendors, and more things dealing with pumpkin than you could shake a stick at. There was a fried pumpkin pie on a stick, pumpkin ice cream, pumpkin ice cream, pumpkin tea, pumpkin coffee, pumpkin juice, and pumpkin just about anything else.

Ira turned to imagine it from Imogene's point of view. "You've never come over for the Fall Festival?" he asked her.

She shook her head, looking wide-eyed at all the banners strung above the booths and tents, colorful banners depicting what was inside. Not unlike the food offering, most were decorated with pumpkins.

"You know, there's so many pumpkins out here, I don't understand why they just don't call it the Pumpkin Festival." Astrid's remark drew all eyes to her. Even Imogene appeared a bit shocked.

Ira chuckled. That was just Astrid.

She gave a small shrug of one shoulder. "Just saying."

"It's a bouncy house!" Mahlon said, pointing excitedly.

He grabbed Imogene's hand and pulled her in the direction of the pumpkin-shaped inflatable "house."

Ira was quite proud of himself in being able to tell the twins apart now. Of course, the scars on their heads helped a great deal. He figured a person deserved to be called by the right name even if they had an identical brother. Or maybe it was especially because.

"Can we go? Can we go?" Mattie jumped in the fray. "Please, Mamm."

Imogene looked at the others, needing confirmation since they had agreed to go together, Ira supposed. Her gaze lingered longest on him.

"It's okay with me," he said. After all, they had come to have a good time, and a pumpkin bouncy house when you were ten was sure enough a good time.

They allowed the children to drag them in the direction of what was officially known as Kiddie Land, a section of the park set up to cater to the younger set. Whoever had come up with the idea had cleverly integrated the park's own playground equipment into the mix adding bouncy houses, bouncy slides, and other inflatable items where the children could play. The whole thing was monitored by volunteers and roped off for the children's safety.

"You can leave us here," Mahlon said. "We'll be okay."

Ira could tell Imogene was a little shocked by the prospect. She looked to the person standing at the entrance of Kiddie Land. "Is that okay?" she asked.

The woman at the front gate nodded. She was wearing a pumpkin orange T-shirt and matching hat. "It's all very secure," she said. "We have plenty of volunteers inside monitoring the children as they play and making sure no one gets into any scuffles. All disagreements are immediately settled. We take down your children's names and give you a pager with the corresponding number. When they're ready to rejoin you, we'll page you and you can come pick them up."

"Really?" Imogene asked. Ira could tell she was completely shocked by the idea.

The woman nodded. "That way the adults get to enjoy the other parts of the festival and the kids get to enjoy themselves as well."

"Please," Mahlon asked, pulling on Imogene's hand as if that was the secret to getting her to comply.

Imogene turned to Ira, as if he had the answers. "You think it's okay?"

He didn't know what to say. They were her children, not his. But he was saved from having to answer as the woman at the gate tried to reassure her once again. "We've never lost a child in all the years we've held the festival."

Not getting an answer from him, Imogene turned toward Jesse.

The young man gave a quick nod, then turned his attention to the boys. "If we allow you this privilege," he said, "you are to be on your best behavior. Remember what we talked about the other day?"

"Man of the house is always honest," Mattie said.

"And trustworthy," Mahlon added.

"And always kind," the two boys said together.

Jesse nodded. "That's right."

Ira stood back and watched as Imogene gave the woman her name and the names of the boys. The lady fixed the boys and Imogene with numbered bracelets, then the lady handed Imogene a pager and a schedule of events and wished her fun at the festival.

The boys didn't look back. They ran pell-mell into Kiddie Land.

Imogene stared worriedly after them.

"They're going to be okay," Ira and Jesse said at the same time.

Ira chuckled. Jesse frowned.

"Let's go," Astrid said, waving her own schedule of events at them. "If we hurry, we can make the pumpkin trivia contest."

Jesse looked at his sister. "No, we don't want to miss that."

Astrid clapped her hands together happily. "Just in time."

"Great," Jesse said.

"Hush," she told her brother. Astrid turned her attention to the rules posted on the booth where the pumpkin trivia contest was being held. "Four people on the team. Fifteen minutes to answer questions. Ten dollars to enter. All money goes to the Baptist Children's Fund." She turned around and looked from Imogene and Ira. "Sound good?"

"Don't you know?" Jesse asked.

Astrid didn't bother to even look at her brother. "No."

Jesse shook his head good-naturedly. He turned to Imogene and Ira. "I don't think you get a vote either."

"I think it sounds like fun," Imogene said. She seemed much more relaxed now that she knew the boys were being cared for and had something to occupy them. And that was just what Astrid wanted. She wanted Imogene to relax a little bit and have some fun. It might've been better if they could have broken up into teams of two. But they would just have to stay in a foursome for now.

Astrid paid the man at the counter who gave them a sealed envelope.

"These are the questions. Here's a pen. You've got five or ten more minutes before we get started. Each team will have ten minutes to answer the questions. After the ten minutes is up, the team who answers the most questions correctly will win." He put a hard emphasis on "correctly."

"What do we win?" Jesse asked.

"Grand prize is dinner for four at La Petite Amie. That's the new small-plate restaurant that just opened up in town."

Ira frowned. "What's a small-plate restaurant?"

"That's when you get a lot of smaller little things to eat and share them with everyone at the table," Astrid explained.

"How you know that?" Ira asked.

Imogene nodded. "I've never heard of such a thing."

Astrid shrugged. "It's the latest thing these days. All the big cities have them."

"I guess this'll put Paradise Hill on the map," Ira quipped.

Astrid laughed. "Don't count on it. Here." She handed him the pen and a blank sheet of paper. "You write down the answers."

The man who had given them their envelope blew three short blasts on a whistle, then waved a flag to get everyone's attention—an orange flag, no doubt. The crowd grew quiet. All the groups were standing around with their envelopes, ready and waiting to hear what he was about to say.

"Contestants," he said into a bullhorn. He held up the stopwatch for all to see. "Open your envelopes in three, two, one." He hit the button on the top of stopwatch, blew his whistle, and the contest was on.

Astrid ripped open the envelope and pulled up a piece of paper. She held it out in front of her so all of them could read it.

"Number one: What are pumpkins?" Astrid read.

"What are pumpkins?" Jesse repeated. "What kind of question is that?"

"The first one," Astrid shot back.

"I think they're squash," Ira said. He had the pen poised above the paper ready to write down whatever they decided their answer would be. "That makes it a vegetable, right?"

"They're a fruit," Imogene said timidly.

"I think you're right," Jesse said. "I think I heard that somewhere."

Ira quickly jotted down *fruit* for the answer to number one.

"Number two," Astrid read. "What colors are the flowers on the pumpkin vine?"

"Yellow," Ira said. "Yellowish orange. Ruthann used to grow them." He jotted down the answer without waiting for anyone to add more to the conversation.

Astrid liked that he was that confident about it.

"Number three: Which of these is not a color of a pumpkin—blue, white, purple?"

"Pumpkins?" Jesse asked. "Have any of you ever seen a blue pumpkin?"

"There are purple carrots," Imogene put in. "And purple potatoes."

"I need an answer," Astrid demanded.

"Skip it," Jesse said.

"I'm putting down purple," Ira said.

"Number four: What percentage of a pumpkin is actually water?"

"Who knows these things?" Jesse demanded.

"You are not helping!" Astrid told him.

"It's like ninety percent," Imogene said.

"Are you sure?" Ira asked.

"Pretty sure," Imogene replied.

"I'll put it down," Ira said. "If we don't hurry, we're going to run out of time."

Astrid turned back to Jesse. "Who knows these things? Imogene does."

"Read the next question," Ira said.

"Number five: According to the nursery rhyme, who put his wife in a pumpkin shell?"

"Peter, Peter, pumpkin eater." Jesse beamed, extremely proud of himself for coming up with the answer. He raised his hand for a high five.

Imogene blinked at it for a second, then bashfully complied.

"Number six: The rock band Smashing Pumpkins is from what U.S. city?"

"How are we supposed to know that? I never even heard of Smashing Pumpkins," Jesse complained.

"Not helping, brother." Astrid shot him a look.

"Just put something down," Imogene suggested. "We can't get it right if we don't even try."

"I put down Chicago," Ira said. "What's the next question?"

"Why Chicago?" Jesse asked.

Ira gave a small shrug. "Why not?"

"Almost through," Astrid said. "Number seven: Before pumpkins came on the scene, what was commonly carved into jack-o'-lanterns?"

Astrid looked up to see if Jesse had a comment. He didn't, but he turned to Imogene. She shrugged and looked at Ira. Ira looked back to Astrid. "I have no idea."

"Guess," Astrid said.

"Watermelon?" Jesse put in.

"Watermelons would've been already played out by October. Something that could grow on into September," Ira said.

"I don't know, rutabagas?" Imogene shrugged. She seemed to be getting a little more confident in her answers, a little surer of herself as being part of the group. Astrid had only a split second to admire it. They had a contest to win, after all. "Gourds? Squash?"

"Put down turnips," Jesse said.

"Why turnips?" Astrid asked.

Jesse arched a brow at his sister. "You have a better answer?"

"Number eight: Who rode in a carriage made out of a pumpkin?" Astrid said. "Cinderella." She looked at Ira. "Write that down."

He did so without question.

"Three more minutes," Jesse warned.

"Nine: Who spent Halloween in a pumpkin patch waiting for the Great Pumpkin to appear?" Astrid looked around. "Anybody got any idea?"

"Two minutes," Jesse said.

Astrid smacked him with the paper where their questions were listed. "Not helping, Jesse."

"What's the next question?" Ira asked.

"Number ten: How many cups of seeds are in the average pumpkin?"

"One cup," Imogene said with a certainty that Astrid had never seen from her before.

"Are you sure?" Jesse asked.

Imogene nodded. "That one I do know."

"Okay, then—" She no sooner got that out than the buzzer sounded again.

"Contest is over, folks. Everybody hand in your sheet. Be sure that your team's number is at the top and good luck."

"That was fun," Ira said. He caught Astrid's eye and she smiled in return. It was fun, and it had been until she realized that the whole point of this was to get Ira and

Imogene together. It should be Imogene smiling at Ira, not her.

Astrid turned to Imogene and nudged her with her elbow. "Did you have a good time?" she asked.

"It would have been more fun if we knew all the answers," Jesse said.

"There was only one that we didn't answer," Ira said. "I think we did pretty good."

"Maybe," Jesse said. "But who knows if even the ones we did answer were correct. I bet all the *Englisch* people got the one about the Great Pumpkin right. And that one about the rock band."

Imogene shrugged. "Maybe, or maybe not. What are we going to do now?"

Astrid picked up the itinerary for the festival and started scanning down. "After the pumpkin trivia contest, there's a pumpkin decorating contest for the young people, a pumpkin toss, and an overgrown pumpkin that we can pay a dollar to guess how much it weighs."

"Let's take the boys to the pumpkin decorating contest," Imogene said. "I wonder if they're ready to leave Kiddie Land yet."

"We could go see, we've only been here for half an hour or so, but by the time we get back over there they might be ready."

"We can always take them back if they want to decorate the pumpkins," Jesse said.

Imogene nodded. "That's a great idea."

"Are we staying until the judging is over?" Astrid asked.

"We should," Ira said. "I don't think we did bad for Amish folks."

Jesse scoffed. "You don't really think we have a chance of winning this thing, do you?"

"Anything is possible," Astrid said.

"I think it's 'with God anything is possible,'" Jesse corrected her.

She shot her brother a look. "And who invented pumpkins?"

Ira laughed. "I think she's got you on that one, buddy."

The whistle blew again, and the moderator of the pumpkin trivia contest waved his flag in the air once more. "Ladies and gentlemen, we have a winner. Team number seventeen."

"What number are we?" Jesse asked.

"Will the team member from the number seventeen team come up and get their prize?"

"That's us!" Astrid said. "We won!"

"We won?" Ira repeated.

"We won!" Astrid said, jumping up and down.

"Whoo!" Jesse cheered.

Only Imogene was composed enough to make her way to the stage to collect their prize.

"That is so great," Ira said when she returned with the envelope containing their gift certificate to the restaurant. "We need to pick a time to go."

"Who's going to keep it until we use it?" Imogene asked.

"I will." Astrid plucked it from her fingers and started to tuck it into her handbag, but Jesse was too quick and snatched it out of her grasp.

He handed it back to Imogene. "You do it, Imogene," he said. "Astrid will lose it before the day is over."

She shot him a look. "I lost one ticket one time."

"You lost two tickets," Jesse corrected her.

"It was for the cake walk and we were six," she reminded him. "You need to learn to let things go, brother."

"Can't," he said with a sad shake of his head. "I never did get that coconut cake."

He was a lost cause, Astrid decided, and turned to the others. "Are you ready to get the boys now?"

As she said the words, Imogene started as if someone had goosed her and checked the pager she had clipped to her purse strap. "There's my boys."

"Let's go get them," Ira said.

He and Imogene led the way, with Jesse and Astrid trailing behind.

CHAPTER SEVENTEEN

The boys were excited to see their mother when the four of them got back to the Kiddie Land entrance. They jumped and skipped ahead, talking about all the things that they had done, about how one little girl had gotten sick and puked after leaving the bouncy pumpkin—it wasn't a house, they had corrected Imogene after the second time she had called it such. And they talked about the games they had played.

"But did you have a good time?" Jesse asked.

"*Jah!*" They nodded simultaneously.

"Good." Jesse clamped them each on one shoulder as they walked.

He was good with them, Jesse. Ira could see that the younger man seemed to have some sort of connection with them. Or perhaps Ira himself had some kind of disconnect. He wasn't certain. He just knew that Jesse jumped in the mix and talked to them. They responded to him, in a way that they had never responded to Ira. Was that his fault? Had he done enough to try to get to know them? Probably not.

Just watching them was making Ira tired. No wonder Imogene was in the market to remarry. They weren't ill-behaved children, they were just . . . a lot.

They rambled on as they walked to the next event, the pumpkin decorating contest. It was a festival-long event with many prizes, including one for the most original and one from every age division.

Imogene directed the boys toward the sign-up booth and Jesse slipped away to get everyone drinks, leaving Ira and Astrid behind.

"They're good boys," Astrid said, coming to stand by him.

He nodded. "They have a lot of energy."

"But they are good children."

"*Jah*," he agreed. He didn't want to sound negative. He surely wasn't about to jump headfirst into a relationship with Imogene, but if it were a possibility, he had to keep in mind that she had two young children. And she was young herself. Young enough to perhaps expect a few more babies in the future.

Now that thought set him back a little.

Was he prepared to have more children? He didn't know. Remarrying could surely lead to such . . . events.

He shook his head.

"What's wrong?" Astrid asked.

"Am I too old for her?"

"For Imogene?" She shook her head. "Of course not."

But somehow he felt old. As sweet as Imogene was and as quiet and unbearable as his house had become, he wasn't sure he was ready for ten-year-old twins. Would he ever be?

He was jumping ahead of himself.

"What?" Astrid asked.

"Nothing." Ira shook his head.

"It's not nothing," she told him. "I can see that it's not nothing."

"Thinking about getting married again is a little unnerving." He hadn't thought about that until now. Really thought about it. Having someone share his house, his dreams. It all sounded well and good, but what if he had lived by himself too long to adjust to someone new? What if he compared her to Ruthann all the time? What if that caused a problem between them?

Jesse came back, bearing four sodas in foam cups as Imogene made her way back over to where Astrid and Ira stood.

The twins headed into the area where the pumpkins waited. The main area was fenced off with a metal railing. Inside someone had set up a number of hay bales each with a large pumpkin perched on top. The children came through, decorated to their hearts' content, then left their offering in the hands of the moderator. All the judging was to take place at the end of the festival.

"And they all get the same package of stickers?" Ira asked.

Jesse nodded.

"How can there be a prize for most original if they get the same kit to decorate it?" Astrid asked.

"That's what I want to know," Ira said.

Imogene pointed toward a table set up at one side of the arena. Ira could see stacks of paper, scissors, markers, crayons, glue, and an assortment of other craft supplies. "They have all sorts of things they can work with."

"Cute," Astrid said.

But to Ira it looked like craft-time overload.

It must have been the same for the twins, too. They were sharing a pumpkin, but Mattie thought they should decorate it one way and Mahlon another. Not five minutes into it, Mahlon went over to fetch the glitter and a tube of glue, and Mattie protested. Mere seconds later they were both covered in a sparkling, sticky mess.

"Heavens!" Imogene rushed around the dividing fence to the inside of the competition area.

Jesse ran in after her and somehow managed to separate the boys, who were both crying with what sounded like raw betrayal.

Astrid looked back to Ira as Jesse and Imogene escorted the twins back out into the thoroughfare. "Boys will be boys," she said with a hesitant smile.

"*Jah*," was all Ira could reply. "Boys will definitely be boys."

"I think it's time to go home," Imogene said, a small grimace of apology dominating her expression.

Jesse could tell that she'd had enough fun for one day. And the twins . . . too much excitement had wreaked havoc on their normally sunny disposition.

"It happens," Ira said.

But to Jesse, his words didn't ring with the truth and understanding that they should have. Just another reason why Imogene didn't need to be marrying someone like Ira. But once Astrid got something into her head, she tended to railroad everyone along with her.

"I'll walk you back to your buggy," Jesse said. Just in case the twins acted up again, he told himself. Yet he even recognized it as a lie. The twins were rowdy, but they weren't inherently bad. They were just working through the injustices of life. He knew they would come out the other side just fine. Now all he had to do was convince Imogene of that. Starting . . . now.

That grimace of an expression deepened. "I got a driver," Imogene said, "but they aren't supposed to pick us up until after dinner." And dinner was hours away.

"I'll take you home," Jesse said. Then he turned to Ira. "That is if you don't mind running Astrid home in a bit."

He could tell his sister wanted to protest. She would rather Ira take Imogene home, and Jesse had ruined it. Now to make a fuss would look odd. At least, that was what he was hoping for.

Ira gave a small nod. Astrid pressed her lips together, but thankfully didn't say anything.

"Come on," Jesse said, and steered them back in the direction of the hardware store.

The boys were still a little miffed with each other and walked silently, one on the far side of Jesse and the other on the far side of Imogene.

"*Danki*," Imogene said as they made their way back to the hardware store. "I really appreciate your help with them. You're good with them," she said.

"It's only because I'm a twin myself," he told her. "I don't know about being an identical twin, but I'm sure it's just more of the same. The dynamics I mean. At its heart."

"What do you mean?"

"There's this person who perhaps knows you better than anyone else can and perhaps ever will. It could be an explosive situation when things go wrong," he explained. "But it is also the best feeling in the world."

She looked up at him. He could feel her gaze searching, looking for something in his expression. Anyone else might have thought she was looking for a weakness, a spot to exploit. But not Imogene.

"I think they miss their *dat*," she finally said.

Jesse shot her a sad look. "I think you're right. But that's something only time can take away."

The boys climbed into the back seat of Jesse's buggy. Imogene pulled herself into the passenger side as Jesse got in and took up the reins. The boys still mad at each other and sat back in their seat, arms crossed, expressions solemn. They were not speaking to each other. Imogene hated when things turned out like this, but at the same time it did allow for some peace and quiet. Until it started up again.

Thank heavens they were so good with Jesse. They responded to him like they had never responded to any other person that she had ever met. Except for perhaps Abner. Why was that? And how could she get them to respond to Ira in the same way? That would be important when the two of them got married.

Not that he had proposed or anything, but he seemed to be content in getting to know each other. And he hadn't run for the hills when her twins acted out. That had to mean something.

She hoped it did.

"What are you doing here?" Imogene asked as he pulled the buggy into the parking lot of the grocery store.

The boys, still not speaking to each other, leaned forward in their seats.

"I just need to pick up a couple of things," Jesse said. "Is that okay?"

She nodded. "*Jah*, sure."

Jesse smiled. He did have a nice smile. "Wait here. I'll be right back."

He climbed out of the buggy and hitched the horse, then disappeared inside the grocery store.

"What's he doing?" Mattie asked.

"He didn't tell her," Mahlon said.

"I wasn't talking to you," Mattie replied.

Imogene turned in her seat. "Sit back and both of you be quiet. It's time to behave." Past time as far as she was concerned. She'd used her *I've had enough* voice and thankfully the boys heeded it this time.

A short time later Jesse emerged from the grocery store carrying two large sacks with the tops folded over. Imogene wanted to ask what was in them, but was it any of her business? No. So she said nothing as he climbed back into the buggy and stored the sacks on the seat between them.

"Next stop, home," he said to her with a smile.

"What'd you get?" one of the boys asked.

Imogene didn't even bother to turn around. "Not your business. Sit back like I told you."

They rode in silence for a moment, then Jesse shook his head. "I can't believe we won the trivia contest."

Imogene couldn't help the chuckle. "I know, I guess we got the question about the rock band right," she said.

Jesse gave a nod. "Ira answered that one, but it was just a guess."

"And your sister knew the ones about books."

"*Jah*, but I think you answered most of the questions. We wouldn't've won if we hadn't had you on our team."

Imogene gave a small shrug. But the compliment burned in her cheeks. She was a bit proud of herself for knowing some of those answers, and then the fact that they beat out sixteen other teams who were *Englisch* was something of a feat. Some of the questions they had simply guessed on they must have gotten right.

"It'll be fun going to try a new restaurant," Imogene said.

"Small plates?" Jesse asked. "I don't understand that."

"I've never heard of it myself," Imogene said. "But I guess we'll figure it out together."

Jesse nodded. "Mattie, what did you like best about Kiddie Land?"

"The bouncy pumpkin," Mattie replied.

"What about you, Mahlon?"

He paused for a minute and Imogene had a distinct feeling

he liked the bouncy pumpkin best as well, but he didn't want to be just like his brother. "The bouncy castle."

Imogene turned just in time to see Mattie nod in agreement. "The bouncy castle was the best," he said.

"Okay," Jesse started. "Mahlon first. What was your favorite part of the bouncy castle?"

"The dragon," Mahlon answered without hesitation. "There was the blow-up dragon in the corner of one room in the castle and if you jumped high enough, you could get on his back. And he was green. And had red flames shooting out of his mouth."

"Flames?" Imogene said.

"Don't worry, Mamm," Mahlon assured her. "It was just like part of the blow-up stuff, but it looked like flames."

"Blow-up stuff?" Jesse asked.

"You know," Mattie interjected. "The stuff that made up the outside part."

"Got it," Jesse said. "What about you, Mattie? Was that your favorite part as well?"

"That was cool," Mattie said. "But my favorite part was the ladder outside. And you could climb it and get into the tower and slide down. And there was a princess."

"You don't say," Jesse said. He was grinning, still watching the road ahead, but he had tilted back so he could better hear the boys. Once again they had scooted up in their seats, but this time their sullen attitudes had disappeared.

"The princess was cool," Mahlon said. "But I still like the dragon best."

"And that's okay," Jesse said. "It's good to like different things from the other and it's okay."

Mattie nodded. "I guess so."

"I know so," Jesse said. "Remember, I'm a twin too."

"But your twin is a girl; that makes it different."

Jesse seemed to consider that a moment. "True, but sometimes it doesn't matter. Like say, when it comes to decorating pumpkins or playing baseball."

The boys nodded.

"Thing to remember," Jesse said. "Is that the same is good, but so is different."

Just like that he had the twins talking once again. Imogene was amazed. Perhaps when the boys got wound up and in a temper over something or another, she allowed her emotions to rise as well. Jesse always seemed to have a clear head. Maybe that was something she could work on too.

They chatted about the other events in the Kiddie Land section. And they discussed strategies for the next day and the best way to make the most of the bouncy castle that they both loved so much.

Imogene sat back and enjoyed the ride home. It was nice not to have to drive, it was nice not to have the boys upset or mad at each other, and it was nice riding beside Jesse.

She supposed the thing that would make it better was if Ira was the one driving the buggy. But then she immediately felt remorse over the thought. She did enjoy driving beside Jesse though she was supposed to be getting to know Ira better. The thing was she just couldn't imagine Ira handling her children the way Jesse had. Try as she might, that image just wouldn't come.

"Turn right up here. That's our house," Imogene said.

"Black mailbox?" Jesse asked.

"That's the one."

Jesse turned his buggy down the packed dirt lane that led to the two-story white house where she and the boys lived.

"It's a nice place you got here," Jesse said.

"*Danki*." Imogene tried to see it as if from his eyes. She

and Abner had worked long and hard to give the yard a pleasing appearance. Each year she planted a row of petunias in varying colors all around the edge of the house. She loved to look out and see a burst of color from every window. The house itself had a wide porch that spanned the length. There was a swing on one end and a small table with two chairs on the other. Since her house faced east, she liked to come out in the mornings and have a cup of coffee and watch the sunrise. Here lately, she hadn't done that. She'd let her life get a little too busy for such leisure.

He pulled the horse to a stop and turned to her, the reins loose in his hands. "I have a surprise for the boys."

Cheers rose from the back seat.

"That's very kind of you," Imogene said. "But I'm not sure a surprise is appropriate given today's behavior."

"Mamm," the boys protested.

She turned and shook her head at them. "You know better." And they did. But these days it seemed they would let their emotions get away from them in times when they needed to keep them in check.

"I understand that," Jesse said. "I do. But I think today's surprise will help ensure a better understanding of today's mistakes."

She thought about it a moment. She trusted Jesse. It was the boys and their acceptance of whatever the surprise was that had her hesitant.

"Please," Mahlon said.

"Pretty please," Mattie added.

"With sugar on top," Jesse put in. He grinned.

Despite her reservations, Imogene felt herself giving in. "*Jah*," she finally said. "I suppose so."

CHAPTER EIGHTEEN

They all filed into the house, one by one, Jesse carrying the two sacks he had brought out of the grocery store.

Once inside, he turned to the boys. "I bought the two of you something at the store."

"Neat," the boys said. "Awesome."

"But I want you to understand that your behavior at the pumpkin decorating stand was not okay. The two of you have to learn to get along."

"We're getting along right now," Mahlon said, with Mattie nodding in agreement. "See?"

"I know you two can do it sometimes, but you need to work on doing it more often. So often that you get to the point where you do it all the time, got it?"

"What do you say?" Imogene prodded.

"*Danki*," they said together.

Jesse handed them the sacks. "Take these to the coffee table," he told them. Then he turned to Imogene. "You might want to get a tablecloth or something."

As he said the words, the boys knelt down around the coffee table and started pulling the items out of their paper sacks. Each contained a small pumpkin, a little bit bigger than a baseball, markers, stickers, even glitter glue. And each twin had their own supplies.

"You think this is going to help them share better?" Imogene said.

"Tablecloth?" Jesse said as Mahlon popped the cap off one of the markers.

"Be right back," Imogene said.

She bustled to her linen closet and pulled out the disposable tablecloth that she used to protect the table when she had any sort of craft going on. Then she went back to the living room. "Everything off the table for a sec," she said.

The boys complied, gathering up their supplies and putting them back into the bags until she got the tablecloth into place.

Then they unloaded everything onto the table once again.

"This is about sharing," Jesse told Imogene. "I guess it's a twin thing, but you share everything. You share a birthday, you share birthday parties, most times you share a room. You share friends and family. It's a little bit easier I think for me and Astrid since we're different genders," he said. "But for them, sharing gets old really fast."

"I never thought about it that way," Imogene said. Not in all of the ten years that she had been their mother.

She had been tickled when she found out she was having twins. *Jah*, it had been a lot more work taking care of two babies instead of one, but she knew they would always have each other. She wanted them to be close. She never thought about them needing to be individuals.

"*Danki*," she said, smiling at Jesse. "I never thought about it that way, and probably never would have had you not brought it to my attention."

The boys chattered on, talking about what they were going to do, giving suggestions to each other, and laughing at their ideas. In general, they were enjoying each other.

But that moment between Jesse and Imogene . . .

Had she imagined it? She must have. But she had thought, for a second, that his green eyes had softened. The light had shone in them, and that moment stretched out until it felt like an eternity. Even with the noise the twins were making behind her, she felt isolated, separated, as if only she and Jesse were left in the world.

Then the moment passed.

Jesse broke eye contact and stepped away. Imogene released her breath, not realizing until that moment she had been holding it.

What had just happened?

Nothing. Nothing happened. It was all in her head.

Jesse bent down next to the boys and started talking to them about their designs and what they were doing.

Imogene merely watched.

Then she realized she was hovering, so she moved farther into the living room and sat down in the chair at one end of the coffee table. Jesse looked up from his place on the rug next to the boys and gave her a quick smile. And that moment almost happened again. Or had she just wished it would have?

"What are you going to do with the pumpkins when they've finished decorating them?" he asked.

"I think I'll put them right there on the mantel with the rest of the fall decorations." Imogene pointed to the place.

Jesse looked over. "I like it," he said. "You must really like fall."

"*Jah.*" And she did.

She had decorated the mantel with a swag of brightly colored leaves in orange, red, and yellow. They were wrapped around a small stream of battery-operated lights that added a little bit of glow to the decor. Three little pumpkins sat right in the center. "I do. I guess because my birthday's in the fall."

"Is it coming up soon?" Jesse asked. "Maybe we can use the gift card and all go out to eat for your birthday. We can call it your birthday celebration."

She shook her head and gave him a small smile. "It's already passed." And there was no one there to wish her a happy birthday. It was something she shouldn't dwell on, and it was something that shouldn't matter. Yet somehow it did. This year anyway. It wasn't like she'd had anyone to make a big deal out of a birthday in many years. That was the problem with living away from a lot of family. Perhaps that was the answer to her problem. Instead of trying to get married again, perhaps she should just move closer to her family. She had a few aunts and uncles and a scattered cousin or two there in Paradise Springs, but her mother and father lived farther north.

But she worried that a move would shake up the twins even more. To take them away from the home that they knew and the places where they had their memories of their father. Would it be worth it to lose that in order to gain a possible relationship with their grandparents? How was a *mamm* to know?

"*Danki* for taking me home," Astrid said as Ira pulled into her driveway.

They chatted some on the way home but not much. It seemed Ira had something on his mind. She only wished she knew what.

"It's no problem," he said.

She waited a heartbeat too long before she started climbing out of the buggy.

What had she expected from him? She had spent the last week and a half trying to get the two of them together— him and Imogene. Yet instead of the Fall Festival being a great place for everyone to get together and get to know each other without a lot of pressures, it didn't turn out exactly as she had planned.

Astrid stopped, peered into the buggy, and met his gaze. "I did have fun doing the trivia with you," she said. "And I think Imogene had a good time too, don't you think?"

He nodded but said nothing.

"You had a good time, right?" Her stomach clenched as he waited to answer.

"*Jah*," he finally replied.

"Is something wrong, Ira?"

"I'm fine," he said. "I'm glad we went today."

"Me too," Astrid said. Then she paused a moment, searching for something more to say, when there wasn't anything else.

"I guess I'll see you then," she said.

Ira nodded. "I guess."

"Tomorrow."

"Tomorrow," he agreed, then he flicked the reins on the horse and started the carriage into motion.

Astrid watched as he pulled back down her drive. She should go in the house instead of standing there watching, waiting to see . . . What? If he would turn around? If he would look back? Why? It wasn't like there was anything between them. No. She was setting him up with Imogene. The trip home was nothing more than that, a trip home. But something seemed off with him. Like he had too much on his mind, and Astrid had to wonder what it was. The problem was she had no idea. And she probably never would.

Ira pulled into the drive at his house, feeling a bit torn. He couldn't say the day went badly, but he couldn't say it went well, either. He climbed down from the buggy and unhitched the horse, then took the gelding into the barn for a brush down and a scoop of oats.

His mind kept running over the burst of confidence Imogene had gotten during their trivia contest. It almost matched the confidence that Astrid walked around with daily. Yet on the way home, she hadn't seemed so confident.

He knew he had been lost in his own thoughts, but he couldn't help it. Somehow, something just wasn't right.

He pushed his buggy into the carriage house and fastened the lock. Couldn't be too careful. Unfortunately, *Englisch* kids and Amish kids alike liked to play pranks. It would do no good to get up in the morning to find his buggy was gone.

He let himself into his quiet, dark house. He had been locking the carriage house for years, and never once thought about the reason why. Why was he so negative tonight? Chances were no one would mess with this carriage and yet he was obsessed over somebody breaking the lock and taking it for a joyride.

He switched on the propane-powered lamp in the living room, then collapsed into the chair next to it. Truth was, he was tired. When the kids had acted out, he just felt tired and old. He supposed he could've stepped in the way Jesse had, but he wasn't a twin and he didn't know that sameness that Jesse had talked about.

Ira supposed he had been a good father. Good enough anyway. But that reluctance was still there. Because he wasn't Matthew and Mahlon's father? Or was it something more? Whatever it was, he needed to figure it out before this thing with Imogene went much further. Did he want it to go further?

He wasn't certain. About the only thing he was certain was that he was tired of being alone.

As he sat there, it felt like the walls were closing in on

him. It'd been that way for a while now, but it seemed worse since he'd been running around with Astrid, Jesse, and Imogene.

He sat there as those walls drew closer and closer. This had to be what it felt like to be in prison. Which was ridiculous. He lived in America, he was a free man, but those walls taunted him. Even in the low light of the fading day, he could see nearly every mark on them. Every scuff that occurred, every nick that happened when someone had knocked furniture against them. Those marks seemed to be a test. Then suddenly he couldn't take it anymore.

He got to his feet and let himself out of the house, then into the barn to get the gelding back out. He pulled the carriage out and hitched the horse to the buggy, then headed into town. First stop was the hardware store. He was going to get some paint. If the walls were closing in on him, they were at least going to look good.

Even as he started slapping on the first coat, he wondered what Astrid was doing this evening.

The sun was almost down as Jesse turned onto the road that led to his house. Just a couple more miles and he would be at the drive and then he would be home. The evening would come to an end.

In truth, the evening had ended the minute he walked out of Imogene Yoder's house. It had been the hardest thing he'd done in a long time. He couldn't figure out why. The boys had decorated their pumpkins with pride. Imogene had displayed them happily on her mantel with the other three little pumpkins that were nowhere near as elaborate. Then she offered him a drink of water and the boys had gone upstairs to play. He and Imogene were left alone.

That moment came back to him. That moment earlier

when they caught each other's gaze and it seemed that time had stood still.

He shook his head at himself. He sounded like one of Astrid's romance novels. He'd only read a couple of them. It was strange, reading them knowing that Astrid had created that story, that she had taken words from thin air and turned them into a book. It was both amazing and perplexing to him at the same time. He had such trouble with the words, and she wove them together like some kind of miracle.

And if he sounded like a romance novel, did that mean . . . ?

No. It didn't. He wasn't falling in love with Imogene Yoder. He'd been in love only once before. And he had married that love. Even before they said their vows, he knew that Amanda was not a strong person. But he didn't marry her because of her health. He married her because he loved her. He didn't know why God limited her time on earth. But they knew that it was coming at some point. Yet he still wanted to spend that time with her, ill health or not. He wanted her as his wife. And she had been, but for such a brief time.

After he buried her, he figured he would never love again. Love seemed so frail, even more so than his poor wife. Love was easily bruised and so hard to give. At least for him it was. So the idea that he was falling in love with Imogene Yoder was complete bunk, as his grandmother would say. Astrid had already vowed to get Imogene and Ira engaged. In fact, Astrid had told him that Imogene was engaged the first time he'd ever seen her.

No, that wasn't it. He wasn't falling in love. Maybe he just needed a good night's sleep.

* * *

"Have you seen Ira?" Imogene asked the following day. "He was supposed to meet me at the hardware store, but no one there has seen him."

Astrid shook her head. Imogene seemed to be in a state. "You don't think anything happened to him, do you?"

"How would I know that?" Imogene asked. "He was supposed to watch the twins. I've got to do my pumpkin thing."

"The secret recipe," Astrid said with a nod.

"That's right," Imogene said. "I can't do my thing if I have the twins with me."

"Can you leave them in Kiddie Land?" Astrid asked.

She straightened the books on the table that sat in front of her. She didn't have to stay at the booth for long, but she knew the boys would get bored if they were just sitting with not much else to do. "Or they could stay with me, I guess. I think they would be much happier in the play park."

"I can't," Imogene said. "I've got to go back home and cook. I just want to know where Ira is."

Then Astrid understood. She was worried about him. Come to think of it he had been acting strange on the ride home and she hadn't seen him all day.

"I'm supposed to stay here for another hour," Astrid said. "If you want, I can run out and see if he's at home."

"Would you?" Imogene asked. "I would feel much better knowing if he's okay or not. That nothing has happened to him."

Astrid nodded. "I understand."

Imogene acted as if to turn away.

"What about the boys?" Astrid asked.

"I guess I'll have to take my chances at trying to cook for the competition with them under my feet."

"Don't you cook when you're at home? Aren't they there then?"

"I do," she said. "I just wanted to be able to concentrate all my attention on the food."

Astrid shook her head and waved for Imogene to send the boys over. "C'mon, you two, you're staying with me."

"Are you sure?" Imogene said. She sounded hesitant, but Astrid could see the relief in her eyes.

"I'm sure. You go do your pumpkin thing," she said. "I'll head over to check on Ira as soon as I finish up here."

"And you'll come back and let me know that he's all right?"

Astrid nodded. "Of course."

"*Danki*," Imogene said. "I'll see you in a bit then."

"Hey, Imogene," Astrid called.

The woman stopped and turned around.

"Good luck."

Imogene smiled. "Thanks."

"Good luck," the boys called after her.

Imogene waved and started back down the street.

Astrid could hardly wait to find out what the secret dish was Imogene was making for the cooking competition. With Imogene anything was possible.

Ten minutes before the hour was technically up, Astrid signed a few of her books and left them on the table along with an envelope for people to put money in. It was on the honor system. But either way she felt like she waited long enough. She hadn't been concerned about Ira until Imogene pointed out that he wasn't anywhere around. Now she couldn't get out to her buggy and over to his house fast enough. Last night he just acted so weird. Not like Ira at all. He was quiet, *jah*, and Ira was sort of a quiet person. But this was different. It wasn't Ira being good thoughtful, it was Ira being *too* thoughtful, as if his thoughts were taking over his evening.

She and the twins ran by Jesse's booth to tell him they were headed out to check on Ira. He offered to come along, but Astrid waved him away. He had so many customers at his booth, and she didn't want to take him away from all that potential business.

Astrid couldn't tell if Ira was home or not when she pulled into the drive.

"Wait here," she told the boys, then climbed out of the buggy.

She tied the horse's reins to the railing and hurried up the steps. Two raps on the door and she opened it. "Ira?" she called. The smell of paint fumes met her nose. "Ira, are you in here?"

She stepped inside and shut the door behind her. The living room furniture was covered with drop cloths and the fireplace had been taped off to protect it from paint spatters. An open paint can and a tray holding a roller with an extendable pole attached sat in the middle of the floor on the bed of newspaper. But Ira was nowhere to be seen. Where was he now?

"Ira," she said louder this time.

He came down the hallway wiping his hands on a paper towel. Paint was splattered on his hair, his face, down in front of his shirt, even on his shoes. "What are you doing here?"

"I came to fetch you. Did you or did you not tell Imogene you would watch the twins today?"

He closed his eyes. "I forgot all about it," he said, opening them once again.

"We were worried about you. She was worried about

you. And today is the pumpkin cooking competition. You want to be there to support her, right?"

"Right," he said. But he looked around as if he couldn't stop the job he had already started.

"This is the time when you can be her white knight," Astrid told him, not knowing if he would fully get the reference.

He shook his head. "I didn't think today's women want to be rescued."

"Don't start getting into that now. Just put on a clean shirt and let's go. The twins are already in the buggy."

"What about—" He raised his hand at the room around him.

"I'll come back and help you tonight if you just come to the festival now."

She stopped. Waited for him.

He stood there just staring at her.

"And hurry."

CHAPTER NINETEEN

Her white knight.

Ira didn't think he'd ever been anybody's white knight before. Ever. Not even Ruthann. It sure didn't feel heroic running into town with the two boys seated behind him in the buggy.

Astrid had said she had an errand to run so the boys couldn't come with her. She said that he needed to take them back to the festival with him.

He couldn't help but think it was a made-up errand just to try to get him and Mattie and Mahlon together and alone for a while. The idea shouldn't have made him feel so uncomfortable. There were two little boys after all. Just two little boys.

What did little boys talk about anyway? He should have remembered from his time when Elam was the same age, but there was that disconnect again.

"So, do you guys have a pet?" Ira asked. Animals were always good to talk about, weren't they?

The twin on the right shook his head. Ira was pretty certain it was Mattie. The cuts they had on their foreheads had almost healed up. It was hard to see the little pink scar in the rearview mirror. Plus it was a mirror, a reflection, so that made it a little bit trickier as well. But he thought it was Mattie. "No. We want a dog, but Mamm won't let us have one."

"A big dog," Mahlon said.

Maybe not the best topic after all. "Dogs are a lot of responsibility," Ira said as gently as he could. He certainly didn't want to get between mother and child on this one.

"Are they more responsibility than horses?" Mahlon asked.

"We take care of the horses," Mattie added. "That's responsibility, right?"

"Well, *jah*," Ira said. "But they're a little different."

"I don't see how," Mattie said. "They're smaller. We do everything for the horse that we would do for a dog."

"You do?" Ira didn't mean to sound so uninformed on the subject.

"*Jah*," Mahlon said. "We walk the horse, we brush the horse, we feed the horse, we give the horse fresh water. That's everything we would do for a dog."

"And there's two of us," Mattie added. "That means we can get the work done double fast."

"And the chickens," Mahlon put in. "We take care of the chickens and there's a lot of them. Surely if we can take care of a bunch of chickens, we can take care of one dog."

"I suppose your mother doesn't see it quite that way," Ira managed to reply. The boys did have a point. If they took care of the horse and the chickens, then they could surely take care of a dog. With two of them doing the looking after, he was certain a dog would be well cared for. Plus, a dog would give the kids another means to run off some of the energy they held inside.

Maybe he would talk to Imogene about it. They weren't like a couple-couple, but they were thinking about it at least. They were getting along fine. Imogene was a good and godly woman. There was just something . . . he didn't know what to call it. But it was there.

"I'll talk to your mother about it," he said.

Mahlon practically jumped to his feet. "You will?"

"I said I would," he said. Though now he was beginning to regret that offer. He might have just spoken out of turn. "Sit down now."

"*Jah*." Mahlon was on his feet, then the next breath he was sitting down.

The boys chatted happily all the way back to the Fall Festival, and Ira wondered if that was all it would take to get them to accept him. Talking to their mother about a dog. He just hoped it wasn't his first mistake.

Ira stopped off at the Fall Festival as he promised. Jesse's booth was still going strong, and Astrid was standing next to him. Further proof that her errand was nothing but a ploy to get Ira and the boys in the same buggy for a while.

"Are you going to get Imogene now?" Astrid said as soon as she saw him.

"It's good to see you, too, Astrid," Ira quipped.

"She was worried about you, you know," Astrid said.

"Worried about me?" Ira asked.

Astrid nodded. "She thought something had happened since you hadn't shown up. I think you should go get her now to let her know that you're fine."

"I suppose I could."

"She's going to need a ride over here with all of the pumpkin stuff, her special secret recipe whatever it is. I was going to go, but since you're here . . ." She trailed off.

"You boys stay here," Ira said. "That way I'll have

enough room in the buggy for your *mamm* and whatever it is she cooked today."

"Maybe you can talk to her about that little thing we were talking about on the way over," Mattie said cryptically. It took Ira a moment to figure out exactly what he was talking about.

"Sure. Right. I can do that." But he wasn't sure today was the day to be talking to Imogene about getting a pet for her boys. He was certain she was a bundle of nerves just thinking about the cooking competition.

"What thing?" Astrid asked.

Mattie crooked his index finger at her and waited for her to bend down before he covered his mouth with one hand and whispered in her ear.

"I see," Astrid said. "Very well then."

She smiled and Ira wondered if she thought getting a dog was just one more part of his courtship with Imogene. One thing was certain, he wasn't certain about it at all.

He left the boys with Astrid and Jesse and started toward Paradise Springs. A little while later he pulled up in front of Imogene's.

"Thank goodness you're okay," Imogene said, bustling out of the house as soon as he pulled up. "Thank goodness you're here. I have to get this all loaded up so I can get back to the festival."

"We'll get it done in no time," Ira said confidently. "Tell me what to do."

The fluttering in Imogene's stomach increased with each minute they were in the buggy heading over to Paradise Hill. To say she was nervous about this competition would be the understatement of the year. Plus, she never put herself out there like this. She had never entered a contest or a competition like this one. She didn't even cook her best dishes for potluck. She simply didn't like to draw attention to herself. But something in her felt compelled to enter this competition today. Mainly because it said pumpkin dishes. It didn't say desserts, and it didn't specify baking. That was when she had come up with the idea of her "something totally different."

She might not have been as nervous if she had some kind of pumpkin coffee cake or cinnamon pumpkin muffins or anything that would serve as an alternative breakfast or even dessert. But instead . . .

"Whatever you got back there, it sure smells good," Ira said.

"*Danki,*" she said. Her gaze fell to his hands, wrapped around the reins as they drove into town. "What's on your nails?"

"Paint," Ira replied. "I started painting last night."

"After the festival? After all that walking around you went home and started painting?"

He nodded.

"Tell me it was a picture of something and not your house."

He shook his head. "Nope. I started looking at all the nicks and things on the house and decided it needed a coat of paint."

"I guess that comes from working at the hardware store?"

Ira shrugged. "I don't know. Now I can't get this paint off my nails. It came off of everywhere else but . . ."

"Surely it will wear off soon."

"I certainly hope so," he said.

They pulled to a stop at the edge of the parking lot. They didn't want to get too close to everyone and not have enough room to get Imogene's goodies out of the back.

Ira hitched up the horse, then went around the side of the buggy. "Let me get your wagon down and then we can load up from there."

"I really do appreciate your help," Imogene said.

"It's no problem," he said. "I'm happy to help today."

He seemed happy. It was just Imogene wasn't good at accepting help. It was the hardest part for her, allowing people to do for her. She needed help and she knew she needed help, but asking for it was something altogether different. Just another reason that she needed to get married.

She needed a helpmate. She would be much more comfortable with that helpmate being a husband than just a friend.

Walking through the festival grounds, pulling a wagon behind her with Ira at her side, felt so much like family. If the boys had been there she wasn't sure she could have been able to tell the difference. But yet there was something missing. Maybe it was just too soon.

She had been crazy in love with Abner, and he had seemed to be crazy in love with her. However, this wasn't crazy love, whatever was growing between her and Ira. But it seemed comfortable enough. It wasn't love, but enough, perhaps. Or maybe it just needed time. Then again, how could she expect that same kind of love now that she'd had then?

Now why had Jesse's face popped into her head at that moment? She knew he was out somewhere in the fray of bustling bodies going from pillar to post. He had a booth today, and according to Ira he was doing quite well. She hoped so. She hoped his business was going fabulously.

Ira walked her all the way to the booth.

"I really am glad you're okay," Imogene said.

"I can't believe you guys were worried about me."

"You said you would take care of the boys for me this afternoon."

He briefly closed his eyes and shook his head. "I'm sorry. I got a little wrapped up in painting and . . ." He trailed off.

"It's okay," Imogene said.

"It's not," Ira returned. "You should be angry with me."

"Well, I'm not."

"Well, you should be," he repeated.

She pulled her wagon a little closer and shot him a be-seeching look. "Wish me luck?"

"All the luck in the world."

A couple hours later, everyone gathered for the judging. Even Mahlon and Matthew wanted to be there to see how their *mamm* did.

Astrid sidled up to Ira and bumped his shoulder with her own. "Did she tell you on the way over what she was making?"

Ira shook his head. "She would not divulge her secret. But it sure smelled delicious."

Astrid whistled under her breath. "Must be something else."

Ira nodded.

"Are you really going to talk to her about getting the boys a dog?" she asked.

Ira's interested face fell and became one of worry. "I promised," he said. "I don't know why I did, but I promised I would ask her."

"All she can say is no, right?" But it was more than that. A part of her thought that it might put too much strain on an already fragile relationship. And that would be a bad thing, she told herself. Because she had promised Imogene that she would get her and Ira together.

She had a book to write. A book about a lonely widow with twins who falls in love with the dashing owner of the hardware store.

But she was beginning to prefer a new idea. An idea about that same dashing hardware store owner falling headfirst for a local romance author.

She did her best to rein in her thoughts, but it was next to impossible. Once she allowed the idea into her head, it swirled around and taunted her with its simple message and complex questions.

Jah, Ira was the first man she had been attracted to in a long time. Maybe even ever. She couldn't pinpoint what it was about him. Maybe the way he tilted his head to one side when he was studying a problem. Or maybe it was the flash of loneliness she could see in his smile. He thought he had it all together. He'd had his love, his life, his family, and he didn't seem intent on asking for more. Yet why shouldn't he have it? Why did it have to be that God had provided and it was all used up now?

It didn't.

Perhaps that was why Astrid thought he would be perfect for Imogene. Not that he was really perfect for her, but that Astrid had seen he deserved more love from this life than what he had been afforded.

Didn't they all?

She had thought herself in a position to provide that love to two very deserving people. She could also argue that she herself was a deserving soul. But a promise was a promise.

Now there was absolutely nothing she could do about it. Book aside, she had pledged another a love, a husband. She surely couldn't take that away for herself. Not and look in the mirror each day.

Why now, Lord? she silently asked. *Why him?*

"The judging is about to begin," Jesse said. He came up on the other side of Ira, the twins flanking him.

Astrid pushed those thoughts to one side as they all turned their attention toward the podium where the moderator stood with a microphone. He announced the judging was about to start, but first he had to explain the rules. The entrants, he said, were all waiting "backstage." Which meant they were hiding behind a curtain that someone had installed around the area. They had had to cook their dish this morning and now were to serve it to the six judges on the panel. While the judges were tasting, the ladies were to tell something about their dish and how it came to be.

"What number is Imogene?" Astrid asked.

"Eight," Jesse said.

"Did you know that?" She turned to Ira.

"No." His voice sounded as if he didn't know why he would. Maybe that was why she kept having crazy little daydreams about Ira Oberholtzer. He wasn't as into this matchmaking gig as he seemed to be.

"We can't see," the twins complained.

"I'm going to take them closer to the front," Jesse said. "Meet me after the judging is over?"

"Will do," Ira said.

Jesse nodded, and Astrid couldn't help but think Ira should be the one taking the twins, not Jesse. At the rate her brother was going, he was totally going to ruin any romance budding between Ira and Imogene. But the truly scary part was that a piece of her didn't care.

It was that same piece that she had acknowledged earlier. She needed to get it under control, that selfish piece that had decided to raise its head and demand a love of its own. Maybe she would find it one day, but it couldn't be with Ira. No matter how badly she thought that she wanted it to be. This wasn't about her. It wasn't even about a book any longer. It was about a gentle woman and two sweet boys who needed a man in their lives. A steady, loving man who could see them through the rest of their days. Ira.

As they watched and waited and Astrid waged war on her own thoughts, the first seven contestants came out with their goods one by one. Each of them gave the six people on the panel the dish they had made and explained it to the crowd. One of those seven was Sylvie Yoder, who had a cream cheese–filled double-layer pumpkin walnut pecan butter cake that she served to the judges. Even from the distance where they were standing, Astrid thought it looked amazing.

Then it was Imogene's turn.

"There she is," Ira said.

Whatever it was she gave to the judges came in a bowl. She also gave the judges a saucer, but again Astrid and Ira were too far away to tell exactly what it was.

After all six judges had been served, Imogene stepped timidly up to the podium where the announcer waited with his microphone.

Astrid could see her knees trembling all the way from where they stood. Imogene just wasn't good about getting in front of people. So much so Astrid was a little surprised she had entered this contest to begin with.

"My entry into the competition is roasted pumpkin soup with toasted pumpkin seeds, rye croutons, and bacon bits."

"Soup?" the moderator asked.

"That goes double for me," Astrid said. "Soup?"

"Shush," Ira said.

"And what's on the saucer?" the announcer asked.

"A slice of toasted sourdough bread served with curry pumpkin butter."

"There you have it," the moderator said.

Astrid looked to the judges to see how they were reacting to Imogene's unusual offering. They seemed receptive, so she supposed it must taste good at least. Though in her life she could never remember making pumpkin soup.

So that wasn't a good gauge. It wasn't like she cooked anyway.

"She did okay," Ira said.

"I think she did great," Astrid returned.

They watched as the next two contestants came across the stage. By then Jesse had caught back up with them.

"Did you see her?" Jesse's eyes twinkled. Wait, why were Jesse's eyes twinkling? This had nothing to do with him.

"We did," Ira said.

Jesse turned to Astrid. "How do you think she did?"

"Hard to say. All the contestants before her made something sweet, and I would imagine that the rest of them did as well. So she's unique in that, but that could work in her favor or against her just as easily. It could go either way, really." About like this matchmaking thing between Imogene and Ira.

Imogene was still bright pink when she came up to them a few moments later.

"I don't think I did well," she said.

Lord, please give this woman some more confidence in herself.

"You did fine," Astrid told her.

Jesse nodded. "You did a sight better than anybody who didn't enter. Now, the important stuff," he continued. "What do they do with what's left over? Can we try it?"

Imogene shrugged. "I guess so. I mean, it's still in my pans and stuff backstage, so I suppose I'll take it home. You really want to try it?"

"It tastes good, doesn't it?" Jesse asked.

"I hope so," she said.

Amend that, Astrid thought. Imogene needed more than a little confidence; she needed a truckload.

"Perhaps we can try at supper tonight," Ira said. "If you're up for it."

She shook her head. "I promised the boys that I would take them to Charlie's today if they behaved for you guys." She looked at each of them for confirmation.

"You'll have to ask Jesse," Ira said. "He really had them more than anyone."

She turned to Jesse. "I think they deserve Charlie's today."

The boys jumped in the air and executed a perfect twin high five. "Awesome. I want to get a Big Chaz."

Imogene shook her head. "I really don't know where they put all this food."

"What about tomorrow?" Jesse said. "Maybe we could try your pumpkin soup tomorrow."

Once again Imogene's color deepened.

Astrid looked from her to Jesse. What was happening here? Jesse kept wedging himself in. He was taking the attention off Ira. How was she going to get the two of them to fall in love if Jesse was constantly interrupting?

"So when are the winners announced?" Ira asked.

"I think in an hour."

"How about we walk around until then?" Jesse said. "Sound good?"

"That sounds like a fine idea," Ira agreed.

CHAPTER TWENTY

They walked around for an hour, looked at this and that, and made their way back over to the judges' stand. Astrid had hoped that the three of them walking around would somehow bring Ira and Imogene closer together, but the boys clustered around Jesse, and Imogene strolled along with them.

The moderator announced that the judging was delayed for a moment and asked if everyone would please stand by.

"What's going on?" Astrid asked.

Imogene shook her head. "I just wish they'd get on with this. It's making me so nervous."

"I'm sure you did good," Jesse said.

A few minutes later the moderator stepped back to the microphone. "Before I announce the winner in today's competition, we have a special prize that we're going to award."

"What's that about?" Jesse asked.

Murmuring, the crowd had pretty much the same questions. A special prize?

"We want to offer an Honorable Mention for the Most Original Entry to Miss Imogene Yoder."

They all five turned to Imogene. Even the boys turned in her direction.

"You won," Mattie said.

"Mamm! You won!" Mahlon added for good measure.

"Will Miss Imogene Yoder come up and accept her prize for Honorable Mention for the Most Original Entry?"

Imogene was standing stock-still, frozen in place.

Astrid grabbed her by the shoulders and turned her so they were face-to-face. "Go get your award."

She turned Imogene back around and nudged her toward the podium. The crowd, seeing her trying to come through, broke apart and allowed her a path to get to the front.

Imogene climbed back up onto the stage, the look on her face a mixture of surprise and terror. For a moment Astrid thought she might burst into tears. Instead she took the certificate from the moderator and smiled at the crowd. Her lips were trembling, even from that distance Astrid could see it. "*Danki*," she managed. Then she made her way back down the steps and over to where they waited for her.

"Thank you, Imogene, for your very clever entry. The board of the festival will be discussing the possibility of having two categories in future festivals—one sweet and one for the savory pumpkin dishes."

The crowd clapped and cheered. Imogene still wore her stunned expression.

"Way to go," Jesse said.

Ira nodded. "You should be proud of yourself."

The moderator tapped on the top of the microphone to quiet the crowd. "And the winner of this year's pumpkin cook-off is"—he paused for effect—"Sylvie Yoder with her pumpkin walnut pecan butter cake filled with cream cheese delight!"

Sylvie must've been waiting nearby, for it took only a moment for her to get to the stage.

"I keep telling her that it was nothing but a square whoopie pie."

They turned as Vern came up behind them.

"But you should be proud of her," Astrid said.

"I'll be even more proud when she starts making them round like they should be." Vern shook his head.

Sylvie accepted her plaque and her award, and the crowd started to disperse.

"See you," Vern said, brushing past them and up to meet Sylvie as she came off the stage. "It's a shame about her not making whoopie pies anymore," Imogene said. "She really did make the best ones."

"I take it losing the competition did a number on her," Ira said.

Imogene nodded. "But that whoopie pie that Sadie Yoder made. It was really something else. A little different than expected. I mean, who would have thought to make them with brownies instead of cake."

Jesse beamed at her and Astrid couldn't help but notice the admiration shining in his green eyes, those eyes so like her own. "You know all about the benefits of being different."

By the time Imogene had gathered up the stuff she had brought for the cooking competition and placed it all back in her wagon, the crowd had dispersed, leaving Astrid, Jesse, Ira, and the twins waiting for her.

"I suppose I should take this home and get it in the refrigerator. If you guys want to try it later on."

"We definitely want to eat it later," Ira said.

"Then I need a ride home," Imogene said. She couldn't

bring herself to look at Ira or Jesse. So she simply stared at the contents of the wagon.

"You said we could eat at Charlie's," Mahlon reminded her.

"*Jah*," she said. "I did. Once we get home, I'll unload all this. Then we'll get our carriage and go to Charlie's from there."

"That sounds like a lot of trouble, seeing as how we have two buggies here already," Jesse said.

"You gotta do what you gotta do," Imogene said.

"And I promised you I would help paint," Astrid said to Ira.

Imogene looked at her. "Paint?" Then she turned to Ira. "You really were painting?"

He nodded.

"He has a real mess at his house still. And somehow I promised I would help him."

"Okay, so here's the deal," Jesse started. "I take Imogene and the boys to Charlie's to eat burgers and then on to her house. You guys go paint."

Imogene turned to Astrid. It seemed to be the easiest way to get everything done and everybody where they needed to be, but it split her and Ira up for the evening. Not exactly a good plan if the two of them were trying to get to know each other. But what? She was going to make Ira eat at Charlie's? Most adults did everything they could to keep from eating at the fast-food burger joint.

She turned back to Jesse. "You don't have to go with us to Charlie's," she said.

Mahlon and Mattie picked that time to break in. "Please, Jesse! Come with us! That would be so much fun."

"I don't think it's fair you asked Jesse to eat that food," Imogene said. Parents ate at Charlie's because their kids wanted it, not because they wanted it themselves, and Jesse wasn't their *dat*, so he shouldn't have to be subjected to that.

She couldn't help thinking about the what-ifs. What if Jesse was their *dat*? Their new *dat*. He did so well with them and he was so handsome and helpful and supportive and—she pulled those thoughts to a screeching halt. They surely weren't the thoughts of someone who was being matched with another.

"I don't mind," Jesse said. "Really."

Astrid pressed her lips together, and Imogene could tell that Astrid did mind. But what was the other solution?

She could almost see the cloud come over Astrid, her thoughts brewing as to how to shift the matchup. Then her expression changed to resignation. Imogene figured they would just have to start again the next day.

"Okay, I guess that's a plan. I'm with Ira," she said. Then she turned to him. "If you'll take me home after we're done painting."

"You are really going to help me paint?" Ira asked.

Astrid shrugged. "A promise is a promise."

"I'll see you at home?" Jesse asked.

Astrid nodded. Then together Jesse, Imogene, and the boys headed for her buggy.

"Do you need me to take care of that for you?" he asked, indicating the wagon.

Imogene shook her head. "I've got it."

"Are you still in shock over your big win?"

"It isn't like I really won," she said. "It was just a special award."

He stopped, so she did as well. "Why do you do that?"

"Do what?" she asked.

"Sell yourself short like that."

"I don't know," she said. "I guess I just don't have the confidence that your sister has about things."

"Astrid has more confidence than any one person should have," Jesse said, starting to back up again. "Just because she is confident and everything, doesn't mean you're not worthy."

Imogene waited a second before starting off again behind him. She wasn't certain, but she thought he slowed his steps for her to catch up. The boys who had been going on ahead also stopped so as not to get too far away from their *mamm*.

"I'm sorry," Jesse said. "That was out of line. I shouldn't have said anything."

She didn't know what to say in return so she just dipped her chin, hoping that would serve as an answer.

"It's just I hate to see someone not reach for something that's right within their grasp just because they don't believe in themselves."

"That's the problem with being friends with Astrid," Imogene admitted. "I think your sister is awesome and I really appreciate her help with Ira, but she definitely takes over and sets the standard."

"That's not it," Jesse countered. "Astrid thinks she can have everything she wants, and sometimes she has to stop and convince herself that it's all right that she wants it."

"I suppose," Imogene said. She stopped as they made it back to the buggy. "You really don't have to go eat at Charlie's with us."

"Yes, he does! Yes, he does!" the boys chanted.

Jesse turned to her, an expressive look on his handsome features. "It seems the masses say I must."

Imogene shook her head. "You really don't."

He loaded the back of the buggy with the food that she had brought for the competition. "What if I want to?"

"You want to?"

A small moment stretched between them as he looked at

her. She wasn't sure what she saw in his eyes, but it was warm and compelling.

"Of course he wants to!" Mahlon said.

"*Jah*," Mattie added. "Jesse likes us."

"And you like him too," Imogene said.

"Got it in one."

"Yes!" Mattie said.

The boys clambered into the buggy, leaving Imogene and Jesse a small moment all their own.

His green, green eyes seemed to see into her very thoughts. She wasn't sure she was ready for him to know what she was thinking. She wasn't even ready to think it herself. But there was something about Jesse. Something that made her want to get to know him better. Was it because he seemed to enjoy her children? Was it because he seemed so kind? She couldn't be sure, but it was there all the same.

"I want to go eat with you," Jesse said.

Imogene swallowed hard and nodded.

"Let's go, then."

The moment was broken as Jesse moved away.

Imogene was grateful for the reprieve. She sucked in a deep breath, went around the buggy, and climbed into the passenger side.

"Charlie's, here we come!" Mahlon cried.

Ira turned to Astrid. "You are really going to help me paint?"

She gave a small shrug, unable to stop thinking about the way they had split up, the two couples who weren't couples heading off together. He was supposed to be getting to know Imogene, yet she was off with Jesse. And she was here with Ira.

"Why not?" Astrid said. What was done was done.

"Then I suppose we should go," Ira said.

Together they walked through the thinning crowd at the festival and out to the parking lot where his buggy had been waiting.

"Are you hungry?" Ira asked.

"Starving," Astrid said.

"What do you say we run by and get a couple of salads from that place off Main? I've had enough fried food to last a lifetime."

Astrid laughed. "Me too. Salad sounds really good."

They went through the drive-through and picked up salads, then headed back to his house.

"I think it's really great that Imogene got the award today," Astrid said.

The two of them were together. Not part of the plan. Time to talk about Imogene. But in truth, she didn't want to talk about Imogene. She wanted to talk about . . . him. Anything else. The weather tomorrow. Something, but not Imogene.

Promise is a promise.

"Really great," Ira said in agreement. "If she can cook like that . . . makes me wonder if we should go over to the Paradise Amish Buffet and eat more often."

"I don't think she cooks there," Astrid said, suddenly realizing she didn't know exactly what Imogene did at the buffet restaurant.

"If she doesn't, then she probably should, if she can come up with something like pumpkin soup with bacon. So delicious."

"Get your mind off that," Astrid said. "We got salad tonight."

"Tomorrow, pumpkin soup." Ira grinned.

Once at Ira's house, they spread their salads on the table

and talked about everything and nothing. For some reason Astrid couldn't bring herself to introduce the subject of Imogene once more.

"Did you ever get anybody to build you a sunporch?" Ira asked mid-salad.

Astrid shook her head. "I really just made that up to come talk to you," she said. "You know, about Imogene." And there it was.

"Why me?"

"Why you what?" Astrid asked. Okay, so she was stalling for time.

"Why did you pick me as a match for Imogene?"

She shrugged, once again racking her brain for an answer. "I don't know. We'd just bought the house and I had been in the hardware store a couple of times. I just thought you might make a good husband for her."

"Why does it feel like there's something you're not telling me about this?" Ira stopped eating and leaned back in his chair, waiting for her to answer.

Waiting for an answer she didn't have.

"That's a very forward question," she finally said.

"It's a very forward plan to try to matchmake two people," he countered.

What sort of answer did she have to *that*?

"I don't know," she said. Truly she didn't. Something had drawn her to Ira. Something that she couldn't name, something that she didn't know, but it was there all the same, like the pull of a magnet. Imogene had asked her to matchmake and the first person to pop into her head had been Ira. Handsome Ira.

"I'm not sure I believe that," Ira said.

It was time to shut down the conversation. Astrid shrugged and met his gaze. "I guess you don't have to."

He studied her, those blue eyes unwavering, but she

managed to put on her best impassive expression. At least she hoped it was her best. She didn't want to have to explain herself to him now. Especially not now that she had begun to think that there was more to Ira. And that more was something she wanted to get to know herself.

"What would you have done if I told you that I didn't want to get married again?" he asked.

Astrid shook her head. "I don't know. It's just I—" She had almost let it slip. She had almost let it slip that the main reason she tried to match Imogene and Ira was simply so she could make notes and write a book. The longer she kept that secret the more it was beginning to eat at her. It was wrong. She never should've done it. She wished she could go back. A promise was a promise.

She looked down at what was left of her salad. She'd been taught her whole life to finish what she started. Yet she didn't feel like she could swallow another bite. It was that lump in her throat. That lump that came when you felt like you had messed up to the point where it would never be right again. She tried to swallow it down. But it refused to budge.

"I'm sorry," she said.

Ira frowned at her. "Sorry for what?"

"For meddling," Astrid said. "I should've never meddled. Jesse's always telling me to leave things alone."

Ira shook his head. "It's okay. You don't need to apologize. I've actually had a good time getting to know her. And you and Jesse, too. With Ruthie getting married and Elam running around, my house is constantly empty. You three have pulled me out and given me something more to do, and I'm grateful."

He was grateful, and Astrid felt lower than a slug's belly. "So you like her?" Saying the words sent a stab of something running from her heart all the way through her stomach. She didn't know what it was, but it felt like . . . jealousy.

No, she denied it, trying to convince herself otherwise, but there it was. She was jealous. Jealous of the match she had made between Ira and Imogene.

People were always going on about how hindsight was twenty-twenty . . . well, this was something else entirely. Maybe she had seen it coming and refused to acknowledge it. Or maybe it had truly snuck up on her like a thief in the night. Either way it didn't matter. It was too late. She had made the match. She had convinced a woman she now called friend and a man whom she was falling in love with that they would be perfect together. And for that, she had no one to blame but herself.

"I like all three of you. I'm glad I made some new friends during all this."

"New friends," Astrid said. *Is that what they are?*

"*Jah*, new friends."

"We should be eating at Charlie's," Astrid quipped, trying to bring the conversation back around to something a little less intense. Personal. Something that didn't have her heart clenched in her chest.

"That's true," Ira said with a chuckle. "Are you finished?" He nodded toward her half-eaten salad.

Once again Astrid wasn't sure she could take another bite. "Store in the fridge for later?" she asked.

"*Jah*," he said.

She put the lid on the to-go container of salad and handed it to him. He took it to the fridge and she gathered up the trash and pitched it in the trash can.

"Perfect," he said, dusting his hands. "I'll change into my painting clothes."

Astrid looked down at herself. She was wearing what was perhaps her favorite dress and there was no way she was painting in it. "I can't paint in this," she said. What had she been thinking?

Ira crossed his arms over his chest and shot her a look of growing disbelief. "So now you're trying to get out of helping me?"

"Take it however you like."

"I'm taking it that you don't want to paint in that dress, and unless I find something that you can wear, you're just going to stand by and watch."

She shrugged. "I guess so."

"I'll see what I can do." He disappeared into the back of the house and returned a few moments later wearing the same clothes she had seen him in earlier in the day, the ones all splattered with paint. But in one hand he held a garment that looked to be a choring dress. "I think this belongs to my daughter, Ruthie. She's a little bit shorter than you are, but I think it'll do for painting."

"Of course he has something," Astrid retorted.

"*Jah*," Ira said. "A promise is a promise."

Indeed it was.

CHAPTER TWENTY-ONE

Astrid came awake slowly the next morning. Without even opening her eyes she knew something was different. The pillow beneath her head was lumpy. Her neck was at an uncomfortable angle, as if she had fallen asleep someplace other than her bed. But it had to be morning. Even through her closed eyelids she could tell the sun was shining. Outside, she could hear the birds singing. A new day. Saturday. *Jah*. Saturday, and the last day of the Fall Festival there in Paradise Hill.

She opened her eyes and looked around. Blank beige walls stared back at her.

She looked down at herself. She was lying on the couch covered in a sheet. The couch was covered in a sheet, and she wasn't covered at all. Just a paint-splattered dress and no shoes on her feet.

From across the room came a snore. A man's snore. She sat up and whirled around, looking over the back of the couch that had been pushed face-first toward the wall she'd been staring at.

Ira's house. She was still at Ira's house. They had painted all night until way past dark and he had promised he would take her home. She wanted to rest. Just for a minute to rest. Now, however many hours later, she was still here.

Ira was asleep as well, stretched out in the recliner, eyes closed, mouth open, every other breath creating a small snore.

She jumped to her feet and raced around the couch over to the recliner where he slept.

"Ira," she cried. She reached out and shook his shoulder.

He came awake slowly. "What?"

"Ira, we fell asleep."

His eyes fluttered closed once more and he nodded. "*Jah*, fell asleep."

"Both of us. It's morning."

He sat up like a shot. "Oh, no," he said. "I'm so sorry."

Astrid looked around, wondering what to do. "What do we do?"

He stood and rubbed his eyes, no doubt trying to get his bearings back. "Nothing, there's nothing we can do. What's done is done."

What's done is done. It was almost as bad as *a promise is a promise.* Look where that had gotten them.

"I can take you home now," he said.

"Okay," she replied. She looked around for her shoes.

"It's not like your buggy's outside or anything. Not anything that would get rumors started."

"Right," she said, finally locating her shoes. She shoved her feet into them, then looked down at her dress. He'd said it had belonged to his daughter. Apparently, she was several inches shorter than Astrid. "I can't go out like this," she said.

He jerked a thumb over his shoulder. "Change back to your regular dress, then we'll leave."

"Right," she said. She made her way down the hall and into the downstairs bathroom. Aside from the dress, Ira had also loaned her a handkerchief to cover her head so she wouldn't get paint on her prayer *kapp*, which was sitting next to the sink just where she had left it. Her dress was hanging on the back of the door, where she had placed it just after supper.

She hurriedly pulled the paint-splattered dress over her head and donned her own. Then she pulled the hand-kerchief from her head and smoothed her hair back as best she could. It would just have to do for now. It wasn't too bad. When she fell asleep she must've been completely exhausted and hadn't moved too much while she rested.

When she got home, she would redo the whole thing to get ready to go out again.

She slowed and took a deep breath. There was no sense rushing around. Hurrying wasn't going to make a difference. Surely, they could come up with some story as to why she had spent the night at his house if anyone questioned it. It wasn't like they did anything other than paint. But sometimes the gossipmongers weren't satisfied with innocent stories like that.

She sucked in another breath, used her finger to brush her teeth, then hung the dress and the bandana on the back of the door. She let herself out and walked back down the hallway, smoothing her hands down the dress she wore the day before.

"How about some breakfast?" he asked.

She shook her head. "I think I should just be going now."

He nodded.

They gathered up their things and started for the door.

What's done is done, she told herself. And this was certainly done.

* * *

Somehow Ira managed to get Astrid back home without incident. There was a lot of traffic on the roads and he supposed he could chalk that up to the last day of the Fall Festival bringing in more visitors than any other day. Hopefully, he and Astrid would get lost among the many travelers, and no one would be any the wiser.

When he pulled up to Astrid's house, Jesse came rushing out. "Where have you been?" he called. "I was about to send the police out looking for you."

"I'm glad you didn't," Astrid said, climbing out of the buggy. She turned back to Ira and he gave her a small smile. "*Danki* for bringing me home."

He gave a quick tilt of his head. "*Danki* for helping me paint. I guess I'll see you later?" he asked.

She nodded. "Later." There wasn't any more left to be said.

"You were really at Ira's house all night?" Jesse asked as Astrid made her way into the house.

Astrid turned and shrugged, acting as if it was no big deal. "It would be the same as if I spent the night with Fiona."

Fiona Lapp owned and operated Hill Yard and Garden Supply and was about the best friend Astrid had. Astrid supposed it was because Fiona was a little like she was, devoutly Amish but a little offbeat.

"That's nothing like spending the night with Fiona," Jesse said. "Aren't you supposed to be getting him with Imogene?"

"Of course," she scoffed. "What's that have to do with anything?"

Jesse frowned at her. "It has a lot to do with everything.

You made a promise to her and then you do something like that?"

She propped her hands on her hips and looked at her brother. "Nothing happened. We were painting. I got tired and lay down on the couch for a few minutes and the next thing I know it's morning."

"It doesn't matter if something happened or not. It can still hurt Imogene's feelings. She's very tender."

"Imogene's tougher than you give her credit for."

"Maybe, but she's not as tough as you think she is."

Astrid stopped. Turned around and faced her brother. "You like her." It was no question.

"Of course I like her," Jesse said.

"I mean like her, like her."

Jesse shook his head. "You're seeing things that aren't there," he said.

"Seems pretty obvious to me," Astrid shot back.

"I still don't want to see her hurt," Jesse said.

"I'm not going to hurt her," Astrid told him.

"You lied to her," Jesse said. "You're not a matchmaker."

"She came to me," Astrid reminded him. She hated the defensive tone in her voice, but it was there all the same.

"You didn't have to lie to her."

"I didn't lie to her," Astrid said. "I just didn't tell her the truth."

Jesse tossed his hands into the air and let them drop back to his sides. "That's the same thing."

"Not hardly."

"You need to tell her the truth."

"She already knows I'm not really a matchmaker," Astrid said.

"I'm not talking about that. I'm talking about how you only did this so that you could figure out your next book."

Astrid stopped still. She'd never said that to anyone. So how did Jesse know?

He shook his head. "I'm your brother, remember? Your twin? I know how you think. I know what's been going on with you and your writing. I figured this out a long time ago. I just hoped you would come clean before now."

Jesse's words stayed with her much longer than Astrid had wanted them to. It wasn't so easy when someone pointed out your faults. It was even harder hiding from the truth. So there was only one thing to do. That was come up with another plot for her book.

But first she had to make certain that she held up her end of the bargain. She promised Imogene that she would find her match and she found that match in Ira Oberholtzer. Now she needed to give them a free pass to fall in love. Which meant tonight . . . no pumpkin soup.

Astrid made her way back out to Jesse's workshop, a little bit grateful that he was nowhere around. She supposed he had gone into the house for a small break and just missed him when she came out. But that was perfect. She didn't need him around for what she was about to do.

Hurriedly she grabbed the phone and called the hardware store. Thankfully, Ira was with a customer. So she left a message with the guy who answered the phone, telling him to let Ira know that she and Jesse wouldn't be coming to Imogene's tonight. They thought perhaps they had eaten something bad at the festival, she had explained. Now they both thought they had food poisoning. Then she coughed for good measure. Like she had to convince Ira's employee. But perhaps he would tell Ira that when she had called she hadn't sounded well.

She hung up the phone and spun around as Jesse walked back to the workshop. "What are you doing here?" he asked.

"I, uh, I called Imogene and she told me that the boys aren't feeling well. So we're not going to eat the pumpkin soup tonight."

"Are they okay?"

Astrid nodded, doing her best not to tally up all the lies she was telling now. "*Jah*, they're fine," she said. "But just in case it's not food poisoning and is perhaps a stomach bug, she didn't want to infect everybody else. But she did say she would make the pumpkin soup again another day." Astrid hoped anyway.

Jesse nodded. "Another time then."

"*Jah*," Astrid agreed. "Another time."

Ira whistled a tuneless little ditty as he hitched his horse up and made his way into the house that evening. He was looking forward to tonight. Looking forward to eating Imogene's soup. He may have spent the last three days in her company, but he was enjoying his new friend. Even if Jesse and Astrid weren't going to be there. He thought she might cancel the whole thing, but he didn't want Imogene to be saddened by the switch. Besides, he was enjoying something other than work and staring at the four walls in his house. Even if they had been repainted recently.

He shut the door behind him and Elam came out of the kitchen. "I thought you would be gone by now," Ira said. "Don't you guys have something planned for tonight?" He couldn't remember what it was that Elam had told him their youth group was going to be doing tonight.

"We were going to the Fall Festival again, but it's been canceled. The outing, not the festival."

Ira chuckled. "That's too bad. So is something else brewing?"

Elam shook his head. "No, but I was thinking you and I might go get pizza or something."

"Sorry," Ira said. "I'm going over to Imogene's tonight to have her pumpkin soup. That one that won the pumpkin cook-off competition. I'm sure she wouldn't mind if you wanted to join us. Of course, there won't be anyone there your age. Just twins. But they're ten."

Elam grimaced and shook his head. "No, thank you."

"Suit yourself," Ira said. "I shouldn't be gone too long." He loped up the stairs to change clothes, still whistling a bit under his breath. Tonight was going to be a very good night.

Astrid stared at the blinking cursor on her computer screen. It was time to come up with something new. A story that didn't have to do with a matchmaker or widows. It's just that she couldn't help think that Jesse seemed to have fallen in love with Imogene Yoder. It couldn't be possible. Perhaps he was just infatuated. Jesse was always a champion of things weaker than him and it was definitely true that Imogene was vulnerable. If it was that sort of thing, perhaps Imogene had spared her brother. Astrid just hadn't spared herself.

She had fallen in love with Ira Oberholtzer, and she had messed everything up. Because after tonight, after Ira and Imogene would eat the pumpkin soup and her special pumpkin butter bread, that prize-winning meal, everything would fall into place. Because Imogene might be a little on the timid side, she might be a little on the plain side, but she was a fantastic cook. She was a good mother, and

Astrid was certain that she had been a good wife. All the things that Ira would want and need for her to be.

But you promised. That was the crux of it all. She had promised. Astrid had promised Imogene that she would match her with someone, and she had chosen Ira. Then she'd gone off and fallen in love with him. But she would hold true her promise to the other woman.

Yet she couldn't help but think that maybe she shouldn't have meddled in all this to begin with. But what was it Ira had said?

What's done is done.

Ira was still whistling when he arrived at Imogene's an hour or so later. He had been looking forward to tonight, looking forward to spending some time again with Imogene, Astrid, and Jesse, but when he'd gotten a message that Astrid and Jesse were feeling unwell, he knew he had to come anyway. He wondered if perhaps Astrid's sudden illness had anything to do with last night.

He shook his head at his own thoughts. Last night hadn't been anything. Nothing other than a friend helping a friend. Being a hardware man he knew that painting a house was nothing special. But he had enjoyed spending time with Astrid. Even if he knew nothing would ever come of it.

Suddenly all that specialness seemed to be sucked out of the moment. She wasn't going to get married ever; he had heard her say those very words. And *ever* included him.

He shook the thought away and tried his best to readjust his thinking. She wasn't going to get married again, but he wasn't going to spend the rest of the days a lonely old widower.

Imogene opened the door, and it hit him all at once. He needed her. He needed companionship and he needed a new start. She needed a husband, a helpmate. There were worse things than mutual need to build a relationship off of and Imogene was a sweet person. He could do a lot worse in getting remarried.

"Ira," she said. She stepped back and smiled, allowing him to enter the house. "I'm glad to see you."

He nodded in return. "I'm glad to see you too."

So this was what it felt like to start over. Ira studied his reflection in the mirror. It was Sunday, an off Sunday for Paradise Hill and a church Sunday in Paradise Springs.

Last night over a bowl of delicious pumpkin soup, Imogene had asked Ira if he would like to go to church with her today. Of course he'd said yes. They had sat down and talked just a little about what they needed from a spouse. In broad, abstract terms not holding each other to a promise, but testing the waters for the future. That was what this was about. It was about his future. A future he did not want to spend alone.

He pushed thoughts of Astrid from his mind. There was no sense in pining over what he couldn't have, but instead he wanted to look forward to what he could. So he was going to church with Imogene today. He would sit across and watch her. He would sit with her twins and monitor them during the service, just like any *dat* would do. Because once he married Imogene, he would be their *dat*.

He never thought he'd be starting over at his age. He had been thinking more about grandkids. Yet he knew there were times when what he thought should be was not the way it fell together. It seemed as if this was what God had planned for him, and he was going to see it through.

Elam was still asleep when he let himself out of the house. He left a note for his son telling him that he'd gone to church in Paradise Springs. He didn't mention Imogene or the twins or anything else. There was time enough for that later.

CHAPTER TWENTY-TWO

Church went off without a hitch, which is to say that Imogene's boys seemed to have taken to him a bit. Ira had played with them some the night before at supper, though they refused to eat their mother's pumpkin soup. He told them that was perfectly fine with him; it just left more for the adults. But the psychology that had always worked on his kids didn't work on the twins. They ate their peanut butter and jelly sandwiches as if they were eating filet mignon.

They really were good boys. But he understood Imogene's need to have someone help. He understood her need for companionship. He needed the same thing himself.

He enjoyed himself, milling around, meeting new people, talking with Imogene. He visited a little more, then headed back to Paradise Hill. All in all it was a good day. A good *two* days. That was when he began to feel like his life was getting on a track to something he hadn't even known he wanted until recently. That was all good as well.

Ira turned his horse down the drive, surprised to see Elam's buggy parked out front next to Ruthie's. He hadn't told his daughter that he was headed over to Paradise Springs for church, and he hoped she hadn't been waiting long. Since it was their off Sunday and she and Lloyd usually went to his parents' house, Ira hadn't imagined she would pop in for a surprise visit.

He walked into the house, a smile on his face, but he felt like he walked into a funeral. Ruthie sat on the couch, her arms crossed. Lloyd and Elam stood by the fireplace staring into the empty pit as if some divine secret was stored there. They all turned to him as he walked in.

"Hey," he said, never taking his eyes off his daughter.

She stood. "Elam said you've been in Paradise Springs for church?"

He nodded. "*Jah*, I thought it might be fun to go visit."

"It's about that woman, right?" Her tone was hesitant yet firm. He couldn't tell how she felt about saying it. That wasn't exactly true; he could tell she wasn't happy, he just wasn't sure how upset she was. Come to think of it, he wasn't sure why she was upset in the first place.

"We've been hearing rumors," Lloyd jumped in.

"Rumors about what?" Ira asked. He continued farther into the room and sat down across from his daughter. She eased back onto the couch cushions.

"About you and that romance writer," Lloyd replied.

"Astrid?"

"*Jah*," Elam said. "Her. And then there's a woman named Imogene," he continued. "Who is she?"

"I believe you've got this all mixed up," Ira said. "First of all, you know better than to listen to the rumors around here. We've got more gossips in this town per capita than any other place in the world."

Ruthie frowned. "That's not true."

"You know what I mean," Ira said.

"That's why we came here to talk to you," Lloyd said. "We want to know the truth of the matter."

"Dat?" Elam asked.

"I don't know what you've been hearing," Ira started. "Truthfully, I'm not sure I want to know. But I will tell you this. There's nothing between me and Astrid." As painful as it was to talk about, it was the truth. "We're just friends."

"Which one is the matchmaker?" Ruthie asked. "Speaking of, why would you hire a matchmaker?"

Ira shook his head. "I think we all need to take a minute and take a breath. I'll explain everything, but I need you three to calm down a bit beforehand. How about some coffee?" He stood without waiting for their answer and made his way into the kitchen.

When the coffee was ready, he took it and some store-bought cookies he had back to the dining table. He thought it might be a little better to be seated around the table and not have everyone hovering in the living room.

When they had gathered round and all had a cup of coffee and a couple of cookies to ignore, Ira sat down as well. "Forget what you've heard," he stated. "I did not hire a matchmaker. I have been making some new friends and I do have a new friend named Imogene. Yes, she's a woman and yes, we've discussed dating."

"Are you going to marry her?" Elam asked.

"I'm thinking about it," Ira said. "I'm keeping my options open."

Tears rose in Ruthie's eyes. "What about Mamm?"

"I loved your mother and I will always love her, but she's gone and I'm still here. I'm only forty-two. Not too old to make a new start."

Ruthie's lips trembled. He knew she was torn between love and truth. She loved her mother, but her *mamm* was gone. Ruthie obviously hadn't thought about her father moving on. Perhaps he should have done this long ago.

"I don't understand," Ruthie finally said.

"I do." Lloyd reached over and squeezed Ruthie's hand where it lay on the table.

She hadn't taken one sip of her coffee since she sat down.

"I wish I did," Elam said.

"There's not been any plans made," Ira continued. "I said it before, I'm just trying to keep my options open. I'm still young and have a lot of life ahead of me. God willing. And the two of you have your lives ahead of you. I'm sure you want to spend it with someone special too."

Lloyd squeezed Ruthie fingers once more and smiled at her. She gave him a trembling smile in return.

"That's kind of what we wanted to come talk to you about today," Ruthie said.

"Tell him." Elam grinned.

"We're going to have a baby."

"That's the best news ever," Ira said. He couldn't help the smile that spread across his face. It was so big it nearly hurt his cheeks. But oh how he wished Ruthann could be here for this. But she couldn't, and it was Astrid's face that popped into his thoughts.

"It's still early," Ruthie said. "But I just wanted you to know."

"I caught her coming out of the doctor's office," Elam boasted.

"So I had to tell him," Ruthie explained. "And I couldn't let him know without telling you."

"Why were you at the doctor?" Ira asked, concern wrinkling his brow.

"He likes one of the girls that works there," Ruthie told him.

"A nurse?" Ira asked.

"Dat." Elam was slowly turning the color of a pickled beet.

"One of the Amish girls who file papers and stuff," Ruthie added.

"I see," Ira said. "So you can see where I'm coming from."

"*Jah*," Ruthie said. "But don't rush into anything, okay?"

"Okay," he said, then, "A baby." He grinned. "I'm happy for you." He really was. Happy for them all. He just wished Ruthann was there to see it. "I'm sorry that my possibly dating again is giving you such angst. It's all good. In fact, why don't we all go out to eat together next week? We can go to the Chinese buffet there in Paradise Springs like we used to."

"I wonder if they still have that orange chicken," Elam said.

Ruthie shook her head. "No oranges." In fact she looked green at just the thought of an orange.

Ira chuckled. "Your mother was just the same when she had you," he told her.

Ruthie gave him a feeble smile. "I never knew."

He supposed there was a lot he never told them about their mother. Thinking perhaps they knew all that for themselves. He would make a point to share those little stories in the future. Now that he was moving on truly, it felt good to talk about Ruthann. It felt good and right. And there was a lot to be said for that.

Once again Astrid was staring at her computer screen wishing for words to appear. She'd been at it all morning. Now she understood why people lamented Monday. She'd never had a problem with Mondays before, but that was when the words were coming. These days, every day was a Monday.

A knock sounded at the door. She was torn between just yelling and telling whoever was there to go to the shop to find Jesse, or just getting up and telling them. Either way, what concentration she had was broken.

With a sigh, she cast one last glance at her computer

screen, the empty Word document with a blinking cursor, then she stood and made her way to the front door. She opened it to a beautiful bouquet of roses and daisies, and for a split second she wondered if they were from Ira. Beautiful flowers.

Then the flowers moved to the side and a young man appeared behind them. "I have a delivery for an Astrid Kauffman."

"I'm Astrid," she told him.

He thrust the flowers at her. "Have a good day, ma'am." He was gone in a shot, back in his little van and pulling out of her drive.

Flowers! When was the last time anyone had sent her flowers? Maybe when their *dawdi* had died a couple years ago? She couldn't remember, and seeing those flowers there filled her with great joy. She took them into the dining room table and set them by her computer, then searched through the blooms for the card.

She opened it and her heart sank the moment she saw who had sent them. Imogene. She shook off that thought. She shouldn't be sad. Imogene had taken the time to send her flowers. Astrid sat down in the nearest chair and read the card.

Astrid, I just wanted to thank you and let you know that Ira and I are making plans, talking about the future. It never would have happened had it not been for you. Here are two coupons for a free buffet. I would love to have you and Jesse come eat during my shift. Hope you're feeling better.

♥*—Imogene*

Astrid didn't know what to make of it. For the last two weeks she had done nothing but try to get these two people together and now that they were . . . it wasn't something she wanted anymore. She had made a terrible mistake by meddling in other people's affairs. She had put things above what they normally valued in the Amish community. She had worried too much about hair and pink cheeks and pretty shoes and handsome men. She'd messed up. She'd messed up big-time.

She tried to tell herself that she made Ira and Imogene happy, and she hoped they would be happy. But she had made herself incredibly sad.

She laid the coupons on the table and put the card back in the blooms. They were beautiful and yet she almost wanted to throw them out. They would be a constant living reminder for the next week or so of the happiness she had given other people but had forsaken for herself.

That was what she would concentrate on. She would concentrate on the fact that Ira and Imogene found the love they were looking for, even if she hadn't.

Jesse came in a bit later, and Astrid was still staring at the computer screen. So she had written the first few pages of it a week ago, but she hadn't written any more on this romance that was due in just a couple of months. She wasn't a fast writer, especially since she'd never learned to type in the correct form and had only in the last couple of years even had a computer. But she couldn't concentrate on the words she needed to put on the page; all she could think about were those beautiful flowers. All she could think about was Ira and Imogene.

"Pretty," Jesse said. "Why the flowers?"

Astrid swallowed hard. "They're from Imogene," she said. "She wanted to thank me. I guess she and Ira are talking about dating."

"What?" Jesse asked. "When did this happen?"

Astrid shrugged. "I guess this weekend. She sent the flowers this morning."

Jesse collapsed into the seat next to his sister. "I didn't—" he started, then he broke off. "I hope you're happy," he said. Then he pushed back from the table and stomped back out of the house. Astrid didn't see him again until well past dark.

Tuesday found Astrid in the same position. Staring at the blinking cursor, no words coming, attention focused more on the beautiful flowers and what they stood for than the work she needed to get done.

"Astrid," Jesse called from the back door. "There's a call for you. It's Sylvie Yoder."

Yet another distraction, something she didn't need, yet was thankful for all the same. Astrid shut her computer and stood. "I'm coming."

She followed her brother out to the workshop and picked up the handheld receiver. "Sylvie?"

"Astrid, listen. I know this is short notice, but tonight is our widows' club meeting over here in Paradise Springs. I was thinking maybe it might be fun to have you come and talk to everyone about your books. I'm not sure that most of the women here know that you actually write those romances."

Right now she wasn't writing at all. But she couldn't tell Sylvie that. As much as she wasn't up for a meeting, how could she say no?

"I would like that," Astrid said. It wasn't a complete lie. Normally, she would love to, just not today, not when the words weren't coming, not when she was so sad about Ira.

But she was going to have to start pretending soon enough that everything was fine. Might as well start today.

"Good," Sylvie said. "So you'll do it?"

"On one condition," Astrid said.

"O-kay," Sylvie slowly replied.

"You have to make whoopie pies." The other end of the line grew quiet. "Sylvie?" Astrid asked. Had they gotten cut off somehow?

"I'm here," Sylvie said. "I haven't made a whoopie pie since the spring."

"That's what I hear," Astrid said. "I think maybe it's time you got back to it."

She could almost hear Sylvie's nod. "Okay. You come and talk about your books, and I'll have the whoopie pies ready."

Astrid smiled a little to herself. "Deal."

The thing about widows Astrid found out over the years she had spent as a writer was that they liked to talk about their late husbands. The good thing about that was she could learn how they met and some of the wonderful courting rituals they had experienced. Astrid would be lying if she didn't say that she thought about just that thing when she said yes to Sylvie, agreeing to come to the widows' meeting. Astrid needed ideas and she needed them badly. If she didn't get something soon, she was bound to start writing a tragedy instead of a romance, and she wasn't sure her readership was up for that. So she got ready on Tuesday, grabbed a bag full of books to share with the group, and headed over to Paradise Springs.

She had vowed when she got up that morning that she would keep a happy demeanor. How else was she going to be able to write happy books? Even if she didn't feel it in her heart, perhaps if she pretended long enough, the rest of her would catch up. She could try anyway.

Astrid pulled her buggy into the back lot at the B&B, then tied her horse to the hitching post and made her way around the building and into the front room. The widows had all gathered in the main room that Astrid thought she had heard Sylvie call the common room. Several of the dining room chairs had been pulled up to accommodate all the widows.

Had that many husbands died in Paradise Springs? She had no idea.

"Astrid," Sylvie said, meeting her between the foyer and the common room. "Welcome! We have quite a turnout."

"I can see that," Astrid replied. She took off her sweater and laid it over her arm. The air outside was chilly with the cool taste of fall, but it was warm inside the B&B, mainly, she supposed, because there were so many bodies crammed into such a little space. "All these women are widows?" Astrid asked. She didn't want to be indelicate, but it seemed excessive.

"Heavens, no." Sylvie flicked her hand in the air as if it was no big thing. "Once word got around that you were coming tonight, the rest of the women started to arrive."

"I hope no one offed their spouse in order to come," she quipped.

Sylvie laughed. "And that's why I like you so much, Astrid. Come on and let me make the introductions."

Sylvie took her around and introduced her to everyone who was there. She paused every so often to let her know who was in the widows' group and who wasn't.

"And you know Imogene," Sylvie said, waving that negligent hand again.

"I do," Astrid said. "Imogene. Thank you for the flowers.

They are beautiful." And a constant reminder of what she had lost.

"It was the least I could do," Imogene said. "I hope you and Jesse are feeling better."

"We weren't—" She stopped herself, suddenly remembering the lie she had told to get them out of supper with Imogene and Ira. She had done that to give them time alone, but that was before she had found out that Ira and Imogene were talking about dating and long before—at least a day—she realized that she was in love with Ira. "*Danki*," she finally said. "We're much better."

"And look," Imogene added proudly. "Sylvie made whoopie pies again."

Astrid smiled at Sylvie over their own little secret. It seemed that she hadn't told anyone why she had made her signature treat, and Astrid wasn't about to ruin it for her.

Sylvie found Astrid a seat and everyone gathered around her.

"So how did you become a matchmaker?" one of the women asked.

Astrid smiled. So this was how the evening was going to go. "I'm not sure what you've heard," Astrid said with an apologetic glance toward Imogene. "I'm out of the matchmaking business."

And unless she came up with a story and soon, she would be out of the romance writing business as well.

CHAPTER TWENTY-THREE

"No."

"But, Jesse—" Astrid started, but her brother was shaking his head before she could get any further.

"I said no."

"But we need you," Astrid tried again.

"You need a warm body that can roll a ball," Jesse said. "Vern has two arms and two legs. He can be your bowler tonight."

"Just like that?" Astrid asked.

"Just like that," Jesse said. "My head hurts. My arm hurts when I bowl. I don't feel good. I think I might be coming down with something." He crossed his arms and raised one brow as if to dare her to contradict any of his excuses.

Astrid could only shake her head. "I think you're being ridiculous."

"I don't care what you think," he said. And that was the problem with her brother. He knew how to set her off more than anyone in the world.

She tamped down her temper. "Fine," she said. "You don't have to go bowling tonight. But I still think you're being chicken." She barely had time to register the red flush that rose into his face before she spun on one heel and made her way out to the waiting buggy.

She told him that Imogene and Ira had been talking about dating during their pumpkin soup dinner. Of course this was later, after she had told him that Imogene had called to cancel their pumpkin dinner. Even after Astrid had told him the truth, that she had only told him that Imogene had canceled so they wouldn't go over and spoil the evening alone between Imogene and Ira. And that they had used that dinner to get know one another better. That Astrid had taken it upon herself to use that time for a little more matchmaking. She just never imagined her brother would be so angry. "Furious" was a better word. He had been downright irate.

Fine, she told herself as she climbed into the buggy and headed into town. She couldn't protest too much anyway. He had himself a stand-in for the evening so it wasn't like they would have to forfeit. But still . . . He was just acting so squirrely.

Astrid did her best to push those negative thoughts from her mind as she drove toward the bowling alley. Tonight was going to be a good night. Though she still thought her brother was being overly dramatic. If she had to sit and watch Imogene and Ira begin their courtship, then she didn't understand why he couldn't be there.

But she couldn't wear that dress. She smoothed down the sleeve of her olive-green dress. It was too much to go matching tonight. Especially when Vern wouldn't be matching. So she would let Ira and Imogene match. Just another show of their solidarity. And that was what she wanted.

Or at least that was what she told herself she wanted.

Everyone was waiting on her when she got to the bowling

alley. She didn't like being the last one to arrive, but her argument with Jesse had put her behind.

"There you are," Imogene said, rushing toward her. "Where's your dress?"

Astrid waved a hand in the air as if that was an explanation. "I got something on it," she said. "It's soaking now."

"What kind of something?" Imogene asked. "It's dark purple. What would show up on dark purple?"

"I've no idea," Astrid said. At least that was the truth. "The kind of stuff that stains dark colors, I guess. Hopefully, it will be ready by next week."

That frown still rippled Imogene's brow, but she nodded.

"Is everybody ready to bowl?" Astrid said. Her voice was too bright by far. She told herself to tone it down a bit before she gave away all of her secrets.

"Is Jesse okay?" Imogene asked Ira as they walked to their buggies. Astrid had bustled off after the last game as if her skirt was on fire, and Vern had hustled ahead, no doubt to spend a little time with the twins before Imogene picked them up from the B&B . That left her and Ira all alone.

Ira nodded. "Astrid seemed to act like he was fine. Almost like he made up some excuse to have Vern take his place," he said.

"I see." She probably shouldn't be as worried about Jesse as she was. But she seemed unable to stop those feelings from rising up inside her.

"You still look worried," Ira said.

Imogene shrugged. "I can't seem to help myself."

"If you want, I can run by the shop tomorrow and check on him."

She thought she might melt with relief. "That would mean a great deal to me," she said.

"Do you work tomorrow?" he asked.

"Of course," she replied.

"I'll call the restaurant and leave a message. After I talk to him. Would that be okay?" he asked.

"That would be fantastic," Imogene replied. "You're a good friend, Ira Oberholtzer."

He smiled.

He was a good man, she thought. One day he would make someone a fine husband.

She pulled those thoughts to a screeching halt as they stopped next to where her buggy was parked. He was supposed to be her husband one day soon. As wild as the thought sounded, that was what she bargained for. That was what she wanted.

She turned to him in the dimly lit parking lot. "Good night," she told him.

"Good night," he said in return.

She watched him walk away toward his own horse and carriage. She could only hope that the union between them would be able to support their friendship. Because he had become such a good friend after all.

Ira was surprised to see Mahlon and Matthew playing in the front yard of Astrid's house when he pulled up to check on Jesse the following day.

"Ira!" the twins called, and ran over to greet him.

"Did you ask Mamm about the dog?" Mattie asked.

Ira shook his head and tied the horse's reins to a nearby

post. "Not yet." That was another thing on the ever-growing list of things to do.

"Aw," Mahlon said. He kicked a clump of dirt with one bare foot.

"What are the two of you doing here today?" Ira asked.

"The teacher got sick and they couldn't find a substitute." Mattie shrugged like that explained the lot of it.

"Imogene called me frantic. Said she needed someone to watch the twins for the day," Astrid said, coming out of the house and standing on the porch. She leaned up against the rail and his heart jumped at the sight of her.

"She called you?" he asked.

"*Jah*. Probably because everyone knows I'm at home."

Still, that didn't explain why Imogene had called Astrid instead of him. He would have watched the boys for her, and it would've made a lot of sense. Seeing as how if things went according to plan, he would be their father soon.

"What are you doing here today?" Astrid asked.

"Imogene is worried about Jesse. So I told her I would come over today and make sure that he's okay."

She all but rolled her eyes. "Jesse's fine. He's just being dramatic."

"Dramatic on what?" Ira asked.

Astrid shook her head. But he got the feeling she just didn't want to answer. "Nothing really."

"Can you stay and play with us?" Mattie asked.

Ira shook his head. "I just came to check on Jesse, then I've got to get over to the hardware store."

"I wish you could stay," Matthew said.

"Me too," Ira said. Though it wasn't the full truth. The truth was the boys made him a little nervous. Especially when Imogene wasn't around. Though he wasn't sure why.

But they were good boys, and it wasn't their fault. So if he had been able to, he would've stayed to play with them. At least, that was what he told himself as he made his way into the leather shop to check on Jesse.

"Ira," Jesse said, looking up from his work. He set aside the tools he was holding and came around the side of his worktable. "What are you doing here today?"

"I promised Imogene last night I'd come by and check on you. She's a little worried about you," Ira said. He rapped his knuckles on the wooden table, suddenly uncomfortable with the idea.

"Me?" Jesse asked. Ira wasn't sure but he thought Jesse looked a bit surprised by the idea.

Ira nodded. "Since you didn't come to bowling last night." He wasn't positive but he thought Jesse's color deepened a couple of shades. "You weren't sick," he said.

Jesse stood stock-still. "Do you love her?" he asked.

It might have been the last question Ira thought the man might ask. Because of that it took him a minute to formulate his answer. "I care for her very much." And that was the truth. He did care for her. She had become a very dear friend to him over the last few weeks. If he wasn't mistaken, they shared a mutual admiration. Truthfully he believed it was enough to build a marriage on . . . eventually.

He wasn't kidding himself that he loved her in the same way that he had loved Ruthann, but it was enough, these feelings he held for Imogene Yoder. It was enough to make a good life together.

Jesse nodded.

And that was when the doubts set in. Was it enough? He had never had a relationship based solely on caring, but he knew many couples who had lived entire lifetimes together based exclusively on mutual admiration and the will of God.

He shook his head at himself. A marriage built on friendship was probably more solid than a marriage built on flighty love. He and Imogene had a common need and he was certain that need would see them through the rest of their days.

"Can you promise me one thing?" Jesse asked.

"*Jah*." Now, why did his voice sound like he was being choked?

"Just take care of her."

Ira swallowed hard. He cleared his throat. Finally, he said, "*Jah*."

Getting out of school was always a lot of fun, Mattie thought. Or it had been when their *dat* had been alive. Before their *mamm* had gone to work at the buffet restaurant. In those times, when school was out they could spend the time with her. At least that was how Mattie remembered it. But these days she was always at work. Now she was spending so much time with Ira Oberholtzer.

Ira was okay, he supposed, just not as much fun as Jesse or Vern.

"I need you boys to behave for Vern and Sylvie today," Mamm said as she stopped in front of the B&B.

"*Jah*, Mamm," Mattie and Mahlon said at the same time.

Vern might be old, old enough to be their *dawdi* or even older than that, but he still knew how to have fun. He didn't fuss when they slid down the banisters, and he didn't put up too much fuss when they wanted to run and play.

Mamm walked them to the front door and into the B&B.

"Look who's come to visit," Vern said, that smile on his face, the one that said he was truly happy to see them.

"I really appreciate this, Vern," Mamm said. "Where is Sylvie?"

Vern jerked a thumb over his shoulder. "She's upstairs getting a room ready for the new guests who are coming in this afternoon."

"Tell her I said *danki*," Imogene said.

Vern nodded. "You got it. Now don't you worry none about these boys here. We'll take good care of them."

Mamm smiled, and Mattie was surprised to see such relief in the gesture. Was it really so hard to find someone to keep them these days? Or was she just stressed out about them being off with someone else while she was at work?

He didn't have an answer for that, so he pushed the thoughts away and turned to his twin. "You want to play checkers?"

Mahlon nodded and together they walked toward the table next to the window, where the checkerboard was always set up and ready to go. They were just sitting down when Sylvie came bustling down the staircase. "I thought I heard you down here."

Mattie turned to see Sylvie smiling at his *mamm*.

"I really appreciate you watching the boys today," Mamm said. There was that worry again.

"It's nothing," Sylvie said. "We enjoy having the young'uns around. So any good news coming our way?"

Mattie didn't hear what his *mamm* said in return, but Sylvie replied loud enough. "I'll tell you, if you want to get a date this year, you probably have to do it quickly. Even into January. Paradise Valley is growing so much all the dates are taken up."

He didn't really understand that comment. Then his *mamm* said, "I don't think we'll get married this soon."

Married?

"Mahlon, listen." Mattie inclined his head toward the adults standing at the edge of the room. "Do you think . . . ?"

"There's no sense in being alone any longer than necessary," Sylvie was saying.

"What?" Mahlon said.

Mattie shushed his brother. "Listen."

"I'm really proud for you and Vern," Mamm said. "But I'm not sure Ira and I are to that point yet."

Vern shook his head as if her words held no value. "Nah," he said. "All that will come with time."

"I'll give it some thought," Mamm said. "*Danki* again."

"It's no problem at all," Sylvie replied. "We'll see you this afternoon."

Mamm said goodbye to them and let herself out of the B&B.

Mattie turned to his brother. "They were talking about Mamm getting married to Ira," he said in a low voice where only Mahlon could hear.

"We don't want Mamm to marry Ira," Mahlon returned.

"I know. So what are we gonna do?"

Mahlon shook his head. "I don't know. But we better think of something fast."

Imogene was more than ready for a break when Callie Raber, the hostess there at the buffet, called her over to the desk. "Phone's for you," Callie said.

Imogene looked at her questioningly. "Will you take a message?" she asked.

Callie shook her head. "It's Sylvie Yoder from the B&B. She sounds frantic."

"The boys." Imogene breathed in and took the receiver from Callie's hand. Table seven still needed a refill on their waters, but they would have to wait.

"Sylvie?"

"Imogene, the boys are gone. I don't know where they are."

"What?" She couldn't be hearing this correctly. "Where are they?"

"I just said!" Sylvie screeched. "They were here just a second ago and now they're gone!"

"They have to be around somewhere," Imogene said. Her heart was tripping in her chest. They had to be around. They knew better than to run off. She wasn't going to let herself get wound up. They were fine. They were somewhere, and they were fine. She just had to keep believing that.

"Have you checked all the rooms?" she asked Sylvie. But even as she said the words a sick feeling came over her. Sylvie wasn't one to jump the gun. Imogene's boys had to be around somewhere, but loose in town could mean anything.

"Vern's still checking, but we already looked once," Sylvie said. "I'm so sorry, Imogene. But I think you need to come. We need your help."

Imogene hung up the phone and looked to Callie, wide-eyed. Callie might not understand. She had never had kids of her own. "My boys are missing," she said. "They were with Sylvie and Vern and now they're gone."

"Go," Callie said. "Go find them."

"My tables?" Imogene was still trying to get her head wrapped around the fact that her boys had run away from Vern and Sylvie's.

"I'll get your tables. Don't worry," Callie said. "The boys are more important."

Jah, the boys were the most important thing. And they would need all the help that they could get. She snatched up the receiver once more and dialed the number to the hardware store.

"Hill Hardware," Ira answered on the third ring.

"Ira," Imogene said, that frantic hysteria rising up in her throat. "I had to leave the boys with Imogene and Vern today. And now they're gone. We can't find them anywhere."

"Are you at the B&B now?"

She shook her head, then as if only then realizing he couldn't see her she replied, "No. I'm still at work."

"You get down to the B&B. I'll be there as soon as I can."

She nodded. "And, Ira," she said, "please be careful."

"Get on now," Callie commanded. "I'll take care of everything for you from here. You just take care of your boys."

Imogene felt like she was moving through peanut butter as she grabbed her purse and ran out the door. For the first time in her life she cursed the fact that the Amish used horses and buggies to get around. If she had a car, she would already be there by now instead of still clomping along the road as fast as her old mare could take her.

Finally, *finally*, she made it to the B&B. She rushed inside, hoping against hope that Sylvie had managed to find the boys. That they had been hiding in the bathtub in an unused room or out back in the shed digging to see what they could get into while they were there. Anything, anything but them still being gone.

"Sylvie?" she asked.

Sylvie shook her head. "We checked all the rooms twice. Vern was just fixing to get in the buggy and go driving around to see if he can find them."

"What do we do now?" Her mind was going in so many different directions she couldn't even think.

"Have you called Ira?"

Imogene nodded. "He said he would be right over." One more person to help them search.

"The police," Sylvie said. "Should I call or do you want to just go down there?"

"Is it too early to involve them?" Imogene asked. Would they really be able to help?

"Of course not," Sylvie said.

"I'll go down there then," Imogene replied.

Sylvie nodded. "I'll stay here in case they come back." But Imogene didn't hold a prayer that they would be found anytime soon.

CHAPTER TWENTY-FOUR

Jesse looked up from the harness he was repairing as he heard a car door slam outside. Must be an *Englischer* come to check out his leather goods, he thought. That was good. Moving his workshop had been nothing if not a chance and a chore, but at least people were finding him once again.

He set the harness to one side and looked up to greet whoever was entering the workshop. But it wasn't an *Englischer*. It was Mahlon and Mattie.

"What are the two of you doing here?"

"You gotta do something, Jesse," Mattie started. "Mamm's going to marry Ira."

Jesse's heart gave a hard pound at the sound of her name. "Does she know you're here?" he asked. "Is she here?"

Mahlon shook his head. "That's not why we're here," he said. "She's going to marry Ira. We heard them talking about it."

Jesse shook his head as if to rattle his thoughts back into place. "You heard your *mamm* and Ira talking about getting married and that's why you came over here?"

He shook his head. "We heard Sylvie and Vern and Mamm talking about Mamm getting married to Ira. Something about dates or something being taken up in the

valley," he said. "We don't care when they get married just
as long as they don't."

He almost smiled at those words, but right now he was
more concerned about the boys standing in front of him,
and whether or not their *mamm* knew they were out running around in Paradise Hill.

"Where is your *mamm* now?" Jesse asked.

"At work," Mahlon said impatiently. "Are you coming
or not?"

"Coming where?" Jesse asked.

"We have a driver waiting," Mattie said. "How do you
think we got here?"

That was one of the questions Jesse had wanted to ask,
but they all seemed to be tumbling around in his head in no
particular order. "You have a driver out there right now?"

"*Jah*," Mahlon said. "He's going to take us back to
Paradise Springs, so you can ask our *mamm* to marry you,
so she won't marry Ira."

Jesse opened his mouth to tell them that he wasn't able
to stop any marriage from happening if the two people who
wanted to get married wanted it. First things first though.

He walked outside into the bright September sun. There
was a hint of October in the air. Fall was upon them and
winter would be there soon. Winter and with it, it would
bring marriage season. Chances were Ira and Imogene
wouldn't get married this year, but they would certainly
plan for the following year. Or maybe not, since it was a
second marriage for the both of them. They might get married sometime after the first of the year. He supposed
Mahlon and Matthew had already worked this out for
themselves, which was why they had a driver waiting in a
small blue car to take them back home. With Jesse in tow.

He walked around the car and over to the driver. Jesse
didn't recognize the man. "I appreciate you bringing the
boys," Jesse said. "How much do we owe you?"

He wasn't about to quiz the man on how the boys had managed to talk him into bringing them into another city. He knew all about twins and the lies they could tell him, the jokes and pranks they could play. He wasn't going to hold that against the man.

The man rattled off an amount and Jesse reached into his wallet. He paid him the cost and gave him a five-dollar tip, then thanked him for his time.

"Why are you letting him get away?" Mahlon said.

"Let's call your *mamm* and let her know that you're here and safe," he said. "Where are you supposed to be?"

"At the B&B with Sylvie and Vern," Mattie replied.

Jesse knew that Vern and Sylvie truly cared about the boys and most likely had already discovered their absence. He would call there first. Then try to track down where Imogene was.

"Are you not going to do anything about this?" Mattie asked.

"First things first," Jesse told him. "You ran away from home," he said. "Let's make sure everybody knows that you're safe before we do anything else."

Mattie frowned. "We've never run away from home."

"*Jah*," Mahlon backed up his brother.

Jesse turned toward them and shot them a look. He didn't have to see it to know that he would have recognized it immediately. It was the same look his *mamm* had given him and Astrid so many times while they were growing up. "You left without anybody knowing. You left without telling anybody where you were going. That's running away."

Their shoulders slumped one after the other as they realized their mistake. "We didn't mean to worry Mamm," Mattie said.

Jesse nodded. "I know that. And she probably knows

that, or she will. But first we've got to let her know that you're safe."

The boys nodded. And Jesse picked up the phone to call the B&B.

"Paradise B&B, Sylvie speaking," the woman who answered said.

"Sylvie," Jesse started. "This is Jesse Kauffman over in Paradise Hill. I'm calling to let you know that Imogene's boys are here with me."

"Land sakes," she said. He could hear the relief in her voice. "How in the world did they get over there so quickly?"

Jesse hid his smile. The boys were nothing if not ingenious. But he wouldn't want them to know that he admired their pluck. What they had done was a serious matter and it needed to be treated seriously. "They hired a driver to bring them over."

"A driver? How in the world . . . ?"

"I don't know," Jesse said. "We haven't got down to the details yet. I just wanted to call as soon as possible and let you know that they're fine. They're all right and they're here with me. I'm sure Imogene knows they're gone," he said.

"She's down at the police station now," Sylvie said. "I'll call down there and let them know that they're with you."

"Thanks," Jesse said.

"And, Jesse," Sylvie added. "*Danki*."

Jesse said goodbye and hung up the phone. Then he turned to the twins. "What you did was serious. I'm sure you worried your mother into a headful of gray hair," he said.

"What if you took us back right now?" Mahlon asked. "That way she wouldn't get mad."

"She's only going to be mad because she's worried,"

Jesse said. "You two mean the world to her and if she thought for a moment that you were in danger . . ."

"We wouldn't want to worry her," Mattie said. "But she can't marry Ira."

"What do you have against Ira?" Jesse asked.

"He's not you," Mattie said with a firm nod.

The last thing Jesse wanted to do was sing the praises of Ira Oberholtzer, but if Imogene had set her sights on him as a husband and he was in agreement, what choice did he have?

He sat the boys down on the bench next to the door and pulled his own chair around where he could talk to them man-to-man.

"You shouldn't hold that against Ira."

"But—" Mattie started to protest, but Jesse cut him off.

"Ira is a good man," he said. "If your *mamm* has chosen him, there's nothing you can do to change her mind. Running away and coming over here trying to convince me isn't the way to do it."

"What is?" Mahlon asked.

"There is no way," Jesse said. He felt the defeat settle around him like a heavy weight, pressing on his shoulders.

"So there's nothing we can do?" they asked.

Jesse shook his head sadly. It was something he would have to learn to accept himself. "No," he told them. "If your *mamm*'s mind is made up, then your *mamm*'s mind is made up."

When Astrid heard the car door slam outside, she managed to keep her seat. The only way to write books was to stay in front of the computer and write them.

She even managed to stay put when she heard Jesse outside talking to someone, a man's voice she didn't recognize. But when she told herself that she really needed something to drink from the kitchen, she peered outside. Mahlon and Mattie Yoder were making their way into Jesse's workshop; she had to find out what was happening.

Somehow she managed to convince herself that it had something to do with her book. Or rather something to do with her attempt at matchmaking, which definitely had to do with her book. She set her glass down near the sink and made her way out the back door around to Jesse's workshop.

"What in heaven's name?" she asked as she went inside.

Jesse was just hanging up the phone. "Matthew and Mahlon decided to come for a visit," he said.

"That's not the whole truth," Mattie said. "We came because we don't want Mamm to marry Ira."

Astrid took a quick step back. The boys had vocalized some concern before, but she thought they'd gotten over their disagreement. Apparently not.

"Why not?" Astrid asked.

"Because we like Jesse. We want Jesse to be our *dat*."

Astrid smoothed her hands down her arms; then she realized it was a nervous gesture and stopped. "Ira is a very good man." *Your* mamm *could do worse.*

"But we like Jesse," Mattie said, enunciating each word so it became almost a sentence in itself.

Never before had she felt like she'd made such a mess of things. Of course, the boys would get over it in time. Right? Well, that was what she was counting on. Once they really got to know Ira, they would see that he was a good man, a loving father. He was attentive and handsome and all the other things that she had attributed to him and all the reasons why she picked him for Imogene.

All the reasons why she had fallen for him herself.

"Maybe she'll listen to you," Mahlon said.

"*Jah*." Mattie nodded in agreement. "Maybe if you tell her that she shouldn't marry Ira, she won't."

Behind the boys, Jesse stifled a cough.

Astrid shot him a look. That *be quiet or you're going to regret that* look. Of course it had worked on him when they were ten, but it surely wasn't working on him now.

"I don't think I have any more sway with your mother than anyone else. If she's chosen Ira, then surely that means he's a good man."

Mahlon stomped his foot, clearly frustrated. "No one said he wasn't a good man."

"That's right. We just said we wanted her to marry Jesse. That's two totally different things," Mattie added.

Okay, so they were right about that. But what could Astrid say in return?

She had no argument for the boys. Only that she had been the one to plant all the seeds to make Imogene fall for Ira. To make Ira fall for Imogene. To make the two of them realize that life without the other wasn't the life they wanted.

Of course, she was stretching it a bit. She still couldn't say that Imogene and Ira were clearly in love, but any fool could see that they were building a relationship. They had an understanding. A friendship. And that was important as well.

Maybe that was what she should concentrate on for her book. A friends-to-spouses kind of story. She thought back. Had she done one of those before? She didn't think so. That might be a good plot. It was the plot that was right before her eyes, so that was helpful.

"So neither of you are gonna help us?" Mattie asked.

Jesse looked to Astrid. "I think sometimes it's better to let things happen naturally," he said.

Astrid did not like the look he was giving her.

So she had dabbled a little bit. So she had manipulated a few things. It wasn't like anyone got hurt. Well, no one but her. She couldn't say she was actually hurt, though she had yet to see Imogene and Ira as officially a couple. But one day soon she would probably be crying in her pillow for a love lost that she never even knew she wanted until she had found it for someone else. But what was a writer to do about that?

"That's it," Mahlon said. "If y'all are done helping us, we're not talking to you anymore."

Both the twins stomped off and made their way over to the porch. They plopped down on the steps, chins propped up on their fists as they pouted and waited for their *mamm* to come. Astrid figured she was coming, anyway. She moved closer to Jesse. "How did they get here again?"

Jesse shook his head, but she could tell he was fighting a grin. "They hired a driver."

"You have got to be kidding me," Astrid said.

"I wish I was. Imogene was at the police station up until a few minutes ago."

"Oh my," Astrid said.

"*Jah*," Jesse said. "Oh my is right. This is your fault. If something had happened to those boys . . ."

Astrid pushed that thought away. It made her stomach hurt just thinking about something bad befalling those precious boys. "But nothing did," she said. "And you know that you were trying not to laugh since they came all the way out here just to talk you into marrying their *mamm*."

"You never should have meddled in this, Astrid."

She knew that now. But sometimes things just happened too late.

They both turned as a buggy started up their drive.

"Ira," Astrid said, shading her eyes so she could see the

driver. She would know him anywhere. That was what love did for you. "What's he doing here?" she asked.

"I think Imogene called him before she went to the police station."

Of course she did. If they were intended, which they weren't officially, but if Astrid were needing to label it, then they were intending to be intended. So of course she called him when her sons went missing. It was only natural.

She and Jesse stood side by side as they waited for Ira to make the trip up the drive. He climbed from his buggy, tied his horse to the hitching post, and came over to where they stood. He looked back to the boys. "Are they okay?"

Jesse nodded. "They're fine."

"How'd they get here?" Ira asked.

Jesse had to relate the story to Ira, the same one he'd told Astrid when she had busted out of the house and wanted to know how the twins had gotten all the way from Paradise Springs to Paradise Hill.

"How'd you find out they were here?" Astrid asked.

Ira gave a loose shoulder shrug. "I just happened to call the inn after Jesse called to talk to Sylvie. She told me they were here."

Astrid nodded.

"I'm glad they're okay," Ira said.

"We're just waiting for Imogene," Jesse said.

"I guess the next question is why?" Ira said. "Why would they hire a driver to come out here?"

Astrid watched her brother. He kicked at a loose piece of gravel and otherwise stared at his feet. "They're still convinced their *mamm* should marry me."

Ever diplomatic Jesse didn't add, *instead of you*. But Astrid felt it hang around them regardless.

"This is not good," he said.

"*Jah*," Jesse said. "I'm sure this is something we're going to have to talk about."

Both Jesse and Ira looked like they would rather be doing something else, like dental work without anesthetics.

"I suppose so." Ira nodded.

Astrid couldn't help but notice that he didn't look up and meet her gaze. Or maybe it was just a coincidence. Either way, it was fine by her. She felt that if she did, she might fall into those blue eyes and never come out again. Yep, that was what love did for you.

Ira was speechless. He had no idea what to say to the situation he saw. He and Imogene hadn't made any concrete plans, and they wouldn't for a while. They were trying to build a relationship on mutual respect and caring. Neither one had fallen head over heels for the other. But mutual need and caring . . . That was still a lot. But he didn't know what to do. Because not only were Matthew and Mahlon having a hard time accepting the change, or even the possibility for change, but his kids weren't very happy about it either.

But this wasn't about the kids. Or perhaps it shouldn't be. This was about him and Imogene needing, needing and wanting companionship as they grew older; that wasn't too much to ask from life. Not as long as he was still living. His wife had died. Imogene's husband had died. And they were both trying to go on. Why was everybody having such a hard time with it? He just didn't know. He felt like they were taking it slow enough. But maybe they needed to slow down a bit more. Or maybe they just needed to speed up and let everyone else figure it out for themselves.

He turned back to look at those two ten-year-old boys, solemn and pouty on the steps, waiting for their mother who no doubt would be in a state of fits when she came to get them. He hadn't done anything to the boys, he hadn't done anything for the boys. He hadn't advised them to come out here. He had done none of that. So why did he feel so blessed responsible? Ira didn't know. Whatever was happening was going to happen soon. A car pulled up behind his buggy. He could see Imogene in the back seat.

CHAPTER TWENTY-FIVE

Imogene opened the door before the car had even come to a complete stop. "Mattie! Mahlon!" she called, searching for her boys.

Never in her life had she been as scared as she was in that hour when she hadn't known where they were or what they were doing. How was she ever going to survive when they grew up and decided to have lives of their own?

They hopped off the porch steps and came running out to meet her. She scooped them up and squeezed them tight. That was when her tears started. She hadn't cried until that moment, and now at last her tears were ones of relief and joy instead of sadness and pain, but remembering that pain . . .

She pulled away and took that moment to look in each of their faces. "Don't you ever do that to me again. Ever! You hear me? I was so worried."

"What do you tell her?" Jesse picked that time to step forward.

"We're sorry, Mamm," they said in unison.

Jesse cleared his throat.

"We're really sorry," Mattie said. This time his words rang sincere.

"*Jah*, Mamm. Really, really sorry we worried you. That was never our purpose."

She hugged them again and they let her, but after a minute they started to squirm and she had to let them go. "What were you thinking?"

Mattie shrugged. "We weren't trying to run away or anything."

"No," Mahlon jumped in. "We just wanted to talk to Jesse."

"So you came all the way out here?"

"It was important," Mahlon said.

"What in the world could be that important?" Imogene asked them.

The twins shared a quick look, then turned their attention once again to their mother.

"We overheard you talking to Vern and Sylvie about how you were going to marry Ira."

"We don't want you to marry Ira," Mahlon added.

Imogene looked up and caught Ira's gaze, then she sent him an apologetic smile and pulled the boys to one side.

"What's wrong with Ira?" Imogene asked, so acutely aware of him standing just a few feet away. Right next to Jesse. "He's as worried for you as I am."

"We like Jesse," Mattie said simply.

"Listen," she started, looking from one of them to the other. "Jesse is a good man. I know you like him. But regardless of whatever happens between me and Ira, the two of you and Jesse can always remain friends."

"But we want him to be our *dat*."

Imogene sighed. "Sometimes that's not the way it works out," she told them. If she could have her choice, she would pick Jesse. Not that Ira wasn't a good man. He was. A very good man.

"But—" Mahlon started.

But Imogene cut him off. "Sometimes things don't work out the way we want them to," she said, coming at the situation from a different angle. "We have to make the best of what we have."

"Like Dat," Mattie said. His blue eyes, so much like his *dat*'s, clouded over.

There was nothing she could do to take away that pain. Nothing she could do to take away that hurt.

She had thought that by getting a matchmaker and finding them a *dat* she would have the help she needed. Maybe, or maybe not. But one thing was certain. Marrying again wouldn't bring their *dat* back, and there would be adjustments. Lots of adjustments.

Imogene nodded. "Like Dat." Her throat was clogged with emotion—her remorse and her love for these children. She would do anything for them, anything at all.

She grabbed them each by the chin and held them steady, looking into their eyes. "Look at me," she told them. "We will figure this out. Okay?"

The boys nodded and she wrapped them in a tight hug once more.

A world-class mess.

Astrid watched the scene in front of her, Imogene and her boys, and she knew then she had made a world-class mess of all this. She had meddled in everybody's lives. She had played with their hearts, only now realizing how incredibly wrong she was for the way she handled all this. She turned to Jesse. It wasn't the first apology that was owed to them all, but he was closest to her.

"I'm sorry," she told him. "I don't know what I was thinking."

Her brother nodded. "I know."

She went over to Ira, biting back the tears that she hadn't realized until that moment were welling in her eyes.

"Ira," she started. She had to stop. She felt weak in the knees from the weight of all her mistakes. "I apologize. I was only trying to—"

He shushed her—gently, easily. "You don't have to say any more," he told her with a sad smile. "I understand. And I'm sorry too."

She didn't ask him what for; she simply moved where Imogene had just risen back to her feet from hugging her boys. She stood, holding hands with them, one on either side.

"Imogene," she started. There came the tears again. She would like to blame them on Imogene's own tears, but she felt so burdened by the choices she had made. She'd been selfish, crying out that she was doing it for other people, when all the time it was for her and her alone.

Imogene shook her head. "Don't say it," she said. "Because I came to you."

"I hope we can still be friends," Astrid finally told her.

"I'm counting on it," Imogene said. She let go of her boys' hands in order to grab Astrid in a tight embrace.

Astrid stepped back and wiped the tears from her eyes. She sniffed loudly, then gave a small watery laugh.

Ira stepped forward. "I guess we can all say we're very grateful that the boys are all right." His voice rose up on the end as if he almost wanted to make the statement into a question. He looked around at each of them.

Everyone nodded, even Mattie and Mahlon.

"I think it's time for us to be headed back to Paradise Springs," Imogene said. She inclined her head toward the driver, who was still waiting, but Ira shook his head.

"I'll run you back home," he said.

Imogene started to protest. "That's not necessary," she said.

He nodded. "I believe it is. How about we go to my house and talk about a few things? Then I can take you from there. Or if you want, you can call a driver."

Astrid watched the moment as it stretched between them. For that small slice of time she thought Imogene might completely turn him down. Instead she nodded.

"Okay," she said. "I'll just go—" She jerked a thumb over one shoulder in the direction of the waiting car.

Ira nodded.

Imogene went over to pay the driver, and Ira turned to Jesse. "I'll be seeing you," he said, reaching out a hand to shake.

Her brother took it, gave a quick shake. Then he took a step back.

Ira pinned her with those blue eyes.

Her heart stopped in her chest. Or at least it felt like it did. Then it gave a hard pound.

"Take care," he said. Then he turned and made his way toward his buggy.

He was untying the reins as the driver pulled back down the drive.

Imogene came to join him and wait for the twins to make their way over to Ira's buggy.

The boys didn't move. They looked over to Jesse, then back over to where their *mamm* and Ira waited. For a second, it looked as if they wanted to protest. But they didn't. A silent message passed between them and they both headed toward the buggy. Halfway there, they turned back and both ran over to give Jesse a hug.

Jesse let out an "Oof" as they squeezed him, then they ran pell-mell back to the buggy. As Astrid watched, they climbed in followed by Imogene and Ira. They both gave a small wave, then Ira pulled the buggy down the drive.

Astrid stood and watched, Jesse by her side, until the buggy disappeared down the road. Then she turned back to her brother.

"Don't say it," she told him, then spun on her heel and headed for the house.

They rode in remarkable silence all the way to Ira's house. For Imogene there was just so much to say, and she rolled the words over in her mind all the way there. What to say first. What he might say next. What was the most important. It all jumbled around until she almost had no words to say at all. But when they pulled up to his house, two oversized, fawn-colored puppies came running toward the buggy. They had just enough rope tied to their collars that they could run from the porch to halfway up the drive.

Their barks drew the attention of the two boys in the back. Matthew and Mahlon rose up in their seats.

"You have a dog?" Mahlon asked.

"You have two dogs?" Mattie added.

"You didn't have any dogs the last time we were here," Mahlon remarked.

In the seat beside her Ira gave an uncomfortable cough. "We can talk about the dogs in a bit."

"Can we play with them?" Mattie asked.

"I'm sure they would love it if you did." Ira pulled his buggy to the stop and got down, and the boys clambered out after him.

They both fell to their knees in the dirt of the hardpacked drive, the puppies dancing all around them, bounding here and there as far as their ropes would let them.

"They're twins," Mahlon said. "Just like us."

Imogene wasn't sure what to say about the puppies. But somehow she had a feeling . . .

"Can we untie them?" Mattie asked.

Ira shook his head. "Not just yet. We have to have a fenced yard to put them in. They don't know this is their home, so if they get lost, they don't know to come back here. We don't want them to run off."

"Okay," Mattie said, clearly unhappy with the prospect but willing to accept it to keep the puppy safe.

"What are their names?" Mahlon asked.

Ira cleared his throat again and that feeling in Imogene's belly returned. "I was kind of hoping you could help me out with that," Ira said.

"Me?" Mahlon asked.

"The both of you," Ira said. "How about you two give it some thought and your *mamm* and I can go into the house and talk."

Mattie nodded knowingly but didn't take his eyes from the puppy he was petting. "*Jah*, I bet you have a lot to talk about."

Ira chuckled. "Son, I believe you're right."

Imogene's knees trembled and her mouth was dry as they made their way into the house. It smelled of paint fumes, but she knew that it would. Though she still had trouble believing that Astrid had helped him paint. Then again, Astrid was nothing if not a can-do kind of person.

"Would you like something to drink?" Ira asked.

She nodded. "*Jah, danki*."

"How about we just go into the kitchen? We can sit around the table."

She gave him a wobbly smile. "Lead the way."

He did, and she followed him into the kitchen. A small walnut table and chairs were pushed back into a breakfast nook, off to one side and strategically placed so whoever was eating could look out a nearby window. The kitchen itself was cheery and airy, with white cabinets and touches of red here and there. Imogene wasn't sure how long it had been since his wife had passed, but she felt the decorative touches in the room were surely the legacy of his daughter, Ruthie.

"I can make a pot of coffee or—"

Imogene shook her head. "Water's fine."

Ira nodded. "Water it is." He poured them both a glass from the tap and placed them on the table, then motioned for her to take one of the seats. She did and he followed suit.

Imogene grabbed up her glass of water and took a hard swallow. She wanted to gulp it all down but knew that she was going to need it. The longer this conversation went, the drier her mouth would become.

"I don't know where to start," Ira said.

"How about with 'I'm sorry to drag you away from work today because of my boys' ill behavior.'"

"Your boys were just being boys," Ira said. He shook his head. "They are clever boys, too."

Imogene felt some of the tension release from her shoulders. There was still plenty left from all the worry she had been through today. "I can't imagine how they got an *Englisch* driver to bring them all the way over here."

"I should've added that they're charming, too."

"I really am sorry that they worried you. That *I* worried you."

"It's no bother," he said. "I'm just glad that they're okay. And what else are friends for if not to share some of that burden?"

Imogene sucked up all the confidence and bravery she could and looked him squarely in the eye. "Is that what we are?" she asked. "Friends?"

He drew absentminded shapes on the table in front of

him with the tip of one finger. "It's the least we are," he said. "But as for anything else . . ." He left his own doubts unspoken; she could tell.

"I'm not sure where this is headed," Imogene said.

"Me either," Ira said. "I never thought about getting married again," he continued. "Not until Astrid came in and started talking about it. She didn't mention any names at first. Just had me realizing that my house was empty and that my kids were moving on with their lives. That I'd been stuck in a rut and I hadn't moved on. But now . . ."

Imogene took another gulp of water. "Say it," she told him.

"I'm unsure," Ira said. "It's not that you're not a lovely person," he told her.

"*Danki*," she said. "I feel the same for you."

"But?" he prodded.

"I think my boys need time to adjust." There, she'd said it. What she might have needed to say all along. But she had said it now.

"The truth is my kids aren't exactly ecstatic over the idea of me getting married again," he admitted. "I think it was just a big shock to them."

Imogene smiled at him. "They love you."

He nodded. "Just as your boys love you."

"So that's it then," Imogene said. She let her voice trail upward at the end as if in question.

"It doesn't have to be," Ira said. "But if we do, let's take it slow," he said. "Give them time to adjust."

"You don't have to do that," Imogene said.

"What?" Ira asked.

"Try to spare my feelings." She shook her head again. "If this isn't something you want," she started. She stopped and tried to regroup. "I'm so glad I found you as a friend," she said. "In a time when I really needed a friend," she added.

"But?" he prodded again.

"Don't you think we deserve a little more than that?"

"Of course," he said. "But there have been marriages built on a lot less."

She nodded. "That's true," she agreed. "But what about love?"

His eyes darkened with something she wasn't sure she could name. Was it love? If so, it wasn't a love for her. Not that kind of love anyway. "I'm not sure love is in God's plans for me this late in life."

She shook her head. "You might be surprised." And that was when she realized Ira was in love with Astrid.

Ira could see the dawning light in Imogene's eyes, but he knew for a fact he hadn't given himself way. Whatever that light was shining in her eyes, she had to be way off base.

This whole talk was necessary, uncomfortable and hard, but necessary all the same. Although he wasn't in love with Imogene, he could perhaps be able to marry her tomorrow and build a good life with her. But only if there weren't so many hearts at stake. But that wasn't the case. They had others to think about. Matthew, Mahlon, Elam, Ruthie. All of their children seemed expressly against their union. Whether that might change in the future, Ira couldn't say. But for now . . .

He reached for the glass in front of him and took a big gulp of water.

"So where did the puppies come from?" Imogene asked, so swiftly switching the subject of their conversation he almost spewed water out his nose.

"The puppies?" How to answer that one . . . He cleared his throat. "I . . . I got . . . It seems I may have jumped the gun a bit," he finally said.

Imogene blinked at him. Then a sudden realization dawned. "Matthew and Mahlon?"

He nodded. "They wanted me to talk to you about getting them a dog."

She blinked at him. "And you agreed?"

He held up his hands in a defensive gesture. "I told them I would talk to you about it."

"We're talking now," Imogene said. "And there are two children and two puppies outside."

Ira shook his head. "See, Jesse gave me this talk about twins and sharing and all that stuff and I just figured—"

"You figured you would get them *each* a dog?" She looked to the ceiling as if some answers were hidden there. "Without even talking to me first?"

"It was my mistake," Ira said. "So I'll take responsibility. I'll keep the dogs here with me. Just consider them my dogs."

Imogene shook her head. "I don't think it's going to be that simple."

She stood and made her way out of the kitchen and back into the living room, where she could look out the window in the front where the boys were playing with the dogs. They had done as he had asked them and left the dogs tied, though he had given them plenty of rope to run around and play.

"If they even suspect that you got those dogs for them," Imogene said.

"I'm sure they already do," Ira said.

She shook her head. "I don't think I can disappoint them on this one."

"I'm sorry," he said. "But really, I don't think you should

take the dogs if you don't think they'll take care of them like they should."

"They'll take care of them, I'll make sure of that," she said.

"I'll come build a fence for them so you can let them outside to play. I think they're going to be pretty big dogs," he said.

"What kind are they?" she asked.

Ira smiled. "Great Danes."

CHAPTER TWENTY-SIX

She should have been sad or something, Imogene thought as she rode home an hour or so later. She might contribute this lack of melancholy to the fact that she was now the proud owner of two Great Dane puppies who were surely going to eat them all out of house and home. But the smiles that her boys wore . . .

She turned in the seat and looked back to where they sat in the back seat of the car, a squirming, giant puppy in each of their laps. "And you are going to take care of them," she told them.

"We know, Mamm," Mahlon said. His puppy, Huck, licked him in the face. Mahlon tilted his head back, closed his eyes, and laughed.

She hadn't heard him laugh like that in a long time.

"Every day," Imogene warned.

"You've already told us that," Mattie said. "We don't mind. We are going to love taking care of our puppies."

Hoss was the name he chose for his dog, and the two were so identical that she wasn't sure how they would tell them apart. Different colored collars perhaps. But that was just what two identical boys needed, she reassured herself. Two identical dogs.

Though she and Ira had left it open, she knew that their

friendship would not go beyond that. Not only because the children were so opposed to them getting married, but because when they did remarry, they deserved more than solid companionship. They both deserved love, and Imogene couldn't help but wonder if Ira would be able to find that with Astrid.

All the way back to her house, she thought about the two of them. Would they be able to get together? They needed to. Though Astrid claimed she wasn't in the market to get married and didn't think she ever would, he and Astrid would make a handsome couple.

That was the only problem with hiring a car to take her back to Paradise Springs, which in itself was a good thing because she wasn't sure how two puppies would make it during the long buggy ride, but she wished she had more time to think. To think about Astrid and Ira. But she put those thoughts on hold as the driver pulled into her driveway. She got the boys out, paid the man, thanked him for his kindness in bringing them all back home.

The boys stood holding their dogs steady as the car backed out of the drive.

Imogene turned to them. "Ira's coming tomorrow to put in the fence. Until then, we will have to tie them up outside, but you boys need to keep a good watch on them. We'll bring them in tonight and put them in the kitchen."

"Awh, Mamm," Mattie said. "We want them to spend the night in our beds."

"Puppies have to get up and go potty in the middle of the night," Imogene said. "And until they're house-trained, they won't be spending the night in the house."

"How can we train them to be house-trained if you won't let them be in the house?" Mahlon asked.

"So the next stop is to the bookstore to get a book on

dog training I suppose," she said. "And that training will be up to the two of you."

"We're up for it," the boys said.

"Until then . . ." She let her words trail off. She couldn't be too specific too soon or they would hold her to that for good. "I guess we'll put the dog food in the barn."

Mahlon toted the large bag of dog food over to the barn as Mattie helped Imogene tie the puppies to the front post of the porch. She had a feeling she was going to lose more petunias to the puppies than she was to the turning weather as they waited for the fence to be built. Fall was certainly coming.

She left the boys outside to play with the dogs and went into the house. It was quiet inside, but she needed a little bit of downtime. A little bit of time to get her thoughts together. The truth of the matter was she was in love with Jesse and she wasn't sure what she could do with that. As far as she could tell, nothing. Jesse was definitely not the person for her to marry. He wasn't in the market for a marriage, despite the fact that her boys loved him so much. That didn't change his past, the things that he had gone through, the things that made him out of reach. But she had learned one valuable thing from all of this. She was stronger than she thought. And she was braver than she knew she could be and she could make it. Just her and the boys. Just her and the boys and the puppies.

She started the kettle to boil and got down a mug and a tea bag. The pumpkin spice tea she had bought at the Fall Festival in Paradise Hill.

It had been another whirlwind day, and she was counting on the tea to take the edge off. That little edge that remained even though the boys were found. Even though she'd just become the owner of two Great Dane puppies, even though Jesse would never be hers. Even though . . .

She still had a lot to be thankful for.

* * *

Monday brought with it the blinking cursor on Astrid's computer screen. She spent most of Saturday in bed, just trying to get her bearings back, just trying to learn to forgive herself for the mistakes that she had made. It seemed the people she had affected and everyone around her had forgiven her, for all her meddling and other transgressions. But it took a day for her to forgive herself.

Sunday was their church Sunday. So she had gone and smiled and sang and prayed and pretended that everything was okay. Even when she saw Ira across the room. So close, but so out of reach.

Then she got up Monday and made the phone call that she'd been dreading all along, the phone call to her editor to say that she had to rethink the storyline for her next book. That she would be in touch when she came up with something worthy to share.

The cursor on her computer screen continued blinking at her, letting her know that she had failed. Where once before it had asked, *Why?* now it declared, *Failed! Failed! Failed!*

She smoothed her hands along the sides of her prayer *kapp* and got a little more comfortable in the chair where she was seated at the dining room table. She pushed the thoughts about having a sunroom to write in from her mind, and that was when she decided to tell the story of a failed matchmaker, a woman who wanted to set up her friend with a worthy man in the district, only to fall in love with him herself. But this time, the matchmaker would end up with the man.

Hey, a girl could dream, couldn't she?

She had just placed her fingers in the ready position, hovering above the keyboard, when Jesse stepped in through the back door.

"Astrid!" he called. "Phone's for you."

Astrid thought for a split second about telling him to take a message, then she decided to go ahead and take the call. It wasn't like she had actually begun writing. And now that she had an idea in mind, it wouldn't be hard to get back to it. But she couldn't for the life of her decide who might be on the phone. She pushed back from the table and walked toward the back door where her brother waited. "Who is it?" she asked.

He shrugged. "Imogene."

Imogene. Astrid had spent the last three days thinking about the woman, silently apologizing to her, and missing her all at the same time.

But then the sound of the woman's name brought a smile to Astrid's lips. She followed Jesse back into his workshop and picked up the receiver. "Hello? Imogene?"

"Astrid," Imogene greeted her. "I hope I'm not bothering you at work," she said.

"Not at all," Astrid replied. "I'm glad to hear from you."

"Good," Imogene said. "Listen, I'm going to make another batch of that pumpkin soup that you guys didn't get to try. So I was wondering if you and Jesse might like to come to dinner tomorrow night."

What could she say but yes? "That sounds great," she replied. It truly did. The best thing for her to do would be to go back to living. Even if she wasn't going to get to do that living at Ira's side.

See, that was the first mistake she made, believing she could convince a man he needed to be married again, when he hadn't had those thoughts before. She had upset the apple cart but good. Now it was time to go back to life as normal, even if that life didn't include Ira, and going to dinner at Imogene's house seemed like the perfect first step. "Did you ask Jesse?" Astrid asked.

"*Jah*," Imogene said. "We got that part worked out. So I'll see you tomorrow at six?"

"We'll be there," Astrid said.

"You promised," Jesse told her come five o'clock the following day.

"But I'm on a roll now," she told him.

Her brother propped his hands on his hips and shot her a look of disbelief.

"I'm already over ten thousand words in this," Astrid said. "I don't want to stop now."

"You promised Imogene you would come over, and you're not getting out of it. A promise is a promise."

A promise is a promise. She said those very words to herself when she was trying to get Imogene and Ira to be a couple. She hadn't made it in the end. She supposed all she could do now was keep up with all the promises she could.

She hit save on her computer screen and shut the laptop, not bothering to move it off the dining room table.

"Okay," she said. "You win."

She went over to the door and slipped her feet into her waiting shoes.

"Aren't you going to change your dress?"

She looked down at herself. It wasn't her oldest dress, but it wasn't her newest dress. And it certainly wasn't a choring dress. It was certainly fine enough for dinner at Imogene's house.

She opened her mouth to protest, but he shooed her toward the hallway. "Go change into something nicer."

"Fine," she said.

It was best not to dispute Jesse when he got in a mood like this; the best thing to do was just go along. If he wanted her in a different dress, then so be it. She would wear a different dress.

She went to her closet and opened it, and somehow the first thing she saw was the pretty purple dress that Imogene had made for their bowling team. Tomorrow night was bowling. How was that going to work?

She supposed they could drop out of the league. Maybe they could find a team to take their place.

She let her fingers trail over that dress and pulled down the one next to it. A peacock blue dress that she'd had made. Truthfully, she didn't know where women got the patience to sew. Of course, some might say that they didn't see where she got the patience to sit down and write a four-hundred-page book, but she supposed that was a perfect example of God's talent spectrum. Everyone had a different talent and that was just how it should be. She pulled on her apron and headed back out of her bedroom door and down the hallway.

"Okay, let's go," Jesse said.

They made their way outside and climbed into the carriage.

"Are you not going to protest about my driving?" Jesse said as he took up the reins and started the horse down the drive.

Astrid shrugged. "No, it's fine," she said. Of course, she usually liked to drive. Jesse had always called her a control freak. This past couple of weeks had taught her that she was not in control. God was. And she would do well to remember that. In all matters of her life, whether it was matchmaking or Jesse's driving, God was in charge.

"Do I need to check you for fever?" Jesse asked.

She rolled her eyes at him. "Ha, very funny."

"Seriously," Jesse said, casting a quick glance in her

direction. "You have been acting really funny the last couple of days. Are you sure you're okay?"

No, she thought to herself. But instead she nodded and gave him a small smile. "I will be."

Jesse's gaze lingered on her for a moment more before he turned his attention back to the road.

She rode quietly while he talked about a few of the orders that he had gotten and how he had managed to finally get his workshop set up.

Astrid listened and made the appropriate noises in all the appropriate places, but she was thankful when they finally reached Imogene's house.

A buggy was parked out in front, a very familiar buggy.

Astrid shook her head as Jesse pulled the horse to a stop. "Ira is here."

Jesse shrugged. "Of course he is. Imogene said she was having a dinner party."

"I didn't think Ira would be here," she said. She wanted to refuse to go in. She wanted to tell Jesse to turn their carriage around and get them straight back to Paradise Hill. But those would be the words of a coward. Never in her life had Astrid Kauffman been a coward.

"I'm just surprised is all," she said, doing her best to make her voice sound offhanded, as if Ira being there was no big deal at all.

Astrid climbed down from the buggy and smoothed her hands over her skirt. Then she took a deep breath. *You can do this*, she told herself, then she started for the house. Jesse was right behind her.

Astrid knocked once on the door, then opened it. "Imogene?" she called.

Imogene came bustling out of the kitchen. "You made it," she said. Her grin was a mile wide.

"I see Ira's here," Astrid said. She was very proud of

herself that her voice didn't waver one bit when she said his name.

"*Jah*," she said. "When I told him I was making pumpkin soup again, he said he had to come have another bowl."

Astrid's heart stuttered in her chest. "You've been talking to Ira?" But she had thought—that was to say, she had *believed*—that Imogene and Ira had parted ways. It was one thing to know that a man wasn't interested in you and quite another to know that he had fallen in love with someone because of your direct influence. Because she had set them up to fall in love.

Stupid. Stupid. Stupid.

"Of course," she grinned.

"Where are the boys?" Jesse asked.

Imogene waved a hand in no particular direction. "They're outside with the dogs."

"Dogs?" It was worse than she thought.

Ira had told her about promising Matthew and Mahlon to talk to their *mamm* about getting a dog. Not only did they get one, they got plural. She wanted to turn around right then and walk back out of the house. But she was brave. Right?

"Come on in," she said, motioning them into the dining area. Ira was already seated at the table. He rose to his feet when they walked in.

He looked a little surprised to see them, and Astrid wondered if Imogene had told him who all was coming tonight. Come to think of it, she hadn't told Astrid, either.

She opened her mouth to ask, but Imogene whirled around and pinned her gaze on Jesse. "Jesse," she said. "Can you help me in the kitchen please?"

He gave a nod and started in her direction.

"I can help," Astrid said. She wasn't handy in the kitchen at all, but she surely didn't want to be left alone in the dining room with Ira Oberholtzer. Not as fragile as her heart felt in that moment.

Jesse chuckled. "I don't think she needs your kind of help."

"Ha, ha," Astrid said.

"Go ahead and sit down," Imogene said. "It'll be ready in just a moment or two." With that, the two of them disappeared behind the kitchen door. Astrid sat down directly across from Ira. "Hey," he said.

Astrid dipped her chin. "Hey." She didn't want to be nervous, but she just hadn't expected seeing him again tonight. She had braced herself and had been ready for the few glimpses of him she got at church. But there were another two hundred people running around church as a buffer. This was something different altogether.

Imogene stood at the door that led from the kitchen to the dining room and peeked cautiously through the crack. She didn't want to open it too much lest Astrid and Ira notice that she was eavesdropping.

"What are they talking about?" Jesse asked from behind her.

"Nothing. I can't see Ira's face," she continued, "but Astrid is rearranging all the flatware on the table."

"What do we do?" Jesse asked. When she had called on Monday, she had called with a plan. A dinner party for two. It was the only way Imogene knew to get Ira and Astrid together. She wasn't sure when exactly she had caught sight of that look in Ira's eyes when he talked about Astrid, but she had seen it. And she realized that somehow, during all the matchmaking that Astrid had been concocting, she had fallen in love with Ira. Somehow in all that matchmaking that Astrid had been concocting, Ira had fallen in love with

Astrid. Truthfully, that hadn't been part of anybody's plan and there were so many bruised feelings floating around that Imogene wondered if they would ever get together without a little help. So she had decided that it was the least she could do to give something back to Astrid, and the dinner party idea had been resurrected.

Astrid had put Imogene through such paces; perhaps she deserved to be put through them herself as well.

"What's happening?" Jesse asked.

"I don't know." All plans had their downfalls, she supposed. But she had hoped, probably the same way that Astrid had hoped, that if she got the two people who needed to fall in love into a room together, maybe even over a bowl of delicious, filling pumpkin soup, that magic might happen.

From the way the two of them looked at anything but the other, she had sadly overestimated the power of that magic.

"Let's take them food," Imogene said. "Maybe if they are eating, they will have something more to talk about." Or at the very least it wouldn't be such an awkward silence. People couldn't very well talk while they ate, so if they were eating, the pressure was off, right? She could hope anyway.

"Okay." She went to the stove and started ladling the steaming pumpkin soup into the two bowls she had laid out. She sprinkled the bacon bits and the roasted pumpkin seeds on top, then set them on a tray where she already had their bread prepared. "I'll just go take this out," she said.

"Do you need some help with that?"

She turned to Jesse and shot him a look. "I do this all day long," she said.

"Silence" wasn't quite the word for what Imogene experienced when she made her way back into the dining room. It was almost chilly in the room, and it was a chill that had nothing to do with the weather.

"Who's ready for soup?" she cheerily asked, hoping she could bring some warmth into the atmosphere.

Astrid looked at her in great relief. "Imogene's world-famous soup," she quipped.

Imogene grinned at her. "I wouldn't go that far. But it's at least Paradise Hill–famous."

"I've already had a bowl," Ira said. "I know how delicious it is."

Imogene served them both their soup and their breads. She refilled their water glasses from the pitcher and started back to the kitchen with the tray.

"Aren't you eating?" Astrid inquired.

Imogene waved away the question. "I've already had something. But you guys enjoy."

Astrid knew in an instant what Imogene was up to. She had set up this date much in the same way Astrid had set up the date between Ira and Imogene. Imogene was giving her the chance to make good on her feelings for Ira. Now all she had to do was get the bravery up to take it.

"I suppose we should pray first," Ira said.

Astrid nodded. She didn't say a word, just bowed her head as they both said their silent prayers of thanks for the food they were about to eat.

And the Lord, please give me the bravery I need to take this step. Please don't let me fall on my face. Please please let him love me in return.

"Amen," Ira muttered.

Astrid lifted her gaze and found him already watching her.

She could do this.

She took a breath, hoping it would calm her, needing the air to say what was on her mind.

But Ira beat her to it. "I think we've been set up," he said.

"I know we have," Astrid admitted.

"It's not so bad," Ira said.

Astrid studied his expression, trying to determine where his feelings lay. Was he upset? Did he think it was funny? Was he grateful?

Please let him be grateful.

"I suppose not," Astrid said. "It's easier being on the other side of it, though."

Ira chuckled. "*Jah*, I suppose it is."

"I seem to remember, though, the time at my house, you walked out."

He nodded. Then he looked up. His blue eyes had turned serious. "I'm not going to walk out tonight."

Had she just heard him say what she thought he had said? "What was that again?"

"I said I'm not going to leave tonight. Not until you promise to marry me."

Astrid looked around the room as if making sure there was no one else for him to be talking to. "What about—?"

He shook his head.

"But—"

He shook his head again.

"Are you serious?"

"I'm as serious as I'll ever be," Ira said. "I think I started to have feelings for you the first time I saw you in the hardware store asking if I knew someone to build your sunporch."

Astrid shook her head. "I've been so deceitful," she

said. "I was only trying to set you up with Imogene so I could get an idea for my next book."

"She came to you and asked you, right?"

Astrid nodded. "She did."

"And did she pay you?" Ira asked.

Astrid shook her head. "I told her I would do it for free. But that was a lie—"

Ira held up one hand as if to stay her words. "It doesn't matter. The fact that you were trying to help her trumps any selfish ideas you had on the matter. After all, that didn't exactly work, did it?"

"Not exactly," Astrid admitted.

"I love you," Ira said.

Astrid could hardly believe he was saying those words. "Can you say that again?"

"I love you, Astrid Rachel Kauffman. You're not perfect, but who is? And I want to marry you, if you'll have me."

"Yes! *Jah*," she said. She came around the table and knelt down next to him. "I've made so many mistakes," she said.

But he shook his head. "We all make mistakes and we all have to learn to get over them. I'm not sure I would even call what you did a mistake; it's just that your actions were a little misdirected."

She nodded.

"Did you ever find a new story idea for your book?" he asked.

"I did," she said. "It's about a meddling romance author who falls in love with the handsome owner of the hardware store. But seeing as how things were turning out the way they were, I had to make up the ending."

He lifted her face to his and planted a small kiss at the side of her lips. "Now you won't have to."

* * *

"I can't see," Jesse said. "Get off your tiptoes."

"If I'm not on my tiptoes, I can't see," Imogene whispered in return.

"If you won't let me see, then at least tell me what's going on in there," Jesse said.

"He just told her that he loved her." Imogene smiled. This was just what she was hoping for. She might not find a new job as a matchmaker, but her match tonight was certainly going to stick. Of course, God had a hand in it. And she couldn't go wrong when she followed God's direction.

"I love you," Jesse said behind her.

"*Jah*, that's what he said."

"No," Jesse started again. "I love you."

Imogene stopped, eased back down flat-footed, and turned to face him, unsure of the moment. Was she dreaming? She had to be.

"Can you say that again please?"

"I said I love you," Jesse said. "I think I have since the first time I ever saw you."

"At church."

"No," he said. "The first day you came to visit my sister and asked her to make a match for you. I saw you then and I think I knew that very moment."

"I don't know what to say," Imogene said. She had dreamed of this moment for so long that now it was here, she wasn't sure if she could separate all of her mind's wanderings with the reality before her.

She reached an arm out to him. "Pinch me."

"I'm not going to pinch you," he protested.

"How am I supposed to know if it's real?" she asked.

He took a step toward her, placed his hands on either side of her face, cupping her cheeks in his big, callused palms. Then he tilted her face to his and planted a sweet, chaste kiss on her trembling lips.

"Is that real enough for you?" he asked.

"Maybe you should pinch me after all."

"No," he said. "No pinching. At least until after the wedding."

Wedding? "You want to marry me?" she asked.

"*Jah*," he said. "Of course I want to marry you. If you'll have me."

"*Jah*," she said. Then her eyes fluttered closed as he swooped down and placed another sweet kiss on her lips.

"Mattie! Come quick! Jesse and Mamm are kissing."

At the sound of Mahlon's voice, Jesse dropped his hands. Imogene took a step back.

Mattie pushed around his brother, who had blocked the doorway to the kitchen. "They're not kissing." He turned to his brother with a frown. About that time the two over-grown puppies came bursting through the kitchen.

"These are the dogs?" Jesse asked.

Imogene nodded, unable to speak she was still so stunned from his earlier caress. "What kind of dogs are they?" he asked.

"Great Danes," Mahlon said proudly. "They're going to be huge."

Jesse turned back to Imogene.

Once again she could only nod.

He shook his head. "I don't know if I really understand what I've let myself in for," he said.

"You can still back out now," she said, praying against everything that he wouldn't take her up on that offer.

Jesse grinned. "Not a chance."

"Does this mean what I think it means?" Mahlon asked.

"It means your *mamm* and I are going to get married," Jesse said.

The boys jumped and cheered, the dogs barking excitedly around her ankles.

"When?" Mattie asked.

Jesse smiled down at Imogene. For the first time in a long time, she felt that life was complete.

"Just as soon as she'll have me."

EPILOGUE

It was the first wedding—Amish or *Englisch*—on record in both Paradise Hill and Paradise Springs where the guests went home hungry because the bride's dogs knocked over the table and ate all the chicken and filling.

Jesse had claimed it was probably a good thing since Astrid had made most of it. And he claimed surprise that Huck and Hoss would even eat it at all.

Astrid didn't think that the least bit humorous. She had worked long and hard to cook for her brother's wedding. And the food was very edible. Even if she did say so herself. But most of all, she was thrilled that he had found his happiness once again.

Jah, Imogene and Jesse had hurried their wedding through, both claiming that they didn't want to make a long engagement of it. The twins needed that family unit, and secretly Astrid believed that Imogene and Jesse needed it almost as much. There was something to be said about being able to come home to those you love and who love you in return. The bishops in both districts agreed that the sooner Imogene and Jesse could get married, the better off everyone would be. Of course, it didn't hurt that Jesse's bishop was also his uncle. In fact, it might have helped a bit, though no one was talking about that. So in between

Henry and Millie's wedding and the one for Sylvie and Vern, Jesse and Imogene and Matthew and Mahlon and Hoss and Huck had all become one happy family.

"At least the dog didn't get the cake," Vern said, working on what Astrid was certain was his third piece. But it was no matter. The cake was there to eat and Vern was always a willing subject. He said would even try some of Astrid's own efforts. He was a brave man.

Jah, she had vowed to learn to cook. But only time would tell if she would master the skill or not. She knew she would never be ready to take on the likes of Sylvie or Imogene, but Astrid was okay with that.

Imogene looked to Astrid. "How about next year?" she asked.

Astrid shook her head. "You shouldn't be worried about my wedding date on your own wedding day," Astrid told her.

It was a beautiful November day. Not too cold for this time of year. And Astrid was happy for her brother and his new bride. Tomorrow they would take over the house that Jesse and Astrid had recently moved into. He needed the shop for all his leather goods and Astrid could write books almost anywhere. She would be moving into the house that Abner had left for Imogene and his sons. It would put her a lot farther away from Ira, but they had decided that long buggy rides would be the core of their courtship. *Jah,* they were getting married, but they hadn't set a date yet. Sometime next year or maybe even the year after. They were in no hurry.

Imogene just smiled and hugged her close. Astrid was grateful that they had become friends. "It's just that if we hadn't met neither one of us would be getting married," she said.

Astrid nodded. "I suppose," she replied. She was still a bit remorseful over all her interference. Sure, it had worked out this time, but for a while there she hadn't been so certain. If things hadn't worked out, there would have been a great many broken hearts in the valley and all of them could have been credited to her. "I just never thought about it that way."

"That's because you've been too busy beating yourself up over all the trouble you think you caused."

"I did cause trouble," Astrid admitted, and thankfully, those involved had all forgiven her. "But my meddling days are behind me now. Nothing like a few close calls to put a woman's mind into the right perspective," she told Imogene. "And don't tell Ira I said that. I don't want him to be getting a big head over all this."

"Ira's not the type," Imogene said. "Which is exactly why you picked him for me."

Astrid laughed. "But who could have foreseen it would end up like this?"

"You should have," Imogene said with a laugh. "If you can't trust the word of a romance author, who can you trust?"

"Truth be known," Astrid said, "I always thought you and Jesse would make a good couple."

Imogene just shook her head. "You just keep telling yourself that."

Astrid nodded. "Of course, because you know, I always know what's best."

Please turn the page for recipes
from Paradise Valley!

IMOGENE'S RYE BREAD CROUTONS

1 small loaf sliced rye bread
1 cup of butter, melted
2 teaspoons Italian seasoning
2 teaspoons garlic powder

Preheat oven to 350°F.

Cut or tear bread into cubes. (How big or small depends on your preference. Varying the size will give a more rustic appearance and will add different layers of crunch to the croutons.)

In a large bowl, mix melted butter and spices with a hand whisk. Add bread cubes and toss. Scatter bread chunks onto a parchment paper–lined baking sheet. Arrange in a single layer.

Bake 10–20 minutes, tossing halfway through.

Imogene's note: Use your judgment. You can always add a little more butter or bread if the balance doesn't seem right. More butter means chewier croutons with a more buttery taste. Less means crunchier and drier bits. You can also substitute olive oil or use a combination of both.

PUMPKIN WHOOPIE PIES
(with Maple-Cream Cheese Filling)

For the Whoopie Pies:

    3 cups all-purpose flour
    1 teaspoon baking powder
    1 teaspoon baking soda
    1 teaspoon salt
    2 tablespoons cinnamon
    1 teaspoon ground ginger
    ½ teaspoon ground nutmeg
    2 eggs
    1 cup granulated sugar
    1 cup dark brown sugar
    1 cup vegetable oil
    3 cups pumpkin purée (or 1½ 15-ounce cans)
    1 teaspoon vanilla extract

For the Maple-Cream Cheese Filling:

    4 ounces (½ cup) unsalted butter, softened
    3 cups powdered sugar
    8 ounces cream cheese, softened
    3 tablespoons maple syrup
    1 teaspoon vanilla extract

Instructions:

To make cakes:

Preheat oven to 350°F. Line baking sheets with parchment paper.

In a large bowl, mix flour, baking powder, baking soda, salt, cinnamon, ginger, and nutmeg. Set aside.

In a separate bowl, whisk the granulated sugar, the dark brown sugar, and the oil together. Add pumpkin purée. Combine thoroughly. Add eggs and vanilla. Whisk until combined.

Gradually add the flour mixture to the pumpkin mixture and mix until completely combined.

Use a small scoop or large spoon to drop dough in heaping, rounded dollops onto the prepared baking sheet. Make sure they are about 1 inch apart.

Bake 10–12 minutes, until the cakes are just beginning to crack on top. (A toothpick inserted into the center should come out clean.)

Remove from the oven and let cool completely on a cooling rack.

To make filling:

Beat the butter on medium speed until smooth.

Add the cream cheese and continue to beat until smooth and ingredients are combined.

Gradually add the powdered sugar.

Add the maple syrup and vanilla.

Beat until smooth.

To assemble the whoopie pies:

Line a clean baking tray with parchment paper.

Turn half of the cooled cakes upside down on tray.

Spoon a tablespoon of filling onto each half.

Place another cake with the flat side down on top of the filling.

Press down gently until the filling spreads to the edges of the cake.

Repeat until all cakes are paired.

Enjoy!

Note: The whoopie pies should be placed into the refrigerator for about 30 minutes to firm before serving.

PUMPKIN BUTTER

3¾ cups pumpkin purée (approximately 30 ounces)
½ cup dark brown sugar
½ cup water
2 tablespoons lemon juice
¼ cup maple syrup
½ teaspoon ground cinnamon
¼ teaspoon ground cloves
¼ teaspoon ground ginger
¼ teaspoon ground allspice
¼ teaspoon sea salt

Combine all ingredients in a saucepan and bring to a boil over medium heat.

Reduce to low heat and cover, stirring often. Simmer for about an hour, or until the mixture becomes brown and caramelized.

Transfer pumpkin butter to an airtight container and store in the fridge.

Will keep without canning for up to two weeks.

Makes approximately 2½ cups.

Note: You can roast your own pumpkin and use it instead of canned if you prefer.

IMOGENE'S PRIZE-WINNING ROASTED PUMPKIN SOUP

1 medium sugar pumpkin (the round, orange kind)
1½ teaspoon sea salt
1–2 tablespoons butter
1 clove garlic, finely minced
1 small onion, diced
½ teaspoon white pepper
¼ cup dry white wine
1–2 cups chicken stock
½ cup heavy cream
Pumpkin seeds for garnish

Preheat your oven to 400°F.

Line a large baking sheet with parchment paper.

Wash the pumpkin and cut it into fourths. Leave the skin on, but scrape out the seeds.

Place the pumpkin slices skin side down on the baking sheet and sprinkle with ½ teaspoon of sea salt. (Set the rest of the sea salt aside for later.)

Roast at 400°F for 25–35 minutes, or until the pumpkin slices are soft and slightly brown at the edges. (If needed, you can check the softness with a fork.)

Once the pumpkin has roasted, sauté the garlic, onion, sea salt, and white pepper in butter for five minutes or until the onion turns clear.

Add the white wine and continue to cook until at least half of the moisture disperses.

Carefully scrape the pumpkin flesh out of the skin and into the pot with the onion-wine mixture. (There should be around 3–4 cups of pumpkin.)

Slowly add the chicken stock. How much you'll add depends on the amount of pumpkin you have. You only want the liquid line to be a half an inch or so *below* the top of the pumpkin. Stir well and cover.

Cook on medium-low heat for 15–20 minutes, stirring regularly.

Remove from the heat and allow the soup to cool a bit. Add the heavy cream and purée with your favorite blender/mixer.

Serve with a sprinkle of pumpkin seeds for garnish.

Note: It's easier to work with the ingredients when they are not boiling hot. If you prefer, you can prepare the soup in advance and reheat before serving.